Where the Driftwood *Meets the* Sand

Betrayal. Survival. Retribution.
DEATH WAS MERELY THE BEGINNING

KELLY WILSON

Death was just part of the journey.
Survival now means seeking those beyond the grave.
But not all spirits can be trusted.

Dedication
In memory of Doug. Forever in my heart.

Timeline

China 1901 – Annabelle was born into the Qing Dynasty, China's last Royal Family. Living in the Forbidden City in Beijing. Annabelle's real Chinese name is Ju.

China 1920 – Civil war continues in China. The Qing Empire collapses. Annabelle (age 19) secretly boards a cargo ship bound for Australia. Chinese family report to the media she is deceased. Captain Patrick has agreed to her safe voyage as a favour to the Qing Emperor in exchange for goods.

Australia 1924 – Annabelle (Age 23) and Captain Patrick marry. They purchase and move into Brambly Estate in the Victorian Coastal town of Brambly Bay. Annabelle meets and befriends neighbour Beth.

Brambly Bay 1926 – Annabelle (Age 25) gives birth to a daughter Charlotte.

Brambly Bay 1927 – Captain Patrick goes missing.

Brambly Bay 1945 – Annabelle's daughter Charlotte (age 19) marries Alex.

Brambly Bay 1948 – Charlotte and Alex give birth to a daughter Georgina.

Brambly Bay 1970 – Charlotte's daughter Georgina (age 22) marries Jack. They live at Brambly Estate with Annabelle.

Brambly Bay 1972 – Georgina and Jack give birth to Isabelle.

Brambly Bay 1986 – Annabelle (age 85) goes missing, presumed dead.

Sydney 2000 – Isabelle (age 28) gives birth to Annie. No father recorded.

Sydney/Brambly Bay 2017 – Annie (age 17) is sent to Brambly Estate for the summer.

Sydney 2015
Annie
Within

I don't know why I do it.

Maybe I like the control.

At *that* moment, the world cannot dictate my pain; it' all on me.

No one, not a soul, can ever find out.

To 'feel something' rather than numbness. I am still existing.

The scars on my skin, a reminder,

that I am not invisible.

Right?

Brambly Cove Beach 1927
Annabelle
Land

Laying face down in the shallows, I let my aching arms rest, let my lungs scream for air. It seemed impossible to push myself above the surface. The many hours at sea had been punishing.

Yet I was not defeated.

A large sea hawk hovered above. I'd noticed the majestic creature's presence at first light, a friend or foe I'd yet to decide.

Pushing and pulling at my weakened state, I felt almost at one with the tide. I willed my numb body to move, I forced myself onto all fours again as the wet sand seemed to draw me deeper into its clasp. Wobbling, my jaw clenched as I began desperately crawling, edging forward once again.

Just one more time, Annabelle.

Survival now meant getting away from the freezing water.

Away from *them*.

Closer to my child. My beautiful little Charlotte.

"Help me, please, someone." My whisper was barely audible over the roar of the ocean, the effort itself excruciating. Not that it mattered, I was the only intruder on this vast stretch of wild desolate beach.

Hardly recognising my voice, I began coughing profusely between my raspy breaths. With chattering teeth, I shivered uncontrollably. My soaking travel clothes weighed me down, making my suffering all the more difficult. My knee-length pleated skirt was filthy and torn. Only one boot remained, and my petticoat and stockings were long gone. I attempted again to tighten my jacket around my chest for protection. Its buttons had been forcibly sliced off with a fishing knife long ago.

My predators had been as unappeasable as the waves over the last few weeks. But I had done what I'd needed to stay alive.

I relished the warmth of the sun's first rays. The inky water engulfing me throughout the night had almost drowned me with its force. But now, feeling the rough sand, I was somewhat restored. To succumb was not an option. Never would I give up on my family.

I dared not look behind. Scanning the vast ocean front, I let a slow, deep breath escape. Feeling my hunched shoulders drop, I hugged my arms around my chest, and let my head momentarily rest on my knees. Relief swept over me; I was alone.

But for how long?

The memories will haunt me forever. Never does one know what the human spirit is capable of until your life depends on it.

Most likely they would have little interest in pursuing me now. They would believe I was of no use to them anymore, and no doubt presumed me dead. After all, I had willingly jumped overboard, into the icy water of the Bass Strait, and was quickly swallowed up into the night. I'm sure they deemed me crazed.

But I couldn't just assume; assumptions were for fools.

Closing my eyes, I tried desperately to get breath deeper into my icy lungs. Time was not on my side. Surviving much longer in the elements would be near impossible. My wheezing increased, and I was losing the battle to cling to consciousness.

Yet for the first time, in as long as I could remember, a small smile formed on my mouth. Lifting my frozen hands, I gently touched the shape of my blistered and swollen lips.

Those bastards underestimated me. My entire life, most people had.

From Sydney to Brambly Bay 2017
Annie
Unseeable

Sometimes I felt like I saw more of my Mum on social media than face to face.

I got it, her career was number one, not me. Like she always said, she was doing it all for *us*. But was she?

I'm sure Mum would say I was being dramatic … again. But days like today, it was pretty clear she had absolutely no idea who I was, nor what I really wanted.

Resting my head against the glass window, the vibrations of the moving bus travelled through my body. My reflection was dull on so many levels. I pulled my beanie further down my head so only the ends of my hair escaped, and I twirled the ebony strands through my fingers. Even my black nail polish was chipped. It almost made me smile to explore the stains on my grey hoodie, rips in my jeans, and scuffed sneakers.

Mum hated the way I looked. She was a true extrovert, polished and proper, screaming importance and glamour.

Me? Well, I wasn't any of those, and most of the time, I was totally comfortable with that.

Our only similarity was our birthmarks. The strange little marking on our left ankles that almost looked like a tiny house if you looked hard enough. Weird how genetics can do that. I remember the day, so many years ago, when my Nan showed me her birthmark too. My eyes nearly popped from my head. Same left ankle, same marking as Mum's and mine. It was near impossible for three generations to have the same birthmark, yet we did.

"We are connected," Nan said.

I missed Nan. Her soothing tone and hugs made me feel so loved. Unlike Mum's. I didn't need to watch Mum on the news to hear her voice; it was well ingrained in my head.

Oh Annie … It's a first-world problem, my girl. What you need is a hobby.

Oh Annie, why must you embarrass me by presenting like that? We have a reputation to uphold you know. Take some pride in yourself chick.

Oh Annie, get involved in life for once.

Was it possible to love somebody and hate them at the same time?

My mum made me think *yes*.

It was my fault. I was always too weak to respond, to tell her what I really felt. It wasn't rocket science. I wanted my mum to be around more. It wasn't like I even knew my dad, not that the famous Isabelle Robinson ever did either. I was the result of a holiday fling, so I'm told. Many nights alone in our apartment I'd wondered, had Mum even wanted to give birth to me?

And right now, I was pissed off, big time.

I still couldn't believe she sent me away. I'd begged to go to the Gold Coast with my friends, have some fun. Last summer we had stayed at Jess's parents beach apartment, it was the best. Why couldn't I just go there again? My friends knew I needed to forget what had happened with Caleb. But oh no, sending me to Brambly Bay was what Mum had decided was best. Surely Mum could see the three of us had been inseparable all year again, obviously we would want to celebrate Year 11 ending and spend summer together.

She is infuriating.

One more year, then Mum can't tell me what to do.

Of course, Abby got to go, and as a result it seemed like every five minutes they were posting from the beach, shopping, cafes, basically doing exactly what I really wanted to be doing, and where I wanted to be doing it.

Jess and Abby understood me. Well, the parts I let them see. Some secrets I could never tell.

Mum's voice rattled in my head.

"You will love it, chick. I just know it. Get you out of your suburban rut, see a different perspective, and meet new friends. You might even meet a boy."

Yep, Mum knew me well. NOT. She has no idea about Caleb, my now ex-boyfriend. Nor the pain he has caused.

I hated it when she used her chirpy fake reporter voice on me.

So far, I'd endured a plane into Melbourne from Sydney and a bus out to Brambly Bay. I shook my head silently in disgust. So, Mum could trust me to navigate my way across Australia alone, but oh no, I couldn't possibly stay at home by myself while she ventured across the world.

I was nearly 18 and knew my city home inside out. I'd been what I like to call a 'key lock kid' for years now. Most mornings I woke to an empty house, and pretty much every night returned alone to our glamorous apartment.

As I said to her yesterday, what was the difference really, whether she was there or not? She was only going to be gone for two weeks. So she'd said.

Yet here I was, packed in like a sardine on this stifling, feral bus.

Mum dropped me off with a quick hug and a fleeting kiss before bustling back out of Sydney airport. "Say hi to Pa and have a blast, kiddo."

Yep, those were her last instructions. *No worries, Mum.* She didn't even look back when she waved. Her bracelets jingled in the air and her red velvet coat floated cape-like behind her. Isabelle always managed to glide in her expensive stilettos.

I'd stood in the middle of the crowded Sydney airport terminal watching her swan away, phone to her ear, as the crowd parted to let her through.

Staring out the bus window now, watching the foreign landscape beyond, a familiar question returned: Was I like my dad? Because I was nothing like Isabelle Robinson, that was for sure.

I was desperate to burn.

How had I let myself get so caught up in Caleb? It was like I became another person around him. A weaker version of myself.

It's been 29 days since he'd ghosted me. Abby and Jess had promised me I'd done nothing wrong, other than been just a little too needy, sometimes. That, and losing my virginity to him. That night was the last time I'd seen or heard from Caleb. I jerked back at the thought, drawing my legs up to my chest.

A flush of heat rose from my neck as disillusion turned to anger. *Bastard.*

He was my first boyfriend after all, obviously I made mistakes. If you could even call him that. I'd only really been seeing him for about six weeks. Does that count?

Tears stung behind my eyes. They threatened to escape and ruin my well-practised deadpan face.

Years ago, I'd felt so empowered reading about a character in a novel having this expression. Someone who didn't show their feelings, the neutral positioning of their features implying a lack of strong emotion. An expression that gave nothing away to an outsider. I'd practised it in the mirror, loving the mask it provided.

It was my way of blending into this world, going unnoticed.

Don't be stupid, Annie.

Then it hit, and the question made my skin tingle with its excitement and possibilities: Would anyone even notice if I disappeared right now?

What if I never made it to Brambly Bay?

It was not too late to disappear.

***Brambly Cove Beach 1927**
Annabelle
*Undisclosed**

I'd had a plan.

Being alone and washed up on what I could only hope was Brambly Cove was certainly not how I'd envisaged my journey would play out.

In the end, I'd been left with little choice. Over the last three months, the days had become muddled as time blurred. I'd ventured across the Bass Strait, heading for Devonport. Now, finally, I was home. Or so I prayed. My crumpled, exhausted body lay somewhere along the Gippsland coastline of Australia.

Despite never venturing to Tasmania in the short few years I'd lived in Australia, this was where my husband had last been seen – according to the one soul I trusted. I'd refused to believe the gossip and rumours that he'd just up and left circling amongst the folk in my small town. They didn't know Patrick as I did. Brambly Bay, our home for the past three years, only saw the façade we presented.

To the people there, we were just farmers, living and working on the land. I was a simple Chinese immigrant who had chosen Australia as my new home after inheriting the wealth that allowed me to buy Brambly Estate.

Nothing more, nothing less.

Yet this was simply fiction. Together, Patrick and I were burdened with a heavy secret. One we would take to our graves. And because of this, the Patrick I knew would never willingly leave me, nor our precious daughter.

There was too much at stake.

The folk of Brambly Bay had been swift to make a judgment and cast aspersions that Patrick was a deserter. After his sudden disappearance, I'd spent much of the first few weeks vigorously defending him, pleading with the town folk to understand. If they'd considered my suspicions of foul play, perhaps they would've helped.

Then I realised my reality. The false pity that oozed out with their fake smiles made me seethe. Not that anyone could have seen it. My face was always cloaked in an impassive façade. I was reminded that people could think what they chose, and everyone had the right to an opinion, educated or not. I knew the truth, and clearly, it would be up to me alone to find him.

The thought terrified me from the first chilling moment I realised Patrick had vanished. Had he willingly left, there were personal items he most definitely would have taken. His pocket watch, glasses, tobacco tin, and identification papers remained at our home, exactly where they were put each night when we retired upstairs.

I wish I had known that was to be our last night together.

How had I not heard anything?

Where had he been taken?

Everything was in its place the following morning … all except for my husband.

This played out again and again in my head as my boat home from Tasmania rocked its crew back and forth, day after day. As the days turned into weeks, the rumination of both the ocean and my thoughts became obsessive with their lack of uncertainty.

So much of the last few months made little sense. Beth, my one and only Australian friend, insisted I go and search for Patrick, that she would take care of my daughter. She even organised my safe passage to Devonport from Welshpool, our neighbouring port. Yet as soon as I'd arrived, I felt a strange sense my arrival was expected. The minute we had ported in Tasmania the authorities had tried to hold me up, claiming they had been tipped off my identification papers were fake.

After one too many arguments with the police and an investigator I'd hired, I was told to leave Devonport, in no uncertain terms. Apparently, there were certain people I was upsetting with my pointed questions. Yet with my identification papers flagged, no passenger ship would take me home.

Had Patrick led a life I'd not known about after all?

I'd been forced to make my journey back to Brambly Bay as a stowaway.

Never, in my wildest dreams growing up in China, could I have foreseen such a scenario. I'd never even seen the ocean.

Life takes its own journey, no matter who you are, or what you had dreamt of becoming.

Over merciless weeks, I had been tortured by starvation, freezing conditions, and severe sea sickness. I remained strong by focusing on my greatest love, my only child, Charlotte. Disappearing into the depths of my imagination, I saw her toddling through the daisy-filled fields surrounding our home. I imagined us laughing as I twirled her in my arms, smelling her sweet scent – that's what had kept me alive.

Charlotte deserved a stable life and a family. She was merely a victim of our secrets, and I was her only chance now.

But in the darkened hours of each savage night, reality and disillusion blurred. Exposure of our truth came with the potential it could prove deadly.

After the first long week at sea, I was discovered. In one way it had been a relief, as I'd desperately needed food and water. I was found in the dead of night and brutally ripped out from the little alcove hiding me at the very front of the boat.

I struggled to decipher if it were in fact a dream. I'd coughed loudly; in my weakened, dehydrated slumber, the very noise that exposed me. Yet my harsh new reality dawned as the men poked and prodded me, impatient to see beneath my clothes and touch my foreign skin. They were thirsty to discover who I was, and exactly how I could benefit them.

The seamen, all six of them, were fisherman well versed in rough conditions. Two of the men were older, one clearly the captain, the other second in charge. They looked like brothers, stooped and slow in their actions. Always with a pipe in their mouths, mostly with a bottle of a dark liquid somewhere on their person. The four remaining crewmen dared not step out of line. If I could win over the older men, I would survive.

They wore heavy hats, coats, and gloves over their dark ganseys and leather sea boots. I longed for the warmth and protection their outfits provided. My intricately detailed lace blouse, skirt and velvet coat were no match for their thick wool.

Initially, the men stared hungrily, towering over me as I cowered on the rough deck. Yet, as my husband had trained me to do, I steeled to my surroundings, forcing my focus. Swiftly I created the façade I needed to survive. I convinced them I was nothing more than a maid, running away from a life of poverty, escaping Tasmania for the mainland. I contrived the tale of the poor widow. I portrayed a woman just wanting a fresh start. This was not an uncommon tale, one which would raise the least concern or interest from the men. I was grateful they appeared easily persuaded, my rugged and dirty state making it all the more plausible. After roughly searching me, the men discovered no personal belongings of any wealth or interest. Except for my flesh, that was.

But there was a price for my stay aboard their ship; I had assumed as much. I was told in no uncertain terms that if I adhered to my assigned chores for the remainder of the journey, I wouldn't be thrown overboard or turned into the authorities on arrival at any of their planned docking stations.

I felt certain that if I just played their game, I would soon be home.

As long as they never found out who I really was.

Over the treacherous weeks, I wondered which scenario would have been better. Being at the men's beck and call, night and day, drunk or sober, one at a time or coming at me in a group – or remaining as the stowaway, starving, chilled, nauseous, sneaking out on the odd opportunity for a morsel of food or water.

No question, remaining hidden would have been safer.

But no strange man, despite what he attempted to do, could ever take away what really mattered.

My daughter was awaiting my return. As were my secrets.

Arrival at Brambly Bay 2017
Annie
Confusion

Finally, I must have slept.

Waking with the jolt of the bus stopping and the brakes letting off their whooshing sound, I sat upright, rubbing my eyes to focus. Instantly my fellow passengers moved about the cabin.

I wished I could scream at everyone to shut the hell up.

I wished I'd never woken.

Irritated, clammy and tired, the air around me polluted my lungs. The kid behind me kicked my seat again. I was not usually one to be confrontational, preferring to let things slide, but right now I visualised kicking the stupid brat straight back, and hard.

My neck was stiff and my brain foggy. My stomach growled with hunger, though maybe it was just nerves. Reaching for the security of my lighter, I felt a little better. As I moved the dusty window curtain aside, I was hit with the final bursts of sunlight traveling low along the horizon.

Nothing looked familiar, but nor should it, really. It had been a few years now since I was last here, and that time we had road tripped in Mum's Mercedes.

How long had I actually slept? Maybe this wasn't even Brambly Bay. We could be in any number of towns.

Should I bail here? Disappear into whatever town this was?

Passengers hastily collected luggage from above and below their seats. Making their way off the bus, most thanked the bus driver in passing. Again and again, my bags, which I'd jammed into the spare seat beside me, were bumped. One boy even knocked my backpack to the floor, not bothering to look back. *Idiot.*

What was the hurry? It wasn't like the bus was going to drive off. Then again, we had all been trapped in our tiny quarters far too long. Most likely the other passengers were actually excited to be here. I checked my phone: 7.15 pm. No wonder I was starving. The trip took nearly three hours.

Mr. Mittens would be wondering where I was by now. I hope old Mrs. Stevenson next door didn't forget to feed him. Cats held grudges; that much I knew from experience. I imagined him sitting tall in his favourite window overlooking the street, cleaning his long orange fur while embracing the sunlight. Such a magnificent feline. I wish I was there too.

No messages from my mum. But too many snapchats from Abby and Jess, first from the SkyPoint Observation Deck, then Surfers Paradise getting spray tans and shopping. I snapped them back, showing my best pissed off face. Flicking my messages open, again I re read my final message to Caleb, I knew it almost by heart.

Look, I know it's rough for both of us, at least I know for me it's been really difficult.

I've left school 3 times in the past 5 days. I saw you today again, you saw me and kept walking. You said you wanted your space at school and not to get in your face or embarrass you, each to their own, but what did I do? The other night meant something to me, you know it was my first time. Did it mean anything to you? You still haven't text me.

Not even looked my way or reached out to see if I'm ok. Why? You know what I'm going through with my Mum, space is the last thing I

*need. Are we broken up? If so, you have dealt with it the wrong way. I
need more of an explanation cause 5 days ago you told me you loved me.*

*Do you even care? Everything reminds me of you and it's controlling
me. I'd appreciate you talking to me. I really don't know what to do now.
I've done nothing to deserve this treatment and your half arse break up.*

Caleb, please message me.

Annie.

What type of person doesn't respond to a message like that?

The same person who has sex before ghosting you I suppose.

Like always, I was the fool. I'd tried too hard to please him. Now
I just sounded like a desperado.

Idiot.

I jumped as a commanding voice booming over the loudspeaker
filled the cabin. "Welcome folks, we have finally arrived in the beautiful Brambly Bay. I hope you enjoy your stay, and travel with us again
real soon."

The driver seemed genuinely excited as he placed his microphone
back in the receiver and stood proudly in his crumpled uniform near
the exit. He well-wished every passenger as if they were stepping off
his bus into the greatest adventure of their lives.

My body suddenly felt like lead.

I spied a familiar Akubra hat despite the flurry of the congregation
surrounding the terminal. People seemed to be coming from everywhere, eager to see their 'person' on arrival. Pa waited just beyond
the entrance of the bus, slightly further back than the rest. He was
smiling and tipping his hat politely as other passengers disembarked.
Chuckling involuntarily, I sighed. Good old Pa. I'm not sure I'd ever
seen him without that hat. Its faded brown leather and the old magpie
feather sticking out the top was as much a part of him as the twinkle
in his eyes and his warming grin.

However, my smile fell as the crowd around him dissipated somewhat. Almost squashing my cheek against my window, I stared. Pa looked so much older than I remembered. He was weathered, stooped and clearly frailer. He wore his standard attire, flannel shirt and jeans, but now his clothes seemed to hang from his frame. And was that a walking stick?

This was not the Pa I knew. I felt the stab of guilt that it had been so long since we had last been here, and even now I only did it under duress.

"Excuse me, miss. Are you getting off me bus? I need to do a sweep of the seats and a clean, if you don't mind."

I gasped – he was right behind me, his polite grin reflecting in the window as he motioned to the exit.

"Yeah, sorry, I'll just grab my stuff. Thanks for the ride, mister."

"No trouble, lassie. You have a great stay. A fabulous little town this one. Every tourist loves it."

I couldn't help myself. "I'm not a tourist. My family has been here for generations. I'm here to visit my Pa for the summer."

"Oh, nice, you might never want to leave, then. The beach seems to have that effect on people." He laughed, and it made his big belly jiggle under his tight blue shirt. His reddened cheeks glistened with a slight sweat. As he reached above for my bag, he was short of breath with this small effort, and his laugh turned into a cough.

I nodded, took my bag, and walked toward the exit, rolling my eyes. My limbs felt like concrete. I looked at the driver one more time. "I won't be here for longer than I have to. My home is Sydney, and I love it there. I actually don't like the beach at all. See ya!"

I didn't wait for his reaction. But I could feel his dumbfounded stare as I strode forward. Taking a deep breath, I headed down the stairs onto the pavement.

Game face on.

"Annie! Annie! Over here, love!

I couldn't help but laugh. Did Pa really think I'd miss him standing there? Without realising it, I'm sure, he was right in the path of every passenger as they wrestled with their bags and belongings.

"Hey Pa, thanks for meeting me. I could have got an Uber back to Brambly Estate, you know."

"Ah Annie, what a sight for me young eyes you are! And all grown up, too."

I blushed. Should I have bothered to brush my hair, and straighten my crinkled hoodie or jeans? And most likely I had food on my face. Oh well, a little late now.

Pa didn't seem to notice as he continued in his animated tone. "And Annabelle is going to be over the moon to see you, love. She's very excited. Been fussing around. She wanted everything in its place, just right for you."

Pa rushed into my space, ambushing me with one of his hugs. He smelt like the sea and diesel. I'd always liked his embraces, but his words made me stiffen.

Had I heard him right?

Annabelle was my great great grandma, and she was well and truly gone from Brambly Estate. A plaque was erected for her some 31 years ago in the local cemetery where many of our past family members now rested.

This kind of talk was not like my Pa at all. I looked over his frail body again, the greys in his hair, and my stomach filled with worry.

Why the hell would he say something like that?

As we meandered up the long driveway toward Brambly Estate, unsuccessfully I tried to push Pa's strange words aside. I opened my mouth to speak, instead pausing to gather my thoughts.

Maybe he had been joking?

Bloody hell, I really hoped so.

Through the open window, I breathed in the warm aromatic air. I watched the trees dance to the summer infused breeze. I had to admit, even though I really didn't want to be here, it sure was a beautiful part of the world.

It was just not *my* world. I fiddled with the lighter in my pocket. I had back up ones in my bag and matches too, just in case. My phone remained silent.

The town itself was small and somewhat old fashioned, but the only place I knew which connected me to my family. Brambly Bay was established in the late 1800s, a place for farmers and fishermen alike. It was typical of many small fishing towns of that era, and the locals had done a great job of preserving its uniqueness. The buildings were historic, but well preserved. Not many new businesses had been set up in the town over the years. Today it had seemed busy, however.

Mum never talked about Brambly Bay. Too busy in her own importance I suppose. She was all about mingling with the right people and seeking opportunities which could help her career.

Brambly Estate was Pa's homestead now, all 300 acres of it. Having stood with pride along the Gippsland coastline since the early 1800's, it'd been a constant source of gossip and intrigue for the town from the beginning.

Annabelle had made sure of that.

I wish I'd known my great great grandmother. I get the feeling I would have liked her.

I remember as a small child thinking Brambly Estate was surely bigger than the entire world itself. But again now, I questioned, what on earth was the point of having all this land? It just wasn't my thing.

I felt miles from anywhere or anyone, despite only having travelled about 4km out of town. We had only passed two cars on the dirt road leading out. Nothing but farmland, sheep, cattle and a backdrop of cliff edges hemming in the sea beyond.

Surely Pa felt isolated out here? Maybe that was the point.

Tonight, it seemed kind of creepy. The sizeable mansion was shaded in the darkness of a cloudy summer night. I had to really focus amidst the dim misty moonlight to see Brambly Estate's looming silhouette. The filthy windscreen of Pa's old pick-up truck certainly didn't make it any easier.

"Pa, why don't you have any lights on?"

"Well, for one, I wasn't at home now was I. Too busy collecting my favourite granddaughter."

Fair enough I suppose. His chesty cough was sounding wheezy.

"Our lights come on automatically. We set the timer in our house, for the heater too. But it is never this dark in Sydney, that's for sure."

Pa braked hard as a wallaby bounded in front of the truck. Instinctively he put his hand out across my body. As we lurched forward, the old engine rattled and hissed at the sudden cessation of movement.

"Bloody wallabies, think they own the joint. Well, I suppose they kind of do! So, Annie, how is ya mum anyways? What is that daughter of mine up to this time?"

My mood instantly darkened, but I refused to let on.

Instead, I smiled watching as he struggled to get the old truck revving forward again. Through the dappled moonlight he muttered under his breath, taking a deep breath, and holding it in. I knew his mood would be brief, however, as he was the gentlest human I knew. I'd always liked his quietude. I got him. Unlike many, I found it reassuring. He used to tell me it drove his wife, my Nan, crazy when he just smiled at her instead of engaging in an argument or debate. He had to miss her gravely.

I'd been selfish, so had mum. Bottom line, we should have visited sooner.

Pa believed listening was more important than just rambling on for the sake of it. We were much alike and both total opposites of my mum. We were happy in our own company, only feeling the need to speak when there was something worthwhile to say. And truth be told, we both were infuriated by mum at times.

Mum is always reminding me I'm missing the point of life. Each time I prefer to observe a crowd rather than become involved, or stay home and hang out with my cat, she says I'm not living.

If people came in colours, mum would be something bright, most likely fluro yellow. Bold and unique. Me, well I would be beige. It's still a colour, but one easily forgotten. Beige just goes with everything and blends in. I think Pa would be an earthy tone. Natural and real, something classic and timeless. I shook off these thoughts.

"Mum is good, Pa. Busy with work as always. She left for Syria this morning to report on their civil war. She was buzzing let me tell you, completely exhausting just to be around. It will be a long flight for the person sitting next to her on the plane…. Thanks for having me by the way. I wanted to stay in Sydney to the honest, nothing personal. Not that I didn't want to see you, I just like my own place."

Pa's hearty laughter filled the small cabin again.

"Now that I understand Annie. No judgment here girl."

I'd always loved the sound of his laugh. He totally understood what mum could be like. I wondered now if we were both imagining the same vision of mum, talking nonstop the entire plane trip to anyone who would listen.

"We are glad you have come Annie. Be nice to have some extra company. The summers are just lovely here, I'm sure you remember. Been a while since we have seen ya. Every day is precious ya know girl. So many memories. Bloody time, it's a thief ya know. Your nan used to say that to me all the time."

Confusion quicky stole any lightness from the moment as I silently fought to process Pa's words.

He had said 'WE. We are glad you have come'. Pa lived alone. Surely, he wasn't referring to Annabelle again.

I clutched at my bag almost using it as a shield from my unease. I waited silently at the base of the veranda stairs for Pa to open the old heavy front door. As the fresh night air consumed the remains of a warm summer's day, I shivered slightly, despite my warm clothes. Even in the dark it was obvious things here had changed. The house looked eerie and unkept. A small crack was in one of the front windows, the door knocker itself dangling with gravity and weeds. They grew in every direction, both in the pavers in the path leading towards the stairs and the guttering barely remaining intact.

Inside, the old mansion felt even chillier like it hadn't been occupied for many months. One of my fondest memories was arriving at Brambly Estate feeling the warmth of the crackling open fireplaces and smelling Nan's baking wafting through the house.

The spacious entrance parlour still had the same chandelier I had always loved. So elegant and intricate, its tiny pieces of glass reflected in the dull moonlight. It always had seemed so magical to me as a kid. I smiled seeing the grand staircase leading upstairs. So many times,

I had raced up and slid down the banister before being told off. And the many hours I had spent, sitting on the landing in the middle of the staircase admiring all the old paintings and portraits along the walls. I always wondered who all the people were and tried to imagine what their lives had been like. Tonight, the paintings seemed menacing.

I sensed something was off. It was more than the darkness and strange chill in the air.

Pa shuffled around me, whistling and humming. What on earth was he looking for? Dropping my bags where I stood in the doorway, I moved toward the switch on the wall. We needed light and warmth, and we needed it fast. But nothing happened as I flicked it again and again. Pa had disappeared further into the house somewhere. I listened for the tick of the old grandfather clock that had stood proudly in this entrance since the early 1900's, but no sound came.

Straining to gather my bearings and adjust to the lack of light, it struck me. The parlour furniture was missing. There seemed to be nothing at all in this once strikingly grand entrance. Wandering further I flicked on my lighter, the contents of the front sitting room gone, too. All that was left in here was the big open fireplace. Marching over to the front dining room directly opposite, I discovered the same. Completely barren. I felt confused and sad and sick all at the same time. Surely there was some reasonable explanation.

Did Mum know about this?

Had Brambly Estate been robbed?

"Here lass, use this to guide you."

I jumped, almost dropping my lighter, startled by Pa suddenly behind me with a thin candle.

"I'm sorry Annie, been having a little trouble with the electricity of late. Annabelle keeps telling me she has the answer I need, but she won't tell me more than that, I can't read her bloody mind, she needs to just spit it out."

I was dumbfounded. He was acting as if nothing was wrong. The flicker of candlelight cast strange shadows around us. I managed my best smile. He met my eyes briefly, and I saw a hint of emotion I couldn't quite place in them before he quickly looked away. Tears began to sting behind my eyes as my mind raced, searching for any type of clarity.

Guilt sent acid through my gut. Pa had lost his mind, been living here all alone in the dark, and my mother and I had entirely abandoned him.

Brambly Cove Beach 1927
Annabelle
Grief

The hawk continued to circle above me, relentless in its screeching. I raised my palm to the sky.

Was I to be her prey?

I thought again of Patrick. He had shown me these powerful birds shortly after my arrival in Australia and told me of their high intelligence. Adaptable survivors he'd called them. Somehow that knowledge seemed to ease my tension as I raised my palm to the sky.

Maybe Patrick had sent her to watch over me.

I stood. Not an easy task. The sand was freezing under foot, and I was grateful the sun had returned, warming the air slightly. It was February and what looked like the beginnings of a hot summer's day. The tropical shower had dispersed as quickly as it had come. I smoothed my damp skirt as best I could, pulling my windswept hair from my face. My precious hairpin had disappeared long ago now. If its thief were smart, selling it would bring him a small fortune. It had been a precious family heirloom. I thought again of Beth, I'd gifted her a similar one.

My dearest and only real friend, she was my lifeline now. Beth had thought of things I had not, as I'd made my hasty and far from planned journey across the sea. Ever since our arrival in Brambly Bay, Beth had been there to help. Australian life had been overwhelming. I was dealing with a foreign land, a new culture and the silent grief of losing my family. Too suddenly I'd found myself a long way from home. Nothing had been by choice.

Beth lived just across the hill from our large portion of farmland on Brambly Estate. We formed a bond quickly despite our vastly different upbringings. I was so grateful for her strength, knowledge and feisty zest for life.

For over a year I had lied to her.

I had wrestled with my conscience for many months, before finally telling her the truth and intimate details about who I was. I believed Beth could be trusted to take this to the grave. However, I never had the courage to tell Patrick she knew my story. For some reason, he had never liked Beth, constantly saying she was not to be trusted. But I had desperately needed a friend, especially as Patrick's ship continued to venture on many long trips out at sea.

On the day I left for Tasmania, Beth had stopped me as I'd rushed to climb the ship's thin walkway. She had placed a small leather pouch in my hand. *Keep this safe* she had said, and remember, trust no one.

This I knew all too well. It had been my life for the last four years. Once onboard, away from any onlookers, I dared open the pouch. Beth had placed money and a note inside.

Annabelle,

Should you run into trouble and are unable to return as a passenger to the mainland, your only choice will be to flee as a stowaway. You must be wise and choose a ship bound for Welshpool. Jump overboard as the ship passes the Brambly Bay Cove, and the tides will wash you in. There I will have supplies waiting, buried under the driftwood erected on the headlands. I will check the supplies every few days until your return. Charlotte will be safe with me.

Godspeed my friend, and remember, 'Where the driftwood meets the sand'.

Forever, Beth.

I'd thought this preposterous at the time, now her whispers of warning ruminated in my mind. Somehow Beth had known things would not go to plan. Now, alone, cold, fragile in every sense, I squinted as the sunlight stretched across the sand dominating the morning. A wallaby darted up in front, racing up the steep bushland beyond the beach. The screech of the seagulls was deafening as they fought for the pieces of a carcass rotting on the sand ahead.

I had been so naïve.

Brambly Estate 2017
Annie
Trapped

I was far from sleep. It was 2am. I felt sad and heavy with loneliness. When last here this kitchen had been the hub of Brambly Estate. I had always loved the long wooden table and wide working benches, the pots and pans which hung from the walls and the old AGA oven which was a source of warmth and delicious smells all year round. At least that was still going, its embers creating a dull glow in the room.

But where was the furniture now?

The previously inviting room was now stark, a white plastic table and two folding chairs were all that remained. Nan had died nearly three years ago now. In her time the cupboards were bursting with an abundance of preserved jars of fruits, pickled vegetables and spices. Now they were almost bare.

Earlier, wrapping myself in the old blanket Pa had left on my bed, I'd crept around the house, tiptoeing on the creaking floorboards. As I had gone from room to room, I'd experienced the strangest sensation I was not alone. I wanted answers, but there was no point in waking Pa tonight.

This was all so weird.

Each room I'd explored had been the same. Most of the magnificent antique furniture was gone. As were the wall hangings and rugs. I knew these were all worth a small fortune and had been in the family for many generations. Many had come from China with Annabelle originally. So where was it all now?

There were six bedrooms upstairs. I always used my mum's old room when I visited. I loved its homely decor, but now only the double four poster bed and an old wooden wardrobe remained. My memories were real, but tonight it was like none of them had ever existed. And to make it all the stranger, Pa was acting like there was nothing amiss.

I tried to call Mum, but as usual her cheery voice mail message slapped me in the face. I knew it by heart. Realistically she would still be in the air somewhere, but I'd had to try. Mum told me she was in for a long flight to the city of Damascus, around 20 hours non-stop. Once landed she would be 7 hours behind Melbourne time.

I sat bewildered on the old white plastic chair. A generator hummed in the corner of the room, my only source of power to charge my phone. Starving I longed for the Vietnamese street food from the café below our apartment. Instead, I found an old tin filled with cream biscuits, that would have to suffice. I filled my mug with more steaming milk from the stove, mixing in layers of cocoa and sugar. Dipping in the biscuits, I wondered had Pa been left with no choice? Was he out of money? Why wouldn't he have told us?

I knew I needed some sleep, at least I had to try. As I climbed the staircase once more, I felt every bit of the weariness and confusion the day had presented. Tomorrow, I promised myself, I'd sort all this out. There was most likely a simple explanation.

Who was I kidding?

A foreign noise intercepted my thoughts. Unsure of its location I moved quietly along the corridor. *Bang.* The sound startled me again. From under the furthest door, I noticed a dim flickering light. I crept closer, listening for even the slightest sound.

Was Pa in there? Was he alright?

Bang. I felt my posture go rigid as the hair lifted on the back of my neck. Pressing my ear against the wooden door which had been locked earlier, I attempted to open it again. To my surprise, this time its handle turned easily.

"Hello, Pa?"

Suddenly nervous, I felt unsure of what I should do next. Maybe I should leave, just mind my own business, go to bed? But curiosity had already won, and I found myself peering through the slight opening in the door. This room was different from any other I'd seen in the house since arriving. It was warm and inviting, filled with furniture and personal belongings. A candle was burning on the little desk under the closed window, another on the table beside the bed. Papers were scattered all over the desk, like someone had just been in here writing. And the smell, it was so enticing.

"Hello?" I dared not move as I spoke. "Is anyone here?"

No response. I crept further into the room, leaving the door wide open behind me. Even at first glance it was obvious it was a woman's room as I moved around silently. Trinkets and vases of flowers, photo frames, even an oriental-like dress was draped over the bed; its linen was exquisite. In one corner was a rocking chair, and a half-completed tapestry sat amongst its cushions. Beautiful rugs and wall hangings laced the room. Bang. Startled again I noticed another window; this one was wide open, its wooden shutter moving with the wind. I shook my head.

See, there is a simple explanation for everything.

Well, at least for the banging sound. But let's be honest, it was weird. Maybe this room was Pa's way of keeping memories alive. After all, I knew long before our time it had belonged to Annabelle, and originally Patrick, too.

But why would he keep just this room as it had been, and not the others?

Suddenly, all the candlelight vanished, then from behind, it sounded like a key was turning in the door lock. Standing in the middle of the room in almost pitch darkness, I consciously forced my limbs to relax.

Surely, I had misheard?

Focus Annie.

I willed myself to breathe. All is good. Obviously just the wind from somewhere snubbing the candles out. With trepidation, I turned to make my way out to the hall. Feeling for the door, I realised it was no longer open.

What the hell?

Frowning, I listened intently. Maybe a breeze had closed it too? Stupidly, I'd left my own candle on the landing just outside the room. As I reached for the handle, its static touch caused a cold shock of electricity to course through my arm.

A hot flush of panic surged.

The door was tightly locked.

Brambly Cove Beach 1927
Annabelle
Betrayed

How long had I slept this time?

Aware I was close to unconsciousness, I floated in and out of reality. Startled at an abrupt screech, my eyes fluttered open. I willed them to focus. There stood the sea hawk, eyeing me suspiciously. She moved around me, then backed away.

How long had she stayed with me?

Fight Annabelle, fight.

I willed my thoughts to be louder than the negative voices within.

Dry retching with the sudden onset of nausea, I grabbed at the stabbing pains in my stomach. As I struggled to my feet, I begged for mercy. To whom, in fact, I did not know.

A series of high-pitched whistling noises broke my thoughts, the bird called to me from further down the beach. My light headedness returned as my eyes widened. Gasping I fell to my knees.

Motionless I stared toward the dunes beyond. Did I dare believe? The large piece of driftwood, in the shape of a gangly branch, stood tall. Someone had buried this in the dune. This had to be the place.

Suddenly exuberant, I surged forward. The sand was heavy underfoot, causing my feet to sink with each step, yet I hardly noticed. I was willing to crawl if needed. Never once did I allow my stare to break as I trudged closer. Through jumbled thoughts I narrowed my eyes, straining to see, desperate for the driftwood to be real.

Gasping, I saw my lifeline: the delicate white ribbon dancing in the sea breeze, tied deliberately to one of the lower branches. Tears welled behind my eyelids causing my vision to blur even further, and an unexpected release of tension almost caused me to fall.

Charlotte's hair ribbon. She had been wearing it when I last held her. I was nearly home.

The embankment seemed near impossible to climb, and the earth fell away beneath me as I clawed my way to the top. As soon as my hand touched the large piece of old wood, new hope surged through my veins. Mesmerised by its touch, I stared at the knots and indentations. It was smooth and worn, faded. Each dent and twist in the wood reflected a story. This huge piece of wood had proven its strength by standing the test of time. Enduring hard years, no doubt, yet had remained strong and defiant against the changes of each season. It had in fact, seemingly become more beautiful and powerful with age.

Shaking myself back to the present I desperately looked around its base for my promised supplies. I began clawing at the sandy earth with my hands, its roughness barely noticeable in my plight. Before long I could feel a hessian bag buried just under the surface.

"Beth, oh, thank you, Beth" I whispered into the wind.

Within minutes I was hastily gulping down water from a canister Then grabbing at the raisin bread like a wild animal, I hungrily devoured the sweet cake-like buns. With each mouthful I felt a little stronger and with a shaky laugh my widened eyes locked onto my source of relief. On my hands and knees, I barely noticed my surroundings as I gorged, my hunger insatiable. I was transfixed with the goodness of the bread, the Anzac biscuits and dried fruit.

Succumbing to the fog in my head, I lay beneath the driftwood amongst the leftover food. I knew I needed to keep moving, but my fatigue was far too great.

I bargained with myself. If I just lay my head down briefly, maybe this heaviness would subside. Then I would have the strength to study the map Beth had left and begin my trek home. The sun danced over my skin, its heat drying my tears and beginning to ease the chill in my bones. I relished its warmth, feeling almost content as it stilled my mind.

As the darkness enveloped my consciousness once more, instinctively I felt the need to get up.

Annabelle, something is wrong.

The hairs on my arms raised. I willed my body to move, to react, to see and hear everything at once.

But I couldn't.

My exhaustion was all-consuming, my eyes too heavy to open, my limbs too dense to move. Vaguely I registered voices. Muffled and distant at first yet becoming louder and closer.

Then the blackness washed over me.

Brambly Estate 2017
Annie
Ghosts

Startled I sat bolt upright, unsure of where I was, or what had woken me. I was completely scattered in thought. The light was blinding, and nothing seemed familiar.

"Annie, there you are! What on earth are you doing in Annabelle's room, lass?"

As the fogginess evaded, I realised Pa stood in the doorway looking as dishevelled and perplexed as I felt. Then it all came crashing back.

"I, well, I don't really know Pa. I was locked in here. Yes, absolutely someone locked me in. Then well, I must have finally fallen asleep. I'm sorry, I was on my way to my own bed last night when…"

Pa lifted his hand for me to stop talking. He shifted uneasily on the spot, looking around the room.

"It's okay lass. No harm done, I'm sure. But no one has had the key to this door since I can remember. Got lost many moons ago. Maybe the old door just got jammed. Anyhow, come down for breakfast when you are ready, got some adventures planned for us today."

I nodded, still confused as hell. Pa was wrong. The door, without question, had been locked on purpose. I knew it in my gut and clearly had heard the key turn in the lock. I wasn't stupid.

But why? And who would do that? Had Pa done it and just not remembered?

Yet I knew better than to argue with Pa, and I didn't want to upset him. After his brief inspection of the sturdy wooden door, he was already turning to leave, anyway.

"Oh, and Annie, be sure to tidy up as best you can in here before you go. Miss Annabelle has one hell of a temper on her when her things get touched or tampered with. I learned that the hard way just last week."

He shook his head before stilling, seemingly deep in thought. Finally, he smiled. I opened my mouth to speak but confusion kept me silent.

"But your hair does look nice, lass. Annabelle used to wear it just like that."

I stared wide eyed at him.

"I never did really understand women, one of life's great mysteries, you females. Why you go to all the trouble of fancy hair dos and frocks I'll never know."

He started to belly laugh as he exited and began his descent down the stairs. I could hear Pa continue to chuckle and prattle on to himself as he slowly shuffled away.

I sat cross-legged in the big bed. Absolutely disorientated, and completely addled.

I wasn't one for imagination, mystery, or intrigue. I was very black and white. Show me facts based on evidence and I'd believe. I didn't even read fantasy or science fiction novels, as it all seemed too far-fetched for me. So, at this moment, nothing at all made sense. But overriding it all, I felt a deep sadness hemming me in whilst sitting amongst the beautiful old linen adorning Annabelle's bed.

I was pretty certain my Pa needed medical help.

What had he meant about my hair?

I jumped up, pushing the heavy covers aside. I stared in disbelief at my reflection in the small mirror on the dresser.

I leaned closer in toward the mirror, turning my head from side to side. My hair was made up in a perfect bun, in which tiny decorative hair pins were placed. I'd seen these before, my nan had worn them. She had said they were precious family heirlooms that Annabelle had brought with her from China.

How the hell did they get in my hair?

My body heat was rapidly rising, and a fluttering sensation dominated my stomach. I fumbled trying to remove the delicate clips, and all the while my rapidly blinking eyes begged for affirmation. I drew a breath, holding it for the longest time before releasing. There was no rational explanation, and that perplexed me to no end.

Maybe I was the one losing it.

Entering the kitchen, sun streamed through the stained-glass windows, dancing across the room. The light was speckled with red, blue, and gold. I stared, momentarily mesmerised by its effect. Pa whistled as he slowly stirred a pot of scrambled eggs. I recognised the tune instantly as Gran would often sing the same song. Pulling my sleeves further down, despite the warm air, I wrestled with my head. It was still early in the day, yet so much had happened.

Should I bring it up with Pa over breakfast? What on earth would I even say?

Pa's old brown hat rested on the small table. His hair seemed thinner and greyer today, but at least he was standing a little taller. A fresh loaf of bread sat on a wooden chopping board, beside it a jar of raspberry jam, butter, and a pot of tea. Suddenly I was ravenous. Too little sleep and brain overload I supposed.

This all seemed normal, right?

Just a family sharing breakfast. Pa had obviously got supplies this morning, so he was thinking straight on some levels. His mood seemed good. So why rock the boat. I lost the courage to question him further, instead choosing to sit and act like he was, like we didn't have a care in the world. He would tell me just what was going on around here when the time was right. Wouldn't he?

As Pa prattled on, he announced we should go surf fishing, a hobby he had loved forever. Me, not so much anymore. Our family had used the beach track often over the years which lead from the back paddock of Brambly Estate, over the dunes, and onto Brambly Cove. I'd loved it once. Together in those early years when we would visit, Pa would take me to explore the coastline. We really did have some great chats in those days. How old had I been? Ten, or maybe 12? We'd built sandcastles and even wrestled in a fish or two, but I'd always insisted he'd let them go.

Could he even walk that far anymore?

Personally, I could not think of anything worse this morning. But I wanted to make him happy. It was the least I could do. Maybe my company was just what he needed to come to his senses a little. They say for humans, reality and fiction can easily become blurred when we spend too much time alone.

The kitchen was warm, and I had to admit the awaiting day didn't seem so bad. Still, I wished I was in Sydney. I wondered what my friends were doing right now. Most likely still in bed. Flicking through my phone I checked for messages I might have missed, annoyed at myself that I still held hope Caleb might have in fact replied.

Curiously I watched as Pa retrieved a third cup from the hutch on the far wall. The design on the fine China cup was so beautiful. I recognised it as a family heirloom that had come with Annabelle from her mysterious life before Brambly Estate. My nan had told me all about so many precious things here Annabelle had cherished. Were we expecting company? Pouring steaming tea carefully and slowly, I noticed his hands were shaking.

"Ok lass, I will go and attend to the fishing gear if you will take this right up to Annabelle. Me old knees don't need another trip up those stairs I do say. Rightio then, see you outside in say 15 min?"

Without looking back, Pa scooped up his hat, waved his hand in the air, and shuffled away.

My lightened mood vanished instantly. I couldn't swallow my last mouthful of toast, fearing I'd gag. I felt the colour drain from my face.

This was getting worse by the second.

I stood reflecting as I stared from the veranda at the distant cliff line and watched the birds dart from one fruit tree to another. At least they still felt content at Brambly Estate.

Typically, I still hadn't had the courage to confront Pa, and that pissed me off.

But I just couldn't, despite rehearsing my speech a thousand times in front of the bathroom mirror. Yesterday had been my perfect opportunity. Pa and I had stood for hours fishing, side by side on the shoreline as the waves crashed around us. But he was so happy in the moment. He, too, recalled the times we had spent together fishing when I was young. He'd hugged me tightly and told me he was so proud of the young woman I'd become.

If he only knew.

Last thing I wanted to do was embarrass him and make it awkward between us. He was such a loyal and proud man. And despite his chirpy nature, I knew he never really recovered when my grandma passed away. It was only 3 years ago after all. People do strange things in their grief.

We should have visited more.

Maybe that was all that was happening, a crazy period of temporary insanity? Was there such a thing?

I was no psychologist, so basically, I had no clue what to do next.

I did know one thing though, I just had to get out of this house before I went crazy, too. Despite its large size, and endless possibilities of things to explore, Brambly Estate seemed to be closing in on me today. It was still early but Pa had already taken off to the sheds. Goodness knows what he did out there, but if it made him happy, all good by me.

All I could see were gardens, trees and paddocks, with not another house or person in sight. The air was already mild and today a strong scent of jasmine travelled with the breeze. As I headed across the grass to the sheds, the sun danced over the land, and the sky was an uninterrupted vivid blue. Birds were scattered in the treetops, almost deafening in their calls and screeches. The ocean was certainly making its presence known beyond the cliff line, the waves must be at high tide. My plan was to take mum's old bike into town, get a few supplies and check out Brambly Cove's small library. Surely that would clear my head.

Mum had finally called early yesterday. About bloody time. She had seemed both excited and preoccupied with her latest adventure, making me promise I would tune into the news tonight. She was reporting live. That led me perfectly to what I really needed to tell her. Tuning in would be impossible without power to the house. And there was no TV here anymore anyway!

I shook my head now recalling how she had fobbed off my queries and concerns for Pa and Brambly Estate. I just didn't get how she could not be concerned about her own dad? And it angered me that I could hear her whispering to a work colleague as we spoke. Surely, she could have given me her undivided attention for just a few minutes. Even if she wasn't really interested, she could pretend. But of course, like always, I said nothing. Again, I chose to continue on as I always did.

Invisible. I was the master of recoiling.

Not daring to rock the boat so to speak.

One day she would see me, hear me. Somehow, I would make her.

I longed for that day.

Was I overreacting about Annabelle? I pondered as I rode a little unsteadily along the dirt driveway. So what if there were strange noises, and a weird chill or smell in the air from time to time. And the things changing place in the house without explanation? Or the strange presence in Annabelle's room? Maybe they were all in my imagination. Old houses have secrets I suppose. But Annabelle's pins in my hair?

I stopped at the end of the driveway to look back upon Brambly Estate.

Did I believe in ghosts?

Absolutely not.

As old and rundown as it now was, I still found it impossible not to get swept up in Brambly Estate's distinctive grandeur. I had so many amazing memories of being here. Mostly before my mum got her high-profile job, and back when my Nan was alive. At least we used to visit more often then.

I wish I understood why mum never wanted to visit Brambly Bay. Some sort of fight between her and Nan was all she would say. I suspected mum carried the guilt of that being unresolved everywhere she went. That's if she had a conscience at all. Some days it was hard to tell. I wondered now if that was partly the reason she had embarked on her crazy, all-consuming career. A busy mind keeps the demons away. That strategy was not going to work forever.

The once white exterior walls had greyed off now, and much of the façade was peeling. A huge double door stood in the middle of the first level, two sets of windows either side. The opened white shutters protecting the windows had seen better days. I smiled now recalling Pa instructing me to shut them tightly each time high winds or storms had come in off the ocean. Those storms had been so exciting. I remember feeling invincible, no matter the elements, protected inside Brambly Estate.

Wide verandas sheltered the house further, both on the ground and upper level. Six more windows and a set of French doors faced the front gardens from above. Each had lace curtains and heavy velvet drapes. I once loved playing hide and seek in them. The chimneys, seven I could see from here, still stood proud. Each bedroom had its own chimney, as did the kitchen, dining room, sitting rooms, lounge and parlour. The servant quarters also had an open fire. It must have been a huge job to keep all going during the harsh winters here.

Moving my attention away from the house, I admired the gardens. These too had been grossly neglected over recent time. Yet they were still magnificent, with huge oak trees and oriental fruit trees planted over a century ago. The driveway was lined with massive pine trees which formed a guard of honour all the way up to the house. The gardens closer to the verandas were now overgrown and mostly weeds, but I remember many times picking the roses, proteas, waratahs and sea daisies. Nan had taught me all about them.

I hadn't realised how much I missed her till now. Seemed like another lifetime.

Did Mum miss her?

I wished I knew what their fight was about. Pa would know for sure.

Sighing, I picked my bike up from the side of the road. It was getting warmer by the second and the quicker I got into town, the sooner I'd be sipping a coke, or maybe an ice cream, anything cold really. Best I got moving.

As my eyes swept over Brambly Estate once more, they instantly locked onto the French doors leading out to the above decking. Suddenly my breath constricted in my lungs and an adrenaline shot raced throughout my body.

I dared not blink.

A young woman had appeared. She was beyond beautiful, leaning slightly over the railing to face the sun. Her black hair swirled around her petite frame as she fought to pin it back against her beautiful ivory skin. She wore an elegant oriental dress. It looked like jade silk. Was she crying?

There had been no one in the house when I had left, had there?

Suddenly the woman looked straight toward me. Stilling, she straightened her back before smiling broadly through ruby red lips. Raising her hand, she waved like she had been expecting me. Instinctively I looked all around, but I already knew. The woman was gesturing to me.

I felt the sweat beading, as my confusion deepened. My hand was trembling as I raised it in a wave of reply. The same tightening in my gut presented. As much as I desperately wanted my rational brain not to acknowledge the fact, I knew her. I'd seen enough family photos.

Was Pa right? Or was I just losing my mind as well? It was Annabelle.

I hadn't been sleeping well. Maybe that's why I was seeing things. I've read fatigue can do crazy stuff to a person; sleep deprivation was even a form of torture used in war. That was good enough for me today; the alternative I refused to contemplate. But Annabelle had seemed so real, and like it or not, the thought was messing with me.

I sat in a familiar booth toward the back of the only café in town. My coke was a godsend. I didn't quite realise how unfit I was and cringed at the thought I still had to ride that damn bike home. The coolness of the room was calming my senses, as was the welcomed white noise of a crowd. Draining the glass, I sucked on an ice cube, and had almost managed to quash the irrational banter in my brain.

Remember Annie, facts speak the loudest. Annabelle died over 31 years ago.

Or disappeared at least. They never did actually find her body.

Time I did some digging. There had to be some locals in this town that knew something.

I'd been to café 'Stay a While' many times over the years. Mostly it had been to drool over the ice cream counter, debating which flavour to have. The café itself seemed to have changed little. Splashes of blue and yellow covered the walls. Big prints of ocean waves and various beach scenes decorated the walls. Even the old wooden tables with their well-worn yellow cushions on the bench seats were the same. The place still smelt of fried food and that sickly-sweet scent I never could place. There were photos of locals plastered everywhere, mostly boasting of the fish caught or waves surfed. I bet I could find a picture of Pa amongst them if I looked hard enough. He had entered many fishing competitions over the years. The cafe was certainly a buzz of activity today, locals and holiday makers from what I could tell.

I was neither.

A strange feeling came over me and I became aware of a figure lurking closely. Unaware my sweat had all but glued my legs to the seat, as I spun around it pulled roughly at my skin. Like ripping a band aid off, its sting made my eyes water.

An elderly lady stood, staring at me. Her broad white sun hat seemed too big for her frame, yet her red dress, belted at the waist seemed uncomfortably tight. She was certainly dolled up with thick make up and heavy jewellery. She held her handbag closely to her chest, as if it were a shield. This old lady seemed startled I had caught her out, yet she remained confounded, almost looking through me, it seemed.

"Hello, can I help you?"

It was all I could muster as I swallowed uncomfortably, waiting for an explanation. I looked around, but no one seemed to have noticed our interaction.

"Hello Annie. My name is Mabel Anderson. I'm a long-time member of this community. May I sit for a moment?"

She looked suddenly frail, and almost confused. Collapsing heavily in the booth opposite before I even had a chance to reply, she plastered a smile on her face, which wrinkled like the action was foreign. I forced myself to relax, no harm done…yet.

"Sure, why not, be my guest."

My sarcasm was more obvious than I intended, something felt off.

"Annie, forgive me, child. I saw you walk in, and I thought for a moment you…well, that you were someone else. But the waitress over there told me you were Jack's granddaughter."

I looked back at the waitress busying herself, balancing used glasses and plates with one hand while trying to wipe up the spilt sauce with the other. She was trying desperately not to look in our direction. I had never seen the waitress before, so how on earth did she know me? But just as quickly it dawned on me. It was a small town, after all, nothing like my beloved Sydney where I could simply blend into the endless crowds.

My new companion was fidgeting with her small clutch bag and smoothing the neckline on her uncomfortable looking dress. She smelt like mothballs and lavender. The thought made me stifle a laugh. Her face was attractive, yet somewhat hardened, and up till now, near impossible to read.

I waited.

"Annie, I am a long-time friend of Jack's. My family have resided here for as many generations as you lot at Brambly Estate. In fact we own the neighbouring land. It's so nice to see a member of Jack's family return. It has been a while, dear. Nearly three years if I'm correct. Have you come to help him, may I ask?"

"Help? I am here because my mother made me come for the summer, or two weeks of it at least. It's not that I didn't want to see Pa. He is great. I just would have preferred to stay in my home."

Why did I even feel the need to explain?

"Yes child, I do understand. Sydney is a far cry from this sleepy town. Goodness, you must find the pace here somewhat slow. Which is very good for our souls from time to time, don't get me wrong dear. And Isabelle, yes, my goodness. We all follow her exciting career. You must be very proud of that mother of yours. I can tell you the folk of Brambly Bay certainly are."

Something was not sitting right. For one, Mabel had lied, she had known exactly who I was right from the start. I couldn't help but take an instant dislike to this woman. Why was she sitting in front of me? Did she actually want something more than town gossip? However, I needed to be polite if this was a friend of my Pa's.

"Can I help you with something Mabel? Because I really must be getting home soon."

"Home? Oh, you mean Brambly Estate?"

I all but rolled my eyes. She knew exactly where I was staying.

"Well Annie, I am merely wanting to ask after Jack. He rarely comes into town, and all but never attends any social gathering. He even missed the last three town meetings. People are somewhat concerned, you know."

I had to jam my lips together to avoid laughing. Was this woman for real? At least she cared I suppose. Maybe I was in luck and Mabel would answer some of my questions.

"Annie, are you listening child?"

Her voice was a little sharper this time.

"Oh, sorry Mabel, my mind was elsewhere. You were saying?"

Mabel frowned, tut tutting me. I gave her my best fake smile, and all my attention. Maybe that would make her leave me alone. She cleared her throat and moved in closer toward me.

She stared intensely, her eyes piercing and suddenly full of malice. "I was saying dear, rumour is, your pa has gone bat crazy. Talks to the ghosts he does. Town folk can only assume it's because he is pretty much dead broke, about to lose the famous Brambly Estate. It's pushed him over the edge, so to speak. Such a shame. Surely you knew, and that's why you are really here?"

I stood and began backing away unconsciously. As her lips formed a cruel smile, I felt sick to my core. What the hell was she talking about?

I had to get out of here. The room seemed to be swirling, and I felt claustrophobic. I was at a loss for words, eager to get away from her. But then a thought tamed my compulsion to flee. Meeting her eyes once again, I blurted out the words.

"Mabel, who did you think I was?"

She shook her head, almost now with a look of embarrassment, waving me off with hands decorated in stone rings, each glistening in the sunlight as she moved.

"Oh dear, all Jack's rambling, it must be getting to me. You will have to excuse my brief moment of confusion."

"Mabel? Please."

"You really don't know, Annie?"

She continued looking up at me for what seemed like the longest time. I wanted to slap the smirk right off her face. Instead, I forced myself to swallow the bitter tang in my throat as calmly as I could muster.

"Why Annabelle of course, dear. Your great great gran. Isn't it obvious? You look so alike, and you are wearing her hair clip. You certainly don't see too many of those around here. It's precious and timeless, I believe. She brought a number of those with her from China on Patrick's ship, so the rumour goes."

I glared, growing angrier by the second. I don't even know why I'd worn the hair clip really, but how was any of this her business, anyway?

"Question is Annie, why would a simple migrant have had such beautiful jewellery? Doesn't make sense now, does it. I have always wondered about Annabelle, such an elusive woman she was. People are not always who they seem to be. Brambly Estate holds some deep secrets, I believe."

I welcomed the balmy darkness surrounding the front steps of Brambly Estate. The stars were so vivid tonight, and the full moon beamed all the way to the distant headlands. A calmness had enveloped the land, but it did nothing to ease the chaos in my mind. With my senses being on overload, barely did I register the distant waves or the cicadas doing their best to serenade the evening.

I flicked my lighter on and off, placing the tips of my fingers over the flame for as long as I dared.

All I could see was Mabel's face. I'd been completely blindsided. Why had she looked so complacent when she delivered her venomous words. Mabel had said she was Pa's friend. Yet without question she had wanted me to feel the sting of our reality.

LIAR.

Mabel had seemed to be gloating over the fact Brambly Estate was in trouble.

Was it?

Mum's phone was going straight to message bank, as usual. Normally when alone, I was content. Rarely did I feel lonely or afraid. Tonight, I felt both. I needed to talk to someone but had not a clue who. My friends wouldn't understand, how could they? Truth be told I didn't.

Releasing a sigh, I pulled my hair down from its bun, inspecting the clip.

What the hell do I do now? Was there someone in town who could help? This situation, the mess of Brambly Estate, had obviously been going on for some time. My heart ached even contemplating the reality that Pa was suffering in any way.

I didn't want to believe Mabel. Could she be misinformed? She had seemed so adamant. Money had never been an issue throughout the generations of our family. Everyone knew that. Mum never elaborated but said Annabelle had taken care of the finances, somehow securing our family's ongoing future. As the story goes, she and her husband Patrick were very wealthy on their arrival in Australia.

And what a spin out Mabel had recognised Annabelle's hair clip. My Nan had given it to me just before she died. Unlike the smaller pink clips that were in my hair this morning, this one was blue and gold. One of my most treasured possessions. Nan Georgina had made me promise never to give it away to anyone but family. Staring down at the heirloom, I made a mental note to google the hairpins design when I had the chance.

Earlier tonight I had crept back into Annabelle's old room, careful to wedge the door securely open this time. I'd looked at the old, framed photos through a different lens. She had been so young, so beautifully exotic when she had first arrived in Australia. What was her real story? Why did she leave her family? What would make a young girl travel halfway around the world to start a new life?

I suppose there were similarities between us. I'd never really thought of it. Come to think of it, my nan used to say I was like her. Same silky jet-black hair and high cheekbones, and my frame was petite like hers.

Nan used to say I was a strong spirit just like Annabelle, named after her for a reason. I disagree. Over the last few years, I'd accepted the fact there is nothing strong about my spirit. That was the simple truth of it. It was never more obvious than right now. Here I was, hiding in the comfort of the darkness, hoping the night would swallow me up, rather than confront my Pa about what exactly was happening at Brambly Estate.

Had mum known the situation here after all? Maybe that's why she had sent me, refusing to deal with it herself.

Nan had told me once, that Annabelle had first met Patrick aboard the ship she had journeyed on. He was the captain no less. I had been captivated by my great great grandma's stories from the beginning. I had always relished the nights tucked up in my big four poster bed here. Nan would come in, sit in the old rocking chair by the crackling fire and fill my imagination with her romantic adventures.

Nan was the one person I felt I could really talk to. She would know what to do right now.

I felt guilty again. Why had I not kept in better contact with my grandparents?

My mum, on the other hand, never wanted to talk about our family. Isabelle believed in looking forward, focusing on the future. Mum had left Brambly Bay as soon as she could at 26. Never looked back so she said. Obviously, her dreams had been vastly different to those of her predecessors. Or was there something I was missing?

Mabel had been adamant Brambly Estate held many secrets.

Jolting, piercing screaming interrupted my thoughts. Loud angry voices sliced through the silence of the night. I stood in fright, straining to see above me. Again, I heard voices, more hushed now, but obviously still heated. Who was up there? Had someone entered the house? Surely, I would have seen them. I'd been sitting in the entrance now for at least the last half hour.

Crash. I could just make out the French doors swinging openly in the night air. Hesitantly, I headed inside and straight up the stairs, toward the voices. The door to Annabelle's room was now shut, but who exactly was behind it? Candles lit the hallway, creating shadows in every corner. Silently I crept along the landing, straining to hear through the door.

"Don't you dare tell me that, Jack. I can fix your problem, but you must follow my clues. The answers you need, lie below. Think Jack, think."

"Woman, stop speaking in riddles. I don't want to let our family nor our reputation down any more than you do, but Annabelle, you are infuriating. Just show me what I must do."

"Open your eyes and make haste for time is running out. There are those in Brambly Bay who would like nothing more than to see the fall of my empire. You must stop this."

"Can you write it down, draw me a map, anything. What am I looking for, woman?"

"The answers will be found, when you choose not to look with your eyes, but with your intuition. Annie is the key."

"What the heck does that mean? Stop, where are you going? You can't leave now. I need your help., come back."

Silence.

Then a gut-wrenching sound, one I will never forget.

Pa was sobbing. His cries echoed through the house. I wanted to go to him, but I could not move. Instead, I stayed, resting my head against the closed door. My own silent tears spilled. That poor man.

And why did Annabelle say I was the key?

The key to what?

Without warning, a deep chill swept through the hallway causing me to shiver. As I looked around for its cause, suddenly I was enveloped in complete darkness.

Once again, all the candles had been snuffed out.

I rode feverishly into Brambly Bay for a second time, intent on getting some answers. How, I had no idea. Maybe Mabel would give me something more, not that I knew where to find her even if I did want to see her again.

A deep heaviness weighed me down, causing the ride to seem tedious and even further than last time. It was only 10am, but already nearly 30 degrees. But nothing was going to stop me. It was better than the alternative, staying home and confronting my Pa about what the hell was going on. I knew the time was coming that I had to face facts and do it. Just not today.

I needed a little more courage. Or maybe some more information. Seriously, I needed both.

I had heard her myself and was certain it was Annabelle. Or at least someone pretending to be her. Was that it? Was someone deliberately trying to make my Pa believe he was in fact crazy? Was someone plotting to drive him out of Brambly Estate? The thought made me desperate.

I was a world away in my head as I walked into Stay-a-While Café. Barely noticing the patrons inside, I headed for the same booth as last time. Falling heavily into the leather seat, once again I welcomed both the comfort and coolness of my surroundings. Closing my eyes, I took in the sounds and smells, just forcing myself to breathe a little deeper for a moment before ordering my drink.

Once again someone had slipped into the booth opposite me.

Why did this keep happening here!

"Annie? Are you okay, hon you look a little peaky?"

My eyes flew open. Directly opposite, sat the same waitress I had noticed the other day. She smiled warmly, and despite being a stranger, her face was reassuring. Suddenly, I had an overwhelming urge to spill my guts right here and now. Carrying this load alone was too heavy and all-consuming. But pulling back, I remembered my encounter with Mabel.

"I'm sorry…. I'm not sure I know who you are?"

I could feel the hot sting of tears threatening to escape.

"Oh, nor should you I suppose. Sorry Annie, I'm Stella. My mum is Mabel. I can bet you remember her! And for all the wrong reasons, hmm. I'm sorry about the other day; she gave you quite a shock I'm tipping. I told her she should apologise. Unfortunately, there has been some bad blood running between our families for many generations now. I wish she would just get over it. What is done is done. Most of it is hearsay anyways. Your nan and I, God rest her soul, certainly wanted nothing more. People all make mistakes. But my mum, well I've come to expect she will be bitter about it all until the day she dies, I'm afraid. We disagree on many things."

Was this why my mum fled from Brambly Bay as soon as she could? At least Stella and I could relate to both having mothers we didn't agree with.

"I disagree with my mum heaps too, Stella. So, I get it."

Another waitress delivered a coke and a large chocolate sundae to our booth. Her smile was equally as warm. I opened my mouth to speak, putting my hand up to gesture I had not ordered this. Stella gently took my hand in hers and gave it a squeeze. I felt myself welcoming the human contact.

"Dear child, this is on the house. It is the least we can do. I'm genuinely sorry about the way my mum behaved."

There was nothing I could do to stop my emotions from exploding now. I felt the silent tears mixing with my sweaty skin. Bewilderment reigned. More than that, I felt so weak in character. Why couldn't I just confront my Pa, then help him sort out this mess? Why did I always have to be a wallflower? I mess everything up, always trying too hard to please.

I'd been in Brambly Bay four days already. We had no power, limited running water, and minimal food. The house was falling down around us. Worst of all, my Pa absolutely believed Annabelle was alive and living at Brambly Estate. Yet still, I had said nothing.

Stella reached for my hand again.

"Annie, you look like you have the weight of the world on your shoulders. Would you like me to fill in a few of the missing pieces for you?"

I nodded, unable to find the words as self-loathing took hold. Stella stood abruptly.

"Let's get out of here for a bit then."

We walked silently out to the furthest point of the pier, opposite the café. Sitting under the shade of the rotunda, the strong smell of salty air and the constant lapping waves consumed me momentarily. It felt almost trance-like.

"Annie, knowing what I do of your mum, I'm tipping you're a smart girl. Your Mum and I were not close, but we did attend high school together before she left. I admire what she has made of herself. You must be very proud."

I nodded half-heartedly, staring at the ground. "Yep, she is very clever, and successful, and of course I love her, but she doesn't have much time for me these days."

"That must feel lonely Annie."

I shrugged, why was I spilling to a stranger?

This was not my usual style. *Be careful Annie.*

"Well Annie, I'm sure you can see, things are not as they should be at Brambly Estate. The place has fallen into ruin and is almost unliveable now. I'm sure Annabelle would turn in her grave to see it as it is. Anyhow, your Pa is a kind and lovely man, but stubbornly proud. He refuses help from the town folk. He is broke Annie. I know he used every last cent in medical bills for your grandma. Georgina was a very dear friend of mine. My best actually, despite our friendship being forbidden as I grew up. She was the mother I always wished was my very own.

Stella seemed lost in her thoughts for a while, staring blankly ahead. I sat, lulled somewhat by the seagulls floating on the waves, and the small boats coming and going. This family stuff was a lot to take in.

Why would their friendship be forbidden?

"Does my mum know about what's happening at Brambly Estate, do you think Stella?"

"I would bet absolutely not my dear. Jack is one private man, and I just know he would be mortified this is happening on his watch. Brambly Estate has been the pride of the region for centuries. That in itself has enraged my mother to the core her entire life. But all this secrecy and worry is taking its toll on Jack, Annie. I am very worried about his mental and physical state."

I looked up at Stella. She seemed so genuine, so different from Mabel. I could see why my Nan had liked her so much.

"I'm worried too, Stella. It's the last thing I expected coming here. I've not had the heart to talk to him about it all yet. I want to, but I just can't. He acts like nothing is wrong, yet the house is barely furnished now. We have no electricity. Not to mention the maintenance issues everywhere you look. I can't just leave at the end of next week and go back to my life in Sydney, pretending nothing is wrong."

Stella nodded, seeming to shift uncomfortably on the seat. She cleared her throat before facing me again.

She reached tentatively for my hand. It was warm and comforting.

"Annie, have you noticed your pa acting strangely? Like he is talking to a ghost? Last time I visited, well….I left quite disturbed. Your pa has always been the most honest, straight-up-and-down kind of gentleman one could meet. Certainly, not one to embellish or tell tales. He is a no-nonsense kind of bloke. You know what I mean?"

I looked into Stella's eyes which darted and swirled with emotion as she blinked rapidly. She was anxious, not wanting to upset me with her revelations. Yet little did she know, her words were sadly reassuring. Relief swept over me. I was grateful someone else knew.

"Oh, you mean Annabelle?"

Stella looked shocked.

"Yes, Jack swears to me she has returned and is trying to help him."

I nodded, staring down at my new thongs and bright red toenails. Assuming in her next breath Stella would perhaps suggest a doctor's assessment for Jack or worse sell Brambly Estate. I held my breath.

"Problem is Annie, and this is just between you and me, as I've not told a soul. Jack is telling the truth. I saw Annabelle with my own two eyes, clear as day. I swear she was standing right in front of me. Annabelle looked as beautiful as the day she disappeared, just as I remembered her."

As I climbed the grand staircase the following morning, an invisible force seemed to be opposing my every step forward. A restless unease causing physical stiffness in my limbs. But enough was enough. I had to know, or at least try to discover some answers, and the best place to start would be Annabelle's room. It was time.

Earlier at breakfast, I had been as brave as I could. I had told Pa all about running into his so-called friend Mabel at the café in town. I left out all of the details of course, apart from her good wishes. Pa had firstly looked perplexed, then I could see his anger rising, a rarity in this placid man. He paced the room before sitting closely beside me. His eyes were weary, yet his fists remained clenched.

"She is no friend of mine, nor this family. Mabel Anderson is a troublemaker and a liar. So was her mother, Beth. The two of them made our lives hell with every opportunity. Please, Annie, stay away from her. I need you to promise."

With that he had left abruptly, telling me he was going fishing should I need to find him, and that I was welcome to join, of course. But I had sat frozen in my spot, watching him shuffle away. It made me sad to see him somewhat scattered and further stooped this morning. He looked exhausted, like the weight of the world was crushing him.

I wanted more than anything to tell him it was okay, that he could share his load with me. But I just couldn't.

I needed to find out what the feud between the families had been about, because my bet, it all lead back to Annabelle. What had been big enough to last generations?

And what did Beth have to do with it?

The door to Annabelle's room was wide open. The window too. A fresh summer breeze filled the space with salted air. But there was another smell. I couldn't quite work out where it was coming from. I'd smelt it most nights since my arrival, and it had been particularly strong the night I was locked in Annabelle's room. Only now did I think to investigate further.

I spied the thin whisp of smoke coming from the ornate oriental pot next to the bed. Of course! Incense! Sitting on the soft covers,

I took in the sweet smell. My gran came to mind. She had told me often how Annabelle had insisted the women of the family be taught about its importance and used it at Brambly Estate throughout the ages. She said Annabelle was very passionate about creating her own oils and incense, and in her time her products were well sort after. Mum had refused to use incense at our home. I never knew why. I'd bought some at a local market once. Mum threw it out declaring it was poison.

A forgotten memory surfaced. I'd been helping my Nan change bed sheets upstairs, maybe even this very room, when she had told me a story about the Chinese women in the ancient Qing Dynasty. It had all seemed so magical and glamorous as she had described their love of incense and floral nectars worn by women. Nan had told me it was very common for noble families to use incense burners near their beds. The women would often even soak their clothes in incense or oils to infuse the smell. She said the Qing women believed there was a deep connection between an aroma and the state of one's mind. I tried desperately now to remember the Chinese word she had used to describe a particular incense.

Heang! That's it! Ha, I remember! Nan told me once 'Heang' has six classifications according to the mood its smell creates: noble, refined, beautiful, tranquil, reclusive, or luxurious.

I smiled, impressing myself for once. Touching the small pot I admired its delicate carvings, all the while wondering why my Pa had left it burning in here. Maybe because he knew Annabelle would approve.

"Annie, Annie dear, we are running out of time."

Startled I jumped to my feet, spinning to face the doorway and scanned the room searching for the voice. I dared not move a muscle, straining to hear even the slightest movement or sound.

Nothing came for what seemed like the longest time.

"Annie, please, I need your help. Brambly Estate is in grave danger of being taken from my family. Your family Annie. Only you can help me now. Others I have reached out but have failed."

The woman's voice was faint yet insistent. Strangely I felt as though its sound was swirling, almost bouncing off the walls, not coming from one particular spot. Yet the fact remained, I was alone in here. I forced myself to breathe, again sweeping the room for a sign. Maybe someone was outside the open window? I tentatively moved to peer out, but nothing but the extensive roofline presented.

"My written words, they will tell you all you need to know Annie. I journaled them for Patrick, one day hoping he would return. Find them hidden where the driftwood meets the sand."

I spun back around. Surely someone was playing a joke.

"Who's here? It is not funny whoever you are. Maybe you're trying to make my pa believe he is crazy, but it won't work on me. Now show yourself."

The incense was no longer smoking. The sweet smell was gone, and the same distinct chill I'd felt the other night suddenly filled the room despite the heat of the day.

Feeling annoyed now I ran my fingers through my hair and for the first time noticed the bangles on my wrist. They were exquisite, a pair of gold and turquoise wire-woven bracelets decorated with gems and carved feathers. I had never seen anything like them.

"There are spirits at play Annie. Beware."

"Where the driftwood meets the sand?"

Despite repeating it all afternoon to myself, I was still no closer to discovering what that meant. That could be anywhere along this coastline. Maybe Pa would know. Should I go down to the beach and find him?

I wandered around the gardens, and sat on the old swing for a while, deeply lost in thought.

I wanted Annabelle to come back. If that really was her, why couldn't I see her?

I'd questioned mum about my great great grandma when she had called, but she'd been no help. At least mum had seemed slightly more interested. I didn't dare tell her I was pretty sure Annabelle was here, trying to connect with us. That sounded too insane, yet I was starting to believe it myself.

"Annabelle had disappeared when I was 15, Annie. Then I got out of Brambly Bay myself 13 years after that. I would have gone a lot sooner if I'd been able, let me tell you. It was like the whole town was caught up in the mystery of her whereabouts from what I remember. She went down to the beach one winter's afternoon and simply never came back. I do recall it being quite eerie in the house after that. Honestly, we never knew if she was going to simply walk back through the door. Nainai was quite a mystifying woman at the best of times."

I hadn't heard mum call her that name for ages. Nainai was the Chinese name for grandma.

"Is that why you left mum?"

I waited out the silence that followed.

"No Annie, I just wanted more for my life. A coastal farming town was never my dream. I wanted to make it big. Make a name for myself. You can understand that right Annie? Nainai always supported my dreams, but both women desperately wanted me to stay, and continue the legacy of Brambly Estate, being the only child and all. Mum never quite forgave me for leaving, I don't think. She never really understood who I was."

I still couldn't tell whether mum was telling me the truth. And I couldn't help but feel history was repeating itself. Mum didn't know who I was either. Did I really know her?

"I'm certain Annie, your great great Nainai held some big revelations close to her chest. There was more to her story. My reporter instincts tell me that. In the nights before her disappearance, she began to share about her life in China. I remember feeling like she wanted to unleash a burden. She had made me swear to keep it all to myself. But then, she simply vanished. I just never quite got to the bottom of what it was. We never did get to finish our conversation."

"It could have been a number of things Annie. Annabelle was devastated that her great love Patrick never returned himself, and then there was Beth's betrayal. That must have stung her deeply. Last thing Annabelle said to me was that she wanted to show me a room. A place that was of great importance to her."

Suddenly mum had my full attention. I couldn't believe what I was hearing. And mum never thought to tell me this? I paced the garden with my phone pressed against my ear. "Wait what? Hang on mum, go back, tell me again? Can you share exactly what she told you?"

"Oh Annie, that inquisitive mind of yours, I love it. But I have to go now. I'm due in the studio soon. And listen, honey, sorry to do this to you, but you are going to have to stay in Brambly Bay a little longer."

"Mum no! mum, did you hear what I was saying before, something is not right here. You need to come back."

"Annie don't be so dramatic. Pa will be just fine. He is a tough one. So, I will need you to stay most likely another month. I think it's a good thing for you Annie. Oh, sorry honey, I'm getting called in by my team. Got to run now, I love you, Annie. Wish me luck and watch me on the news!"

With that, the phone had gone dead.

Even though that was hours ago now, my mind still reeled.

What happened to Annabelle's husband?

What betrayal was she talking about? Did mum mean Beth, as in Mabel's mum? Nan had spoken of her a few times.

Had that been the beginning of the feud between the families?

I placed the ornate hair clips and pair of bangles in the middle of the plastic table and waited. I'd made a salad for dinner, despite my lack of appetite, I hoped Pa would be back from his fishing trip soon. Typically, I was dictating the worst-case scenario in my head as I waited.

How much should I say? Was overstepping?

I desperately didn't want to upset Pa. But too many strange things were happening here. Surely, the jewellery would serve as a conversation starter. Not that I had a rational explanation as to how the pieces ended up on my body.

I spend so much of my life second guessing what I should say, or how I should act. It was infuriating. I shook my head, determined from this moment things would be different. It was time I grew up.

Soon Pa wandered in, windblown and tired. I poured him a cup of tea and found some chocolate biscuits. He sat heavily, letting out a sigh. But still, he smiled at me, winking.

Maybe I should wait?

No. I need to be brave. I'd been here a week now, and the air between us was getting thicker. Was it just me who noticed?

"Pa, can I ask you about a few things?"

He looked up at me for the longest time, then cast a long glance at the jewellery on the table. Silently he picked up the bangles, clearly confused.

"Annabelle's mother gave these to her when she journeyed to Australia. Annabelle wore them all the time. Where on earth did you find these? We never saw them again after Anabelle disappeared."

Although still offering a weakened smile, his dull eyes said it all. Pa's chin began to tremble. I reached over for his hand, and he began to sob.

"I don't know what to do, Annie."

Never had I imagined this moment, yet here we were. It almost felt like a turning point for me. Normally I would back away from a situation like this, but not today. Instead, I felt suddenly empowered rather than fearful of confrontation. Perhaps it was out of protection for this dear man. Pa was my family, and he needed me. For the first time in my life, I saw myself as stronger than my mum. I wasn't going to run away as she had.

I took a deep breath. Guess I might as well dive right in.

"Pa, I can't understand it, and it doesn't make any rational sense, but I think, well somehow, Annabelle is trying to help us sort out the problem here at Brambly Estate, I mean. I need you to trust me and tell me everything you know. I believe she is trying to show us a way out, save us from losing Brambly Estate. I want you to know Pa, you are not alone in this anymore."

Pa covered his face with his hands. His frail body shook violently, his tears seemingly releasing years of pent-up anguish. Finally, he stilled, sinking further into his chair. I sat quietly, picking at my nails, chewing on the inside of my gums, hoping I'd done the right thing. I couldn't look at him.

"So, you believe me then. No one else in this town does. They all think I'm crazy, Annie. Don't blame 'em. I don't know when it first started. A few weeks back now, maybe more. Annabelle's visits I mean. She is back all right. Sometimes I see her, sometimes I just feel her presence or hear her calling to me. I've never been one to believe in all that ghost mumbo jumbo, so I've been a little slow accepting it meself to be honest. But Annie, I know she is here."

I clasped his hands in mine again, relieved we were finally talking.

"I totally believe you, Pa. I saw her myself, and I heard her the other day, upstairs. I didn't want to believe all this, but it's happening alright. And this jewellery, somehow, I think she wanted me to have these for a reason. Pa, what has happened to Brambly Estate? Why haven't you told mum?"

"I'm a proud man Annie. I didn't want to worry you lot, and well, I never meant to let the property get to this state. I'm so ashamed. I've run out of money. I'm too old to farm our land anymore, and I've nothing left to employ anyone to help. When your nan had her cancer treatment, we used every last cent to keep her alive. It is a bastard of an illness that. Was it not enough to take my dear Georgina? My best friend was stolen, just like that. Your nan was my life Annie, my greatest love. But her cancer didn't stop with just her; it took both our lives."

Again, Pa began to cry, silently this time. He didn't seem angry, just simply defeated. I felt the ache in my throat. Fumbling for words, I felt helpless to know what to do next. Yet as completely contradictory to this moment as it was, I also had a strong sense I was meant to be at Brambly Estate right now. That somehow, I was part of the solution.

"I sold everything I could trying to keep this place. I made a promise to Annabelle. She said I must keep Brambly Estate and its treasure in the family. She knew one day you would return and love it like your own. Not that you had even been born then, so it was bloody confusing let me tell you. In the days before she disappeared, she told me as much. I thought her bat crazy back then to be honest. Yet a part of me knew the truth about her. She was a spiritual woman, who stated often she could foretell the future. She was the bravest, toughest yet most mysterious woman I'd ever met. So loyal to her family. None of us knew her real story, I'm sure."

I sat up a little straighter, then I leant in, eyeing Pa more closely.

"Me? What have I got to do with this? Are you kidding? And what treasure do you mean Pa?"

"Steady on there, girl. I don't think there is any treasure, Annie. Annabelle was very evasive, never telling us exactly what it was, but she was adamant it existed. After Annabelle disappeared, we searched relentlessly. There were always rumours Annabelle had brought a fortune with her from China. Maybe she used it all to buy Brambly Estate. Who knows, Beth could have made it all up. She was once Annabelle's best friend you know, before she became the worst possible enemy. I hate that family. I know that much. Bloody troublemakers the lot of them. Mabel made me another offer, just a few days before you arrived to buy Brambly Estate. You mark my words lassie; I'll burn this place to the ground before the likes of them get their paws on it. I know Annabelle would support me on that, too."

I sat wide-eyed. This was a lot to take in, a lot to comprehend. Was Pa rambling now, or was there truth to this whole treasure thing? Why would Beth know about the treasure? And what the hell did Pa mean when he said Annabelle told him I held the key to the resolution.

"And now Annie, she is back. Annabelle keeps telling me she has the solution. But her messages are too cryptic for an old bugger like me. I need your help, Annie. Please."

I stared down at his old leathery hands, squeezing them reassuringly in the hope of offering him some peace, not that I felt any myself. He squeezed mine back.

"Pa, where does the driftwood meet the sand?"

He froze, then suddenly looked up intently at me. His piercing blue eyes had instantly come to life, and his cheeks flushed. He searched my face with silent questions, all the while nodding with increasing enthusiasm.

"I know the spot, Annie. It's the place that saved Annabelle's life before she nearly lost it again."

Adrenaline and excitement kept us moving. For the first time since coming here, I felt completely present. This was exactly where I wanted to be and despite the circumstances, it felt really satisfying. Was it because I felt valued? I knew Pa believed in me and needed my help. So did Annabelle it seemed. Yet did I really know enough about Annabelle to trust her? I wanted to, that much I knew. But something still didn't sit right.

My lighter had remained in the pocket of my jacket all night. I felt alive without the sting of a burn for the first time I could remember.

I dared not even imagine being the one to find the right clues to help us save Brambly Estate, yet truth be told I could think of little else. I was filled with nervous but hopeful energy.

What was it I was even looking for?

I was running on basically no sleep from last night, as was Pa by the looks of him. I'd done everything in my power this morning to persuade him to rest, to convince him I could go alone. But I knew my words had fallen on deaf ears. Pa was a stubborn old bugger.

Not that I blamed him, nothing could have kept me away either.

It took us nearly an hour. The track heading through the bracken and low scrub was overgrown and at times it seemed like not a track at all. But Pa had insisted he knew the way. I trusted him. I wished I'd worn long pants as he'd advised. The sword grass was cutting my legs, and the marsh fly bites relentless.

"No one much has used this here path for a long while Annie. Some people say, on the day Annabelle disappeared, she was last sighted making this very trek. Who knows really? What say we ask her when she decides to show up again ha?"

I tried to imagine what Annabelle must have felt. Had she stood in this very spot?

Pa's laughter swirled around us with the wind, mixing with the squarks of the seagulls. For a moment I felt at peace but just as quickly my smile faded. His laughter took a dark turn into a raspy cough, making him unsteady on his feet as he gasped for breath. Lunging forward I caught him just in time before he fell. I held on tightly despite his attempts to push me away.

"Pa, let's stop for a sec. Nothing is worth you getting sick. Just tell me the way and I will keep going. It's really hot, maybe you could rest here a bit?"

I handed him the water from my backpack, all the while never letting go of him as he shook.

"I've lived here me whole bloody life girl, I know it like the back of me hand. I also know today is not the day I'm carking it. I intend to find this bloody treasure first, buy me self a big fat steak, some beer and see Brambly Estate secure. Then I'm happy to fall off the perch. You got that Annie? Now stop ya fussing."

Pa stood taller; I could tell his bravado was false. I loved this man. He deserved a good life. He deserved to find Annabelle's treasure. I removed my hands from his arm, smiling warmly as I nodded, gesturing him to lead us on.

Keeping a close eye on Pa, we navigated the steep terrain down the cliff edge onto the rocks and sand below. The sea was wild today, its white capped waves and ocean spray spasmodic and its noise deafening. We stood side by side, mesmerised by its power. A sea hawk circled above us; it too looking for its prize.

How Annabelle possibly could have survived jumping overboard, then washing up on this shore all those years ago, was simply mind-blowing.

'Over there Annie'

Following Pa's sight line, I saw it. A huge piece of driftwood, as big as a small tree, firmly standing tall in the beginnings of the dunes.

'Where the driftwood meets the sand.'

My words were but a whisper and swiftly dissipated in the wind before barely being voiced.

Pa was away, moving quite quickly now. I followed him closely, struggling in the uneven sand. I never was one for the beach; it just was so uncomfortable on every level to me. Again, I tried to imagine Annabelle's elation when she had first sighted this driftwood. The day Annabelle had first touched the sand here was early hours in the morning, so Pa had told me. She had been on the small ship for nearly 2 weeks prior to jumping overboard. Then she endured hours in the pitch-black, unpredictable ocean, being thrown around in every direction by the sea.

Could I ever be that brave?

Standing here now in the very spot she had been, fighting to keep her family safe. I felt a deep kinship and almost obligation to Annabelle. It suddenly became important to me that I could be. Somehow, I wanted to connect with her, make my great great Grandmother proud. Was that weird? I wanted to show Annabelle I was as bold as her. That I would fight to honour her legacy.

Did these qualities even exist inside of me?

"So, I suppose we dig hey Annie. I should have asked Annabelle to bloody get whatever it is we are looking for, herself."

Pa was smiling, scratching his head, wiping the perspiration away from under his hat. I pulled myself back into the present.

'My bet, Pa, is that we are looking for her journal. She told me we would find the clues we needed in there. Did you ever see her writing in one?'

'All the bloody time Annie. She would sit up in her room for hours writing. Must be a collection of them somewhere I'm tipping.'

Searching avidly for any clue that might help us, I scanned every inch of the driftwood. But reality was, if there was something Annabelle had hidden out here all that time ago, it was either long gone or very carefully hidden.

'Just going to rest for a bit first Annie, I'll be back in business soon love. I just need to sit me bones down here for a few shakes.'

Watching as Pa headed over to a shaded dune, he sheltered himself from the wind, laying back against the grassy slope, before pulling his hat down over his face.

I knelt in front of the wooden structure, touching the smooth wood with anticipation, trying to imagine what Annabelle must have felt in those first moments of being here. I closed my eyes, all consumed with wonder and the roar of the ocean surrounding us.

'Annie'

Startled, jolting from my thoughts, my eyes flew open. Right behind her circled a sea hawk letting out a shrill call.

Frozen, I stared at the beautiful, magnificent, timeless woman, close enough to touch.

Annabelle.

She smiled at me. Her stance was strong against the swirling wind. Her ivory silk dress so striking, like nothing I'd ever seen. Her glistening ebony hair danced around her sparkling eyes.

'Dig here Annie. Deep below you will find a large tin. I buried it here before I left, for Patrick, should he ever return. But I understand he has travelled beyond this world now. Very soon I will join him. You are the one Annie; it is you who needs to read it now. Hurry child, Brambly Estate is running out of time, I am afraid, so is our dear Jack.'

I looked away from Annabelle for the briefest moment, following her gaze over to my Pa. He slept peacefully unaware she was here at all. A million questions filled my mind. There was so much I needed Annabelle to explain. But as I turned back to face her again, she was gone.

What did she mean Jack was running out of time?

"The spirits are calling him home Annie. They are calling to Jack".

Annabelle's voice swirled in the wind.

The old, rusted tin had captured my full attention. With no particular markings, and similar in size to a shoebox, it adorned the table space between us. A small padlock still secured its metal façade, despite its years underground.

'Well Annie, you ready?'

How could I not be? I could hardly sit still so high was my anticipation. Pa had his screwdriver ready to break the lock, his boyish grin making him appear 10 years younger. I silently prayed that this box contained the answers we so desperately needed.

"Go for it, Pa."

A harsh knock on the door abruptly pulled us from our moment. We both jumped, staring at each other for a long second before Pa nodded.

He stood, grabbing the box, and stashing it swiftly under the kitchen sink. Shuffling out, he headed down the long hallway toward the entrance palour, screwdriver still in hand. I followed, annoyed at the interruption.

'Hello Jack, hello Annie. Sorry for the unannounced visit Jack. I was wondering if I could come in for a chat?"

I had no idea who the men in cheap suits dominating the entrance were, but something told me they were not here to admire the view. I watched Pa stiffen. The larger man fiddled uncomfortably, fumbling to retrieve some papers from his briefcase. The other younger man craned his neck to get a glimpse inside. Pa folded his arms, blocking the door further. I copied his stance protectively.

'You have no business being here Mr Stanton. My time is not up yet. I've received the letter you sent. I'm aware I have till the end of the month, and that's still 9 days away.'

What the hell was he talking about?

Pa's chin lifted, his jaw visibly tightening. His face reddened as he continued to stare, moving his glare between Mr Stanton and the nameless man. Mr Stanton's plastered smile remained, yet his colleague looked at the ground. I edged closer beside Pa. Whatever was going on here was my business too now and suddenly I felt very defensive.

"Jack, please. You need to be reasonable here. We have it on good authority you will be unable to make your payment by then. We just wanted to offer you a solution. Put your mind at rest that we are on your side mate. Can we come inside to chat?"

I watched Pa step further into the man's personal space; his agitation radiated. He cleared his throat, flexing his fingers repeatedly.

"Mr Stanton, we both know you are not my mate. All you people want is to run us off this land. You always have. I know you are friendly with the likes of the Anderson family. Mabel has been in my face about buying Brambly Estate for years. Never will they set foot on my land. Not after what Beth did to Annabelle all those years ago.'

I could see Pa waning; his anger was causing him to shake now. He was rolling up his sleeves and loosening his collar. Just what was he planning to do?

The man took a step back and put his hands up defensively.

'Jack, please just hear us out. We have a very substantial offer here. In fact, it's more than generous. Does it really matter if it's the Andersons who purchase it? Just think, your worries will be over Jack, don't you think that's what your daughter and lovely granddaughter here deserve?"

Mr Stanton smiled broadly at me, the most insincere gesture I'd ever witnessed. His colleague fumbled in his attempt to hand over a contract of sale.

Then I saw her. Just beyond, resting by the shade of a pillar on the veranda, graceful yet purposeful in her presence. Annabelle was watching the men, then stared directly at me, nodding like I would understand what to do.

Was I the only one who could see her?

I don't know how, but meeting her eyes instantly empowered me. This moment brought powerful clarity and somehow, I knew.

I was courageous enough; I had been all along.

I stepped in front of Pa, snatching the paperwork from the dweeb's hand. He went to speak, but remained silent, mouth agape.

"As my Pa has told you, we will not be selling Brambly Estate gentlemen. Not now, not ever. So, here's what is going to happen. You're going to get off our land immediately. Then you can go directly and tell Mabel we will not be selling. We will contact you at the end of the month, Mr Stanton."

With that, I ripped the paperwork into shreds. My mouth formed a smile, but my eyes did not. I pulled Pa back inside and slammed the door in their faces.

Nothing had ever felt so right.

It had to be close to midnight as I crept toward the kitchen. Again, sleep would not come. Pa had been a mess after Mr Stanton had left. He retired hastily to his room and asked me to leave him be. His sagging posture and unsteadiness portrayed his defeat and wounded pride.

I had a monster headache, no doubt caused by my relentless internal conflict and my inability to focus on anything else. It sucked, I felt exhausted yet totally wired all at once. I slumped down at the kitchen table, shoving a biscuit in my mouth.

Flicking my lighter on, I scorched the edge of a fresh biscuit before shoving it into my mouth, barely tasting its sweetness.

Was Pa going to survive this? Let's face it, the situation was escalating so darn quickly.

Barely noticing my actions, I took comfort in the sting of the flame as I moved my lighter along the tips of my fingers. Back and forth the tiny flame danced, just long enough for me to feel its scold.

Angrily, I pushed the lighter across the table.

Focus Annie, surely, you can at least do that.

Pa had known about the eviction date, so why had he agreed for me to come here over the summer? Perhaps he really had believed Annabelle when she had told him I was the one to save us from this mess.

Grabbing the box we'd stashed under the kitchen sink, I placed it again in the middle of the table. Bloody hell, it better be good. The turbulence all this was causing, was nothing short of torment.

Stuff it, I could stare at it no longer. I decided to open it right now. No time like the present. Picking up the screwdriver Pa said would do the trick, I jammed it into the rusty lock.

The stiff lid took some pulling to open, and when I finally pried it ajar, rust crumbled and flaked across the table. A damp, earthy smell filled the kitchen. I was crazy nervous and excited.

It was now or never.

Carefully I pulled out the box's contents one by one, placing the items on the kitchen table. A pocket watch, some paperwork, tobacco tin, reading glasses, some photos and a small leather-bound book. A surreal stillness hemmed me in as I focused on Annabelle's belongings. Surrounded in just a flicker of light, my heartbeat pounded in my chest almost making me feel like I vibrated from the inside out.

There was no way I'd be sleeping tonight. I had to admit, this was one of the coolest things I'd ever done. I was energized and awake, buzzing with adrenaline. Picking up the photos I was mesmerised at the sight of Annabelle, her arms were linked tightly with her beloved Patrick. He looked so handsome in his dark double buttoned sea uniform. They stood proudly at the front of a ship, Patrick's vessel no doubt.

I continued to flick through the memories. Wedding photos and baby Charlotte, she was my great grandmother. I recognised all of them from the portraits which adorned the walls of the staircase at Brambly Estate.

How had their love story gone so wrong?

Nan had told me when Patrick disappeared so suddenly, he had left his personal belongings behind, which obviously added to the mystery and weight of the theory it was foul play. Annabelle had kept them safe all these years.

Why was Annabelle so sure he would know to find them at the Driftwood?

Then another thought struck me. The day she had buried this tin, had that been her last alive?

The book felt cold and smooth, sparking a chill of anticipation to course through my veins. It was bound with a thin leather strap, holding its precious contents safe. I was busting to burst it open, yet apprehension waned.

If this very book had the information Annabelle wanted me to find, then I couldn't back out, could I? It really was all on me. And that felt like a lot. But then, out of nowhere, I sensed her presence. Annabelle's familiar scent suddenly surrounding me, helped me relax a little.

Getting overwhelmed now isn't going to help anyone, Annie.

The pages were stiff, they smelt earthy, almost mouldy, yet still laced with the spicy infusion of incense. Turning the paper carefully, I caught my breath as I focused on a single image, the only marking on the first page. Curiously, the 'house looking' symbol was similar to my birthmark, no mistaking it.

How was this possible?

Then to my absolute horror, looking further into the book I realised the script was written in Chinese. Annabelle's handwriting was scrawly, black ink inscriptions filling page after page. None of it made any sense to me. I only knew the smallest amount of Chinese, always promising myself I'd learn more but never quite getting around to it.

"No! What the hell"

I knew my voice was too loud as I jumped from my chair and began pacing. I dare not wake Pa, but this was ridiculous. Tension reigned, tightening my neck and shoulders. Unconsciously I began to rub my brow as if that would somehow ward off this headache.

Staring out the window, another still starry night enveloped the land. I pulled the journal to my chest and closed my eyes.

Think Annie.

Suddenly my eyes flew open as I felt the book being pulled from my grip. Flinching, I stumbled back, clutching on as best I could.

"Give it to me Annie, I shall read it to you child."

And just like that, there she was again, smiling at me like this was all normal and part of the plan. I blinked rapidly, just to make sure she was real.

'Hello Annabelle.'

I whispered, my voice real enough, but my mind still somewhat disbelieving. Fixated on her, time seemed to slow down. When she smiled, Annabelle glowed the softest yellow, almost sparkling around the edges of her frame. Was that her aura? It made her look different to the last time I'd seen her. Annabelle seemed peaceful, mesmerising and confusing me.

'You have done well, Annie. Now let us save Brambly Estate shall we.'

January 1986

'My dearest love. I have failed you and never shall I forgive myself. I have searched day and night for you, but to no avail. I write this in the hope that someday you will return to us and this, my journal will help you understand events since your disappearance. Patrick, Charlotte and I will remain at Brambly Estate until the day you come for us. My dearest husband, I hope that day to be soon. Danger surrounds us and I fear for our lives.'

Annabelle looked so sad as she read aloud. The dim light of the candle seemed to magnify the intensity of her black eyes; her voice was soft, barely more than a whisper, laced with raw emotion.

I sat, cross legged, hanging on her every word. My rational brain still battled to cope with all this as I fought to quash the internal questions.

I had little choice but to believe at this moment I was in fact, face to face with a ghost.

Annabelle all but caressed her journal as she continued.

'Annabelle, I don't mean to interrupt, but can I ask questions along the way? What lies beneath? Beneath where?'

My great great grandma stared vacantly at me for the longest time, almost trance-like. It was eerie as her eyes became smoky in appearance then appeared to glisten. Without answering she continued.

'You were right from the beginning Patrick. Beth had betrayed us. She was not to be trusted. I told her about our real story Patrick. Please forgive me. I thought she was helping me, but all along she was the enemy. I believe now it was Beth who had tipped off whoever has taken you, that we are of such wealth. Then she took our child.'

Raising my eyebrows and leaning in closer still, I knew I needed to rein in my impatience. This sudden revolution had left me fighting to maintain my composure, but I had to make sure I didn't scare Annabelle away.

'Is that what this generational feud is all about? What did you tell her that was so significant?'

Again, Annabelle stared forward and smiled sadly. Obviously plagued with painful memories she appeared to be halting her speech to gain control of her own emotions before continuing to read.

'Patrick, Beth led me back to the spot on the beach. The one you had once told me about, where the driftwood meets the sand. I was barely alive when I finally found it, but that was nothing compared to what was coming. I was being watched that day, easy prey. Men grabbed me, swiftly bundling me into the very same horse and cart which had delivered me to the boat heading for Tasmania only weeks earlier. Beth's cart. Yet this journey was far different. This time, I was a prisoner. Beth watched as the men tied me up in the cellar of Anderson Estate. She acted as though a stranger, never once meeting my eye. Yet soon I was to see a side of Beth I never thought possible. She demanded our jewels and treasure, in exchange for Charlotte's life. Beth said we owed her. She also said, should I attempt to cross her, Charlotte would suffer the same fate you had.'

Unconsciously bringing my knees to chest, I was gripping myself so tightly my knuckles had turned white. Almost staring without seeing, every word she spoke swirled inside me. Then blinking rapidly, I found myself suddenly straining to see Annabelle. Was her presence fading? She seemed more like a silhouette of wispy smoke.

'The memory, it is just too distressing Annie. I cannot continue. You my dear child, you must take it from here.'

Then Annabelle was gone. Her journal remained open beside me, her candle barely flickering.

What was I supposed to do now?

So, Beth had betrayed her best friend, for money no less. But there was more to it, I was sure now. Why on earth would Mabel believe this was all on Annabelle? She must have known Beth was delusional.

Was Beth also responsible for the death of Patrick? That's what she insinuated all right. But Annabelle had never given up hope he was still alive, so it seemed.

And what was it Annabelle gave her in exchange for Charlotte?

I felt like I was going to explode.

I needed to see Stella again. Mabel would be even better, but she wasn't about to help, this much I knew.

Erratically, unable to sit still, I went up to Annabelle's room, pacing and reliving each word she had spoken. Once near the open window I suddenly noticed the dawn birdsong had begun drifting in, and the rosy hue now blanketing the early morning sky. That was all the motivation I needed.

Almost running down the stairs, I raced outside, grabbing mum's old bike from the shed.

Sighing, Stella sat heavily. I couldn't help but wonder, was it the intense morning heat, or the long-term exhaustion of this saga causing her to appear so depleted? I hoped I wasn't bringing up too many bad memories. I had little choice, however.

"I'm not sure I can help you, Annie. As I said, this feud runs deep. Been going on for as long as I can bloody remember. Whatever really went down between Annabelle and Beth, well, truth be told, I've come to accept we may never know.'

Frustrated I kicked at the sandy pier flooring, splintering the wood. We sat together in the exact spot we had last time, yet today the wind swirled uncomfortably around us, and sand particles felt gritty in my eyes. Surely there had to be something Stella knew which would help. And where the hell was Annabelle? She seemed to only appear as it suited her. Well, it sure wasn't suiting *me* right now that she was nowhere to be found. How did the ghost thing work anyway? Was it similar to a genie? Could I summons Annabelle? The thought made me chuckle with its insanity. I knew my great great gran well enough to know, no one summoned her, ever.

Stella continued to stare ahead, unrattled by the wildness of the elements.

"The hate in our family toward Annabelle, well, it was intense. My mum, good old Mabel was adamant she was solely responsible for cursing our family. Beth had purchased more land not long after Patrick had disappeared. How she afforded it, I will never know. That land backs onto Brambly Estate to this day. Beth had grand plans to build her empire from potato, barley, and wheat crops. From what I can gather, she was very envious of the wealth and prestige surrounding Brambly Estate, their crops were thriving and business booming. But year after year disaster struck, burnt and poisoned crops, locust plagues, and suspiciously just on her parcel of land. Other farms were not affected…… She believed Annabelle was the cause. She told everybody who would listen that it was Annabelle who had cursed her."

'It doesn't make sense, Stella."

"Who knows Annie. There were some pretty serious rumours, and some even more damaging accusations to follow. But it was all so long ago. Things get twisted and turned, embellished, and forgotten. Maybe it is best we leave it alone.'

"I wish I had that choice, Stella. I sure didn't ever imagine my summer like this. I don't know what to do honestly.'

Stella forced a smile, but her eyes spoke her truth. "I get that Annie. I remember Mabel saying after the incident between her and Beth, if we can call it that, Annabelle used to recite the same words over and over each time they crossed paths.

'*May you live in interesting times, Beth.*'

I stood, almost pacing in front of Stella, my thoughts were running wild.

If only I could turn back time.

And if that were the curse…it sure didn't sound that bad to me.

Stella was squinting, attempting to block the strong morning sun as she followed my movement.

'Georgina, your Nan once told me she believed the feud, or the incident as such, was not all about wealth. Both Annabelle and Beth loved Patrick…… so the story goes."

Shuffling back a step or two, for a split second my breathing was suspended. With a sudden racing heart, my skin tingled.

Nothing was more powerful than a woman scorned, so they say.

Anderson Estate 1927
Beth
Black Envy

I watched with pure delight, as Charlotte played contently on the picnic rug I'd placed so carefully in the shade of our oak trees. How they had grown over the years, seemingly made for a little child to be under.

This perfect child.

She was much like her mother. Her porcelain skin flawless, ebony hair which gleamed in the dappled sunlight, and those eyes. Just like Annabelle's, they were almost black, fanned with thick long lashes, and wildly luminous.

Unlike them, my own strands of mousey hair swirled around my plain aging face. This land, and the harshness of farming life, mirrored my appearance. Attempting to tame my curls, I pushed them back into my bun; they too, like me, wanted to be free to dance in the wind. I brushed my hands over the hair clip securing it tightly. This little treasure had been an unexpected gift from Annabelle, not long after she had arrived at Brambly Estate. Dear naive Annabelle.

I would never have owned something so lovely without this gift; why was it to be her who had the riches? Were the rest of us undeserving?

As a little girl, I had dreamt of a life entirely different.

I longed to look like Annabelle. Exotic, mysterious, so very powerful it seemed, and sure of who she was.

Everything I was not.

Much like the entire town, I was captivated by Annabelle from the first moment I saw her. To outsiders, we had grown to be best friends over the years. Honestly, I had wanted so desperately for this to be the truth of it. Living on the land can be lonely, and a new friend seemed like just the antidote.

But the truth was, I hated her.

Despised everything she was, and all she had.

Why did she come to Australia? And why did she have to pick my town?

I was town darling before her. Even Patrick was starting to warm to my charm. Those pitiful town folk traitors. We'd had a long history of anti-Chinese prejudice before Annabelle. Yet that all seemed to be forgotten when she swanned in and cast her spell.

Well, I haven't forgotten.

Annabelle had become like a thick tar running through my veins, blackening me from the inside out. How much longer could I prevent the cracks from appearing, the seething hate to erupt from within, I dared not think.

These days, my thoughts both unsettled me greatly, yet kept me alive, and with purpose. How I relished the secret plans to destroy Annabelle and her empire. Evil plots I'd never thought possible by Beth Anderson.

Elimination. On this land, only the strong survive.

Annabelle didn't belong here.

Shaking my thoughts aside, I forced myself to focus on the present moment. Surveying my surrounding property there was no question, it was beautiful, peaceful, almost perfect. Yet it would never be enough for me.

All just a shadowy façade. People were so easily fooled.

Distantly I could hear the roar of the ocean, and closer in, the screeching of the cockatoos forever fighting over my fruit trees. Despite not being able to see it, I knew Brambly Estate and all its grandeur was nestled just a little further beyond my land. I could smell its wealthy stench.

'You should be my baby, shouldn't you dear Charlotte. You would like that, wouldn't you, my love.'

I knelt beside her, as she grinned up at me, snatching the rattle from my hand. I had collected so many baby goods. Instantly the familiar ache in my stomach returned. My mind led me to the vacant upstairs bedroom. The one I had so meticulously created for my baby's nursery. For so many years now, I had lived silently with heartache, longing for my own child.

I blamed my husband. He'd promised me the world. Stupid man. Behind closed doors a greedy and selfish man, a closet alcoholic. Yet he presented to the world as our town's prestigious, and powerful mayor. Most of the time he barely noticed me. I hated the way he looked and smelt. I revolted at his every touch. All secretly of course. I had appearances to keep up. I wanted the lifestyle, and I would do as I needed to get it. As far as the world was concerned, onlookers would be sure to marvel both at our happiness, and success as a couple. We were the leaders, the influencers, the elite of Brambly Cove. Annabelle was threatening my power.

'We just need to convince your daddy, dear Charlotte. Patrick, I want as my own. He is the man for me. Worldly, charming, handsome. He would surely take me away from this town. I could sail the world, see new places, live the life I've always dreamt I would. I am working on it beautiful girl, soon he will adore me. Captain Patrick will come around. Once I rid the world of your mother, and my disgusting husband, everything will be just perfect. I have such grand plans for us my child. My dear Charlotte, you will see.'

Despite my venomous words, I deliberately kept my tone light and airy, almost song-like, so as to not upset this perfect child. We needed to build trust after all.

Sitting close to Charlotte, I took in her sweet scent. I'd been quick to bath her, ridding the terrible incense smell Annabelle cherished so much. Now the breeze caught the aroma of lavender and lemon. The oil creation sourced from my very own garden. Much more fitting to our Australian landscape I believed.

"We are not in China now, are we, dear Charlotte. So, we don't need to smell like that foul country, do we now. Luckily you are only half Chinese dear little one. The rest we can certainly rid you of over time."

I tickled her and she giggled again, rolling onto her side, chubby legs dancing in the air. Oh, how I loved the sound of her happiness. My own laughter was perhaps a little too malicious now, but Charlotte seemed not to notice.

My sweet baby girl would never even remember Annabelle.

Brambly Estate 2017
Annie
The stranger

Agitated, I moved from room to room. Searching for something, anything that might help me find this stupid treasure. That's if it even existed.

I'd not seen Annabelle for two days now.

Mum had been no help. Finally, she had picked up the phone, after I'd left about a dozen messages. But again, it was like she wasn't listening. She openly detached from my situation every time.

Why?

Even from the other side of the world she could manage to make me feel unheard, like I didn't matter. I rubbed at my itching and irritated skin. Earlier I had counted to 10 as the small flame had tortured my forearm; its intense pain voided mum's voice in my head.

I didn't want to be weighed down by resentment.

Were other parents like her? Was my mum really so self-absorbed she could not see her family needed her here? As I wandered around this morning, mounting frustration was fogging up my brain.

Maybe, I should have told her as much, voiced the words I fought to keep so carefully tucked away.

'Annabelle, if you are here, it would be a really good time to show up.'

I looked around. Defeatism surged as I spoke aloud to no one in particular. This sure was one big house when you were all alone. Now it echoed as so much of the old furnishings had been removed. Room after room of nothingness. I wanted so much more for Pa. This was not a home anymore.

He had gone into town for supplies. Or so he said.

Stepping out through the French doors on the lower level, I let the morning sun warm my skin. Eyes closed, I breathed a little deeper, stretching and letting the ocean's scent fill my lungs. Releasing some of the oppression from within felt good.

'Annabelle, please. Please come back. I really need to talk to you.'

'Hmm, I hate to tell you, but she hasn't been seen for around 30-something years. Don't know if she will be home today either.'

Reeling back, my eyes flew open in shocked surprise. As they adjusted to the light, they locked onto the lone figure leaning casually against the entrance pillar. How had I not heard him approach? I felt the sting of intense heat creep up my body and flush my face. He smiled, with a questioning smirk, his eyes dancing with amusement. Clearly, I was the butt of his joke.

I wanted to speak, but as usual, nothing came to mind. I felt annoyed, embarrassed, yet strangely curious. Brushing his shoulder length blond hair out of his face, I was drawn immediately into the intensity of his blue eyes as he looked at me. His tanned muscles glistened with sweat under his black tank top. And that smile, it seemed to light up his chiselled features.

I considered my own appearance, daring not to look down at myself. Jean shorts, old Nivana tank top, bare feet, crazy bun hair. I felt my red face gain more heat. If only I could be swallowed up right now. Aware my hoodie was inside, and my burns could be exposed, I kept my arm protectively behind my back.

"You have just got to be Annie! I'm Tommy. I hang out here a bit helping your Pa. Is he around?"

For the first time in my life, I stuttered. His voice was smooth as honey.

"I'm, well, I'm obviously aware Annabelle is long gone. I was just, well, kind of venting. I'm not crazy if that's what you're thinking."

"Not my business, Annie. You can talk to whoever ya want, chickee. No judgement here."

He waved his hands casually in the air.

I wanted to wipe the smirk from his face yet found myself swept up by his immediate charm. Typical surfy type. So different to any boy I'd dated. How clichéd. Small town surfer boy meets city girl. I forced my focus, rolled my eyes and stood a little straighter, willing my brain to de clutter and come up with a clever reply. I was normally better than this.

'So, is he?"

Startled from my thoughts, our eyes locked on like magnets. He continued to smile, his body language relaxed, his curls dancing in the breeze. I, on the other hand, felt like a rigid soldier, heading into battle in a foreign land. Suddenly I didn't know what to do with my hands. I unfolded my arms, shoving my clenched fists into my jean short pockets.

"Sorry, is who? What?"

Tommy threw his head back with laughter. "Am I that boring Annie? I was asking, is your Pa was around? I told him I'd help him with his boat today.'

"I, well, sorry, who are you again? I don't know where my Pa is at the minute. He did say he was heading into town, but I'm really not sure. He hasn't mentioned you to me."

I was rambling, mortified. I willed my mouth to stay shut. He must think I'm a complete idiot. I focused on the ground, hoping it would swallow me up.

'Cool, no stress Annie. I will hang out till he rocks in. You cool with that?"

I met his eyes again, their intense blueness reminding me of the ocean. Blinking rapidly, I willed myself into rational thought. I was not one of those girls who flaked at the sight of some strange player just because they battered their gorgeous lashes. I forced myself not to look at his sun kissed dimples.

Get it together Annie. Bloody hell!

Clearing my throat, I threw my shoulders back, and placed my hands on my hips, willing false confidence.

"Actually Tommy. I'd feel better if you leave. I really don't know who you are. And from what I've seen over the last week, there are some pretty screwed up people in this town. You could be just another snake trying to get your hands on Brambly Estate. I haven't been here long but met my fair share already. Or maybe you 're a serial killer, never can tell these days.'

I waited for his reaction. My heart was pounding, I dared it not to expose me. I'd bravely spoken more of my real thoughts to this stranger in the last few minutes, than I had dared speak to anyone for as long as I could recall. What was happening to me?

Tommy burst into laughter, doubling over, slapping his hands on his knees. It infuriated me. I crossed my arms tighter and continued to stare.

"Oh chickee. You sure are from a big city, hey."

He shook his head turning to leave, still smiling broadly. What the hell was that meant to mean?

"And as you know, my name is Annie. So don't call me chickee....ever thanks!"

He stopped, spinning on the spot to face me again, looking me up and down. His raised eyebrows and bemused smile said it all. I cringed at the way this stranger could enrage me yet make my heart flutter at the same time.

"No stress Annie, you need to chill out I reckon. Just let your Pa know I came over, like he asked me to. Maybe tell him you scared me off."

Grinning like a proverbial Cheshire cat, he saluted me.

"Depart I will, but may we meet again soon. You are kind of gorgeous in your own salty way."

"Oh, and Annie, my mum says hi. She said to ask if you wanted to come for dinner. Stella, you remember her, right?"

With that he winked before swaggering away. Swallow me now, I willed the earth. Blinking rapidly to regain composure, my mouth was agape, but no reply came.

OMG! Could he not have just explained that from the start? I had a compulsion to flee, yet stood like stone, staring at the back of his head.

Why did I speak to him like that? Idiot.

"Nice boy that Tommy, don't you think Annie?"

Now she chooses to show up!

Despite refusing to turn around, I knew it was Annabelle. Instinctively pulling my hood further over my head as I sat, I curled my hands protectively around my middle.

"Look at me when I speak Annie. It is the least you can do."

Was she for real? The least I could do! Eyes rolling and letting out a long sigh, I stood and faced her.

My annoyance turned briefly to amusement. I didn't know whether to laugh or cry. I was actually pissed off at a spirit! How was that even

a thing? I'd worked too hard over the years to stay away from drama.
I didn't need this shit.

Annabelle rested gracefully against the same pillar Tommy had
done so only minutes earlier. She smiled down at me.

"Relax Annie, you didn't know who he was. Let it go now, I've got
a feeling Tommy will be back."

"I don't want him to come back. He is so full of himself. Makes me
sick actually. Boys like that are nothing but trouble."

Annabelle moved closer toward me as I stood, offering a bemused
smile. Her eyes glowed attempting to reach deeply into mine. They
twinkled with mischief. I hadn't seen this side of my great great
Grandmother before.

I wondered what would happen if I touched her.

"That's not what I saw Annie. Not by a long shot, dear girl. You
remind me very much of myself you know."

Whatever. I wasn't interested in small talk, I was too agitated, feeling protective of myself right now. She didn't know anything about
me, nor Tommy for that matter. I needed to change the subject fast.

"Annabelle, please. We need some answers, some direction. Can't
you just lead me to the treasure or show me a way out of this mess
right now? I want to help you Annabelle and Pa obviously, but enough
with the games. Please."

She gestured for me to sit, and for the first time I noticed she once
again was carrying her leather journal. Annabelle's style was so graceful, almost regal. So captivated by her, my annoyance dispersed. She
had the power to completely spellbound me, as I bet, she had others
too. Clearly, we were poles apart in this way.

I wondered how often she had sat in these very chairs, perhaps
marvelling over her Brambly Estate in its finer days. Her sweet smell
of incense enticed me again. Annabelle appeared so real today, like a

perfectly normal, living person. Last time she had come, her presence was almost vaporous. She wore the same ivory gown, yet today her hair was different. It was pinned up in swirls around her porcelain face, revealing for the first time an obvious scar.

I stared.

It was thick and jagged, running all the way down the left side of her neck, disappearing into the neckline of her dress, long since ingrained, yet still noticeable. How had I missed this before? Could this injury be related to her death?

"Patrick, I did what I must to save our child."

Pulled from my thoughts, I realised Annabelle was reading again. Her lashes fanned her lowered eyes, her cheeks glowed as her ruby lips breathed the powerful words once more.

"Beth seemed suddenly crazed, Patrick. Like a woman possessed. She was rambling and pacing, demanding I hand over enough of my jewels to allow her to buy more land. She said she *was the chosen one, not me. That it was* she *that should have the greatest wealth, the most influence,*

and be the most admired woman in Brambly Cove, not me a Chinese lower class citizen.

I tried desperately to reason with the woman whom I thought to be my best friend, yet she appeared suddenly a stranger to me. I told her she could have it all. Everything Patrick, all I wanted was Charlotte. I begged Beth to let me have her. I was so desperate to know our child was alive, but her men had tied me up in the basement. Then something changed in her eyes, Patrick. They darkened, as if they suddenly reflected an onset of insanity, almost like she was possessed. But there was more.

Beth whispered to me then. She stroked my hair, dug her nails into my scalp. As she lent in closely, I could smell the evil radiating out of her soul. She muttered, almost spitting her words, telling me you belonged to her Patrick, as did Charlotte.

It was then I changed my tactic, Patrick, just as you had taught me. I pretended to submit. Rather than fight her with my words, I assured her she was right. I apologised for coming to Brambly Bay. Convincing her going forward things would be different. I could relocate, remove myself from her life. I persuaded her to first return Charlotte in exchange for my disappearance and jewellery. The rest we would work out between us once we had found you, Patrick. I assured her, you would also agree to her terms.

She allowed me to return home, chaperoned by her men. I retrieved some, but not all of our precious treasure and handed it over in exchange for Charlotte. That was a risk, but I chose to take it. Beth was not as smart as me, and I knew that. She spat at me as she grabbed the bag of jewels. Then her demonic laugh, so horrible, it is one I will never be able to erase.

From that day my darling Patrick, never did I feel completely safe in Brambly Estate again. Yet I've been wise in anticipating the worst and putting measures in place to ensure our safety. Barely do I venture from Brambly Estate these days, never without Charlotte.

But my dear Patrick. You know me well enough that I would not waste the years that have come between us. While I remain hopeful of your return, I have dedicated much of my time to ensure Beth never felt safe again either. I made a silent promise to Charlotte and you that day Patrick. That I would take care of things, and that I have done my love. Beth and her descendants will continue to suffer my curse. Much of our fortune remains safe, as does the future of our precious Brambly Estate."

My chest tightened. Realising I was holding my breath, I let it release slowly.

Was Annabelle as innocent as we had thought?

Bass Straight Ocean 1927
Beth
Captured

Patrick tossed about, moaning as he moved involuntarily from one rough surface to the next at the mercy of the ferocious waves. He had no idea I was watching, nor how he'd come to be at sea. Patrick remained tied at his hands and feet.

My crew had certainly done a job on his handsome face. One eye was swollen shut, and some of his teeth missing. Dried blood caked his face and torn jacket.

Instinctively he attempted a jarred movement away from the men as they poked him, throwing a bucket of sea water over his head to bring him around.

"Not so grand and mighty now are you Captain Patrick, hey lad."

They laughed as they circled and ogled their prey. One flicked his cigarette into Patrick's body.

Silently I gestured to the men. As commanded, they grabbed Patrick roughly, hauling him up onto the ship's deck. I ventured closer, adopting a pondering pose. My heartbeat fluttered, rapidly beating wildly.

'We hope we haven't inconvenienced you too much, Captain. Our boss just needed to borrow you for a while. We are going on a little trip."

Fighting to regain composure, Patrick glanced around, attempting to speak for the first time.

"Where are you taking me?"

I barely recognised his raspy voice and slurred speech.

"Ahh that would ruin the surprise, Captain Patrick. But here's the deal. You be a compliant guest on this here boat, and we might even consider returning you to that pretty little Chinese wife of yours. However, should you cause us trouble….well, we are always looking for good bait out here. Looks to me like you might be just the answer we need to get us a big catch…"

Again, the men laughed. I smirked looking at this once powerful man now crumpled against a wine barrel. Despite loving him, he needed to be reminded just who held the power.

"Can you untie me? I will comply, you have my word. Perhaps then we might discuss what exactly this is all about, and why you have me here. I am willing to offer you a very good deal, but I must be returned to my wife and child. It is imperative."

Patrick was speaking directly to my captain, who crouched beside him. He reeked of booze and tobacco and wheezed as he laughed. The other men joined him, sniggering and jostling about like it was their biggest catch ever. These men were fools, low life scum, but I needed them for now.

"Thank you, men. I will take matters in hand from here."

I waved my hand in dismissal, jutting my chin skyward.

As the men parted quickly allowing me through, I marvelled in Patrick's confused and bewildered stare.

"Beth?"

"My darling Patrick, I do hope you are okay. I am a little disappointed my men manhandled you so. I will take care of you my dear. Your Beth is here now. Everything is going to work out just fine, you will see. We will get you all fixed up and return to our new life Patrick. Just you, me and our dear baby Charlotte, of course. Won't that be so lovely hmmm, just perfect. Just the way I know you wanted us to be."

Patrick's body was so cold to my touch, he began shaking his head in denial. I stroked his face, humming and smiling as he tried to scramble back from me.

"Beth. Please. Help me. I don't understand. What is happening here?"

Brambly Estate 2017
Annie
Revelation

Pa was still not home. Brambly Estate was eerily still, not a sound, not even a breeze. What on earth could be taking him this long? He never stayed out on his boat into the evening. I'd fixed us some dinner nearly two hours earlier. Dusk itself was now almost gone; its diffused light had all but disappeared below the horizon.

I'd searched this house from top to bottom today. I would almost put money on the fact there was no treasure here. Even the attic and cellar were all but bare. Unless there was some sort of secret room I'd missed?

Completely over it, I slumped back in the chair on the veranda. This was all too hard, impossible. Frustration had set in big time.

Who was I to even think I could help here?

I wanted out. I wanted to go home, yet I knew I couldn't. I wouldn't dream of leaving Pa now.

Without warning the evening birds began to screech. Their calls were consistent and near deafening, but strangely tonight I found this more comforting than the silence. Cockatoos flew over my head into the tall trees. Fixated in the moment, I became absorbed in my surroundings, sighting a pack of wallabies grazing contently in the nearby paddock. A baby joey bounced around them, excited to explore his new world so it seemed.

"We meet again Annie! Hi ya!"

Nearly jumping out of the chair I snapped back into the present moment. My heart sank seeing it wasn't Pa, yet instantaneously seemed to flip. Tilting my head to one side, I raised my eyebrows.

He was back.

"Hi Tommy."

Such simple words, yet they struggled to leave my suddenly constricted throat. All I could think of was my embarrassing behaviour the last time we met. Oh man, and now he was back, this was going to be torture. And he looked even more gorgeous tonight.

OMG where had that thought come from?

Tommy threw his old bike aside and leapt up onto the deck, crashing down into the chair beside me. He'd raised quite a sweat under his tank top in the evening heat.

'Do you want a drink? I can go grab you some water maybe?"

That was all I could muster up as a peace offering. Tommy was acting as if nothing had ever happened. He sat back relaxed, stretching his arms above his head smiling broadly and nodding.

"That would be bloody awesome Chick…I mean Annie. Thanks."

I smiled fleetingly before bolting inside. I rushed to fill a glass. Checking my appearance in the mirror, I rolled my eyes. Why did I even care all of a sudden? I forced a slow exhale before heading back outside.

"Sorry to hassle you two days in a row Annie, but I still haven't heard from ya Pa. He always needs my help this time of year, so mum agreed I should come back over."

Tommy gulped down the drink. I found myself staring at the water dripping down the sides of his mouth. I wanted to reach out and touch it.

Bloody hell Annie, get it together.

"He is not back yet actually. He left really early to take the boat out. Honestly, I was just starting to wonder if everything was okay. So, maybe, if you don't mind, um, maybe you could help me look for him? Just in case, you know. I'm sure nothing is wrong, but I'm just.."

Tommy put his hand on my shoulder. The electric shock stilled my stuttering. I stared at the ground unable to meet his eyes.

'No stress. Yep, let's go. It is a bit late to be out actually. He normally is back before the tides turn mid afternoon. Gets a bit dangerous out there after that. But don't freak Annie, Jack is a tough old bugger, he knows what he is doing."

Following Tommy away from Brambly Estate and onto the beach track leading to the boat ramp, I wondered what would happen to Brambly Estate if Pa passed away? The same protective feeling began rising up through my veins. This was our family home. As Annabelle had insisted, I was here for a reason. I just wish I knew exactly what that was.

Tommy abruptly haltered, causing me to crash into him. It was impossible not to notice his body was lean and strong. Pointing toward the jetty, he was clearly unaware of the fluttering sensation he was causing within me. The waves crashed against the shoreline. It was nearly dark now.

"Hmm. Well, he is not out on his boat as you can see."

Once on the jetty, Tommy investigated more closely, jumping aboard Pa's moored vessel. He pulled at boxes and containers in the small compartments inside the cabin. Should I join him? I felt so awkward just standing up here. It was cold now, too. Shivering, I felt a sudden unease.

"Hey Annie, looks like your Pa never went out in the boat at all this morning."

Tommy poked his head up through the cabin entrance.

"All his stuff is here, including fresh bait. Yep, this old girl has been moored here all day I'd bet."

I stared down at the boat.

"Then where is he? Does he usually go to other places you know of? Pa hasn't really gone anywhere much since I arrived."

Disappearing again, Tommy continued to look around, leaving my question unanswered. It was then, bending down, I saw it. Flinching as my blood pressure dropped, my heart leapt and began beating rapidly. Wedged into the rough planks on the small dock was Pa's watch.

"Tommy, hey Tommy, I think something is really wrong."

Tommy jumped up beside me. We crouched silently, staring at the evidence in the palm of my hand and then questioningly at each other. Pa's watch face was smashed, and the leather band broken.

Turning away, Tommy began pacing, searching the area. He flexed his fingers repetitively, rubbing the back of his neck.

"There! Look Annie!"

He took off toward the entrance of the jetty, launching himself over the side into the shallows. I ran after him, desperate to know what he had seen. Wading in the shallows, Tommy retrieved Pa's Akubra which had been wedged under the jetty.

Pa would never leave his hat behind willingly.

Bass Strait Ocean 1927
Beth
Hysteria

Propped up against a wall inside the small cabin of the ship, Patrick's bodily functions were clearly still noncompliant. He shivered relentlessly and sweated profusely.

Still tied at the hands and feet, he remained at my mercy. I felt almost weightless with power yet aggravated in the same breath. Patrick tracked me as I paced, a little unsteadily. The seas were rough, as was my mood.

I stilled, suddenly overcome with empathy for my greatest love. Attempting to gain control over my mind at this point was a relentless inner battle.

"So, Patrick. We have a few matters which we must discuss. I felt the best place to do that was away from Brambly Cove, and well, its certain distractions."

I pulled up a wooden stool, sitting heavily beside Patrick. I was sweating profusely. For the first time, I noticed my hands shaking. Racing thoughts had me a little addled, but this I would never reveal. I stared at him for the longest time, lips pursed. Then like the flick of a switch a smile formed, and I could see this was more unnerving for Patrick than my anger. It had been far easier to fool my dear Annabelle with this façade.

"Please Beth, just tell me what we are doing here. This can all be forgotten. I can give you whatever it is you want."

Instant elation filled me to my core.

"Oh Patrick, I knew you felt the same. I just knew it."

I beamed down at him now, clasping his hands and attempting to move them over my heart. He pulled away from me abruptly.

"You felt it too, didn't you? The undeniable spark between us Patrick, from the very first moment. I knew you would appreciate me taking some action, to speed things up. Best Charlotte is young when we transition into our new life. That way she won't remember Annabelle. It's for the best. It really is."

Awaiting his response, I watched in dismay as his eyes bulged, and heard the audible intake of his breath. Smiling sweetly, I knew it was only a matter of time until he awoke to his senses. I had complete authority at this moment.

"Beth, dear Beth."

He tried to sit up and lean in toward me. I took in his sweet scent.

"I appreciate the gesture of you bringing me here. Obviously, we have much to discuss. How in fact did you get me on board, and perhaps you can be so kind as to tell me where we are going?"

My hysterical laugh filled the small space. I moistened my lips, running my fingers along his jawline.

"It was easy Patrick. Remember the tea cake I dropped off yesterday for you and Annabelle to enjoy for supper? I served it right up for you both myself, remember? It was laced with sedatives. My men simply came in the night and whisked you away. Your sleeping beauty was none the wiser."

Breathless I lay my hand over his heart.

"My plan was to vacate with you in Tasmania. We could relax, wine and dine, spend some quality time getting to know each other. What a beautiful way to begin our life together is it not?"

Patrick attempted to pull away, as I gripped more tightly at his jacket.

"I can arrange for Robert to disappear, don't be concerned about that. And you, dear Captain Patrick, can be in control of returning Annabelle to where she belongs. Far away from here is all I ask. Then we will become the most powerful couple. Oh, my darling Patrick, doesn't that sound wonderful? I will be the wife you need, the wife you deserve. With your wealth behind us, and my fine taste for living we will be the envy of the land. Our life together will be long and prosperous. We will be rid of the scum who presently brings us down. No longer will Annabelle and Robert hold us back."

I stood, applauding my own brilliance and grinning ear to ear. Then Patrick began to thrash, edging away from me, he spat in my direction.

"Beth, how dare you! How dare you speak of Annabelle that way. You have betrayed her. She trusted you. Why would you do this? Annabelle is the one I love, and she always will be. Do you hear what I am saying Beth? You are deeply confused, certifiable indeed."

I felt my eyes flash wildly like a lightning bolt. Leaning in, I slapped him across the cheek and then began to scream, my rage escalating beyond my control.

"You will rot in hell Beth before I ever touch you. You are clearly mad, heinous, and I will certainly make sure you pay for this horrendous crime against my family."

I quietened, calming myself by breathing deeply. Never once did I break his stare. Squatting over his body, I ran my fingers over his head, chest and down his legs, ignoring his flinches at my touch.

"This is far from over Patrick. One way or another, I will get Annabelle's precious jewels. I deserve them. If I can't have you Patrick, then neither can she. Annabelle is nothing. She will be sorry she ever set foot in Brambly Cove."

He kicked at me, I stumbled back slightly, still on all fours. Turning to face him again, I rolled my head back and began to laugh. Grabbing fistfuls of my hair, I pulled and scratched until I bled. Then covering my ears, rocking in a ball, I attempted to block out my confusion and torment.

"Men……men! Come in here. Men!"

The small space began to fill immediately as the crew rushed to my side.

"Captain Patrick wishes to be thrown overboard. Leave him tied and weigh him down well. Do it immediately. Now!"

I stood gingerly as the blood rushed to my ears. Straightening my hair and sea clothes my adrenaline raged uncontrollably.

"And men, after Captain Patrick has been taken care of, turn this boat around. We have a change of plans."

Brambly Bay 2017
Annie
The Prophecy

"Annie, hey Annie."

I looked back toward his voice.

"Time to call it quits. No point looking around much more, it's too dark. The tide is getting really high, and we've covered every bit of the cove I can think of. He's not here. Let's go back up to the house, maybe Jack's there."

I let out a long, slow sigh before nodding. My head was spinning anyway. Watching him intensely as he caught up, even in the semi darkness Tommy's face said it all. His tense features told me he didn't believe his own speech. If Tommy was worried, then I knew something was very wrong here.

Pa was not home at Brambly Estate. The house felt emptier than ever before, and that strange chill seemed to be running through the hallways again. Was Annabelle here? Did she know Pa was missing? Or even better, where to find him? I'd decided not to call mum just yet. She probably wouldn't pick up anyway. Even if she did, she would tell me I was overreacting. Was I?

Silently we sat in the candlelit kitchen, chewing and swallowing like robots, I couldn't taste the food anyway. Barely finding the energy to speak, Pa's hat and watch on the table between us felt like an elephant in the room.

"I can't leave you here alone tonight, Annie. It wouldn't be right."

Mid-chew, I stared up at Tommy. Swallowing sharply. My heart skipped a beat.

"I'm fine, really. Go home, you have helped heaps, but I'm good. I got it from here."

Did I sound convincing? That couldn't be further from the truth. Internally every fibre of my being was screaming for him not to leave me alone in this creepy house. But I wouldn't show him that, I just couldn't.

Tommy simply smiled. His response was firm.

"I'm staying Annie. I will sleep in your Pa's room, no arguments, Okay? We will head out again in the morning. We're going to find him, Annie I promise. There's gotta be some simple explanation for all of this."

I wasn't so sure.

Tommy got up to leave. Like me, he had hardly touched his dinner.

"Night then, and thanks Tommy, I owe you one."

Taken aback, Tommy grinned down at me for what seemed like the longest time. Those blue analysing eyes, near impossible to escape, somehow penetrated my hidden world. Yet his smile felt so non-judgemental. Very different from the way my mum made me feel. Around Tommy, I didn't perceive myself as a bother or burden at all. I attempted to smile back, but instead broke his stare awkwardly, studying the lettuce on my plate.

"You know where I am if ya need me, Annie. But try to hold yourself back tonight hey, we need to get to know each other a little better before you crack onto me."

Startled, I sat bolt upright, unsure of what had woken me. Momentarily thinking I was back home in my bed in Sydney, I reached for my bedside lamp, which didn't exist here. Unbalanced I nearly crashed to the floor. As my eyes adjusted, I registered the moonlight streaming in, followed by the familiar silhouette sitting at the base of my bed.

"Annie, we are running out of time. I need you to be smart now."

Why couldn't she appear before I was finally in the deep sleep I very much needed?

I sat further up, wondering what time it was as I rubbed my temples. My head pounded. Annabelle's aura appeared almost like vapour and not as yellow tonight.

"Annie. Your Pa, where is he?"

"I was hoping you could tell me, Annabelle. You're the supernatural one. I'm really worried, he's missing, and we think he may be hurt. Tommy and I were going to try again in the morning to look for him. We've searched all day."

I felt sick at the thought of Pa out there alone somewhere. Annabelle walked over to my window, staring into the darkness.

"I think I might have given your dear Tommy a bit of a fright. I went into your Pa's room just now."

I stifled a laugh, wondering just how Mr Cruisy had felt about that.

"He is not *my* Tommy, Annabelle. I barely know him. He is confusing and annoying, but nice too, I suppose. Anyway, please, let's just focus Annabelle. What do you want me to do now?"

Annabelle faced me again, leaning on the window she seemed wistful and lost in thought as she lightly stroked her throat.

"I'm sure Jack will show up tomorrow. I helped raise that boy from birth, so he knows this land better than anyone. And as for Tommy, he is keen on you, Annie, I can tell. Maybe if you let your guard down a bit, you would see. Has your mother taught you to be this protective of yourself? Isabelle was always a little different from us, a little absent and removed so to speak."

How did I answer my great great grandma at this moment? I really didn't know Mum any differently from the way the world did. The feted news reporter, always so full of glitz and glamour. I moved uncomfortably in my crumpled bedsheets, knowing the way Annabelle was looking at me, there was no hiding from her questions tonight.

"I, well, I am not like my mum. I'm not the person she wants me to be, at all. Actually, I'm everything she's not really. I'll never be confident like her. I don't even think Mum really likes me, to be honest. She loves me, but only because she has to. Mum knows I'm weak, and it infuriates her. I'm just a bland kind of person."

Annabelle stood abruptly from the end of the bed. She moved closer, eyeballing me. Taken aback, I wondered was she angry at me all of a sudden? Her aura had deepened and sparked around her frame. I began biting the inside of my bottom lip, flustered and feeling trapped.

Then the strangest sensation coursed through my body. I caught my breath, not quite knowing what was happening. Looking down I saw Annabelle was holding my hands. I stared back up at her softened features. Her steady eye contact was less invasive now and had become almost comforting. She looked so real, so alive again.

"Annie. You must listen. I'm not leaving until you promise me you have comprehended what I've got to say. I've made that mistake before with your Mum. She never quite understood me. Given, it was a lot for her to comprehend at the time. This is very important.

Her voice was serious, almost authoritative now. Wide eyed I tried to imagine what was coming. She didn't budge.

"Like it or not, you are the one, Annie named after me as the matriarch of this family, I came to Australia to set up an empire that would serve our family for generations an preserve the memory of my people. Now it is up to you to continue. You must never speak of yourself that way again. Your mind believes what the mouth utters. And you are very wrong. Do you hear my words, child?"

I tried to pull away, beyond disbelief. What on earth was she rambling about? Annabelle cupped my chin, raising my face to meet her eyes again. Her hands were electric, leaving my skin tingling, the instant connection between us undeniable.

"There is nothing bland, boring, or weak about you, dear child. You have everything you need to be powerful and successful in this life. There is only one person holding you back, and that is you. Annie, remember, often the loudest people are the most insecure. Trust me, your mum knows how special you are. Isabelle knows you are everything that under her cleverly prepared and hardened surface, she is not."

I hadn't realised I was crying. Annabelle's words were more powerful than anything spoken over me before. Did I dare imagine? I wanted so desperately to fit somewhere in this world. I felt the rush of relief at finally having been validated. I'd longed to feel appreciated my entire life.

But why did Annabelle believe in me this much?

Maybe she was right. But even if it did all start with me, I honestly didn't know how to be any different than I was right now.

"Whether you see it or not Annie, we are very similar. That's how I know."

I wiped my tears away roughly; I was getting agitated with my confusion.

"Know what Annabelle?"

'That you, Annie, have the courage, the power, to save Brambly Estate. You just need to have the will and belief.'

My mind was racing, desperately trying to process all she had said. Annabelle stood, pulling her shawl further across her body. I wondered how she had returned as a spirit. Was that a choice all dead people could make?

I desperately wanted to ask her how she had died. And what had she meant when she'd talked about the conversation she'd had with mum all those years ago.

I remembered now, a heated debate I'd had in school last year. I'd cited so many facts rebuking the notion of ghosts and spirits. Yet here I was, communicating and holding hands with a woman who had supposedly died some 30 years ago. Not only that, but this spirit also believed I was the 'chosen one.' What the hell was I supposed to do with that little nugget of info?

This was too much. Madness. Was I going insane?

"Annabelle, Pa says our family never really knew much about your story. He said you came from China obviously, but the circumstances remained kind of a mystery all these years."

She turned, smiling, yet stayed by the window. Her yellowish glow was strengthening, appearing almost misty once again.

"Would you like to know Annie? Patrick and I decided from the beginning to keep my previous life a secret. We felt going forward, it would be safer for our generations of family to come. You would be the first in our family to know my truth. Are you ready for that Annie?"

Was I? Did I really have a choice now? Annabelle was willing to trust me. Despite my reservations, deep down I knew I longed to be invested. It was just a matter of believing I could. Nodding vigorously, I watched Annabelle's face light up.

"It is to be then."

With that, her presence now barely more than a mist-like vapour again, dispersed. All that remained in the darkened room were her swirling words.

"Remember Annie, with this knowledge comes great responsibility. Danger lies ahead. But she who remains inside of you is greater than she who is in the world."

I felt mentally numbed. Almost frozen, I remained cross legged amongst the bed sheets. Glancing around without really seeing anything, completely lost in deep thought I twirled the thin cotton sheet around my fingers.

"This just can't be real. It's impossible," I whispered.

"What is?"

I jumped, suddenly crashing back into the present moment. Tommy stood sheepishly in the doorway, candle in hand. What was it with lack of privacy in this house? Annoyed I moved further under the quilt.

"Don't you knock?"

He shrugged. Wearing only a pair of boxers, I tried not to stare at his six pack which was equally as golden as the rest of his muscly body. Was that a tattoo Tommy had just above his hip bone? I wanted to reach over and touch but didn't dare.

OMG Annie. Stop.

Quickly shaking off the intrusive thought, I cleared my throat.

"The door was open, and I heard voices. Thought maybe your Pa was back. No such luck hey. You okay Annie?"

Never had I felt under such scrutiny. I dared not look down to see I'd covered up enough of my singlet top. And my hair, I dared not think what it was doing right now.

"I'm fine….you?"

"Yep. Had a bit of a strange dream just before though. I thought Annabelle was in my room. How trippy is that hey!"

Tommy laughed but I could tell by the way he shifted his weight uncomfortably, he was a little rattled.

"She looked exactly like the picture mum showed me of her, taken just before she disappeared, or died, or whatever happened. There is some strange shit happening in this house, Annie."

That was the understatement of the century. If only he knew.

"Yep, that's for sure. Sorry we woke you Tommy…I mean, me, I mean sorry I woke you. Sometimes when I talk out loud it helps me make sense of stuff…you know?

"It's cool. I'll go back to bed for a few more hours then. You should try to sleep, too, Annie, maybe quit reading for now, hey. We need to be fresh in the morning."

"I wasn't…what? Reading?"

Tommy pointed to the brown envelope in my lap. Up till this moment, I'd had no clue it was there.

'Is that from your boyfriend hey? Aww is he missing you, Annie? See you in the morning then. Sweet dreams."

Tommy sniggered as he left. My mouth opened to voice a smart-arse reply, but no sound came. Tommy, I decided, managed to calm me, then piss me off in just a split second. Shaking his annoying voice off, I inspected the letter.

Where on earth had this come from? My bet, it was another mysterious Annabelle clue. Why the hell did she keep making everything so cryptic?

Leaping from bed, I quietly lit the small remaining candle on the desk before tiptoeing across the room to shut the door. I didn't need Tommy poking his nose in at this point. Reality was I hadn't made up my mind if he could even be trusted yet.

The discoloured envelope looked old. It had browned over time, and its edging water stained. No stampings or markings were apparent, and it was tightly sealed with wax. I was hesitant to even open it for fear of destroying its delicate façade.

Nervously I unfolded the brittle paper inside. Straight away I knew its author. The smell of Annabelle's incense was well ingrained. The date on the top read March 1920. I shook my head perplexed. If that were correct, then how was it possible this was addressed to me?

Unlike Annabelle's diary, this was written in English.

Without reading further, I turned to the last of the 3 pages. All were filled with beautiful black cursive writing. It was signed 'Ju'.

Why?

17th *March 1920.*

Dear Annie,

This letter serves to tell you my story, and perhaps in time, make a connection to your own. I can only hope you know some of your family's history and can understand the political tension I've lived through in China. To fill in any gaps, I have written to you.

Generationally and spiritually entwined, forever we will be.

My name is Ju, which means daisy.

I intend to plant these flowers in my new homeland of Australia. Other than in books, I've never sighted, touched, nor experienced their smell. But daisies symbolise new beginnings for me. Somehow give me the strength to embark on the unknown.

Earlier today I left my homeland forever. Filled with both trepidation and pride knowing my journey will keep our family legacy alive.

I am 19 years old, born in 1901 into the Qing Dynasty in China, a descendant of the Manchu people.

The Qing Dynasty, was formed in 1636 and demolished in 1911. A Dynasty that for 263 years, right or wrong, has been marked by social structure, separating people by ethnicity and class. It is said we will be the last line of royalty to exist in China. Many of our own people have grown to despise us, and our wealth. Perhaps our failure to reform and modernise China has led to our collapse. These decisions were never something I was privy to. Women are excluded from such matters.

I have lived an extremely sheltered existence in the Forbidden City in Beijing. In my 19 years, rarely has anyone been permitted entry, with the exception of my family, loyal advisors and staff. Therefore, I grew up without friends or the freedom to explore the world beyond. Despite longing to experience such things, I am both terrified and excited at the prospect of my enforced future.

All females living in the Forbidden City were restricted to the inner court and prohibited from venturing out from the imperial quarters deep inside the palace. I have, however, been privileged in education and was strictly tutored in all subjects from a very young age. I am fluent in 3 languages and am well-versed in martial arts, as well as many forms of creative expression.

At present, Civil War continues to worsen in China. With a large population growth over the last few years, there is simply insufficient farmland and jobs to support communities. Rural poverty and famine led many to rebel against the Qing Dynasty.

Foreign powers have also impacted trade with China greatly, causing further war and treaties which have deeply harmed our royal status. In 1912 a new republic was established. This saw the Qing Dynasty overthrown. It was the most frightening time in my life, up until now I will admit.

For the last eight years, we were granted permission to remain in our palace in Beijing. Rumour is, under the new laws, my uncle, Puyi, will be the last Chinese Emperor. He was granted the right to maintain his imperial title in the Forbidden City until 1924. However, we recently had word this favourable treatment has been overturned. My family is being forced underground as I write.

I know Annie, my revelations must be near incomprehensible. But it is my duty to impart to you what was foretold to me by trusted Qing scholars.

You, Annie, are the chosen one. You will save our family's empire in the year 2017. To date, it is predicted you are to be born in the year 2000. I will become your great great grandmother. I understand how fictitious these statements must appear. I assure you; I write with a sound mind.

At present, I sail from China to Australia under the protection and guidance of Captain Patrick Robinson, aboard his ship Grace's Voyage. Since the civil war and famine began, Captain Patrick's ship is just one of many that have regularly brought much-needed Australian produce to our shores such as wheat and butter. We exchange them for Qing coins and heirlooms, tea, silk, and opium.

I've been warned this journey will be long, and even at times haz-ardous with varying weather conditions. I am aware the ship's living conditions will be vastly different from what I have known. My quarters thankfully are pleasant. I have been assured of food, water and medical attention if required. However, it is imperative I remain unseen by all other passengers and crew.

Captain Patrick is well known to my uncle the emperor of China, Puyi, yet a stranger to me. It is my first day at sea, and we have barely exchanged a word as yet. His brief smile upon boarding was somewhat reassuring, however. Puyi arranged for me to discreetly leave China with the intention I will not return, nor be traceable. The most harrowing part for me is that I must never contact my family again. This is all very much against my wishes. My pleading and defiance did me no good. I was simply reminded that just as the prophecy foretold, it was my birthright.

Once in Australia, my new identity will see me becoming Captain Patrick's bride. I will enter a new land as Mrs Annabelle Robinson. Unaccompanied Chinese women travelling away from home is strongly disapproved of currently. It is said Captain Patrick is a very kind and upstanding gentleman. My mother says he will take care of me, but I cannot help but be filled with concern and wonder. Despite my tenacious spirit, Annie, I will need to draw on much inner strength to endure.

I am aware Captain Patrick has been compensated well for this long-term business arrangement. Secretly, however, I do hope perhaps one day we would find love and companionship if our forced marriage is to remain.

I am frightened, Annie. Overwhelmed and distraught at both the thought of leaving my family and becoming a wife to a stranger and foreigner. But I do understand it is my duty to rise and protect the legacy of the Qing people. These are my people.

I am determined to triumph despite adversity no matter the cost.

Bestowed upon me has been a great honour. I travel with the purpose of protecting a large portion of Qing coins, heirlooms, and jewellery. These ancient treasures of the Qing empire are priceless. It is feared they will be stolen or sold off, as our civil war escalates. Especially now with foreign countries becoming actively involved. Only Captain Patrick and I know the treasure travels with us.

Secretly I question how Puyi knows Patrick can be trusted? But this I must have faith in, as his knowledge of the world is far greater than mine. Puyi is a wise ruler.

It has been told to me Annie, that in fact over a century from now, you will be the only one who can find the long since hidden treasure and save our family's legacy and future.

I was instructed, once on the ship, to write this letter in English and keep it guarded until the time was right.

Such time is now, Annie.

Godspeed my child. And many blessings over your journey.

Annabelle.

穀倉

Letting the letter rest on my lap I sighed, releasing the longest breath. My thoughts blanked then swirled so quickly, it was impossible to keep up. I unconsciously untied and re-gathered my bun.

I jumped off the bed, reminding myself to be quiet as I paced. I totally did not need Tommy butting in again.

This is bloody inconceivable. My rational brain was screaming all the impossibilities of this situation, as a strange emotional numbness seeped through my veins. Even the symbol on the bottom was identical to the one I had been marked with at birth, just like in Annabelle's journal.

'So let me get this straight. This letter is suggesting Annabelle was told of my future existence in the early 1900's? Yeah right.'

Insanity was kicking in.

I needed to talk to my Pa.

The walk had cleared my addled brain somewhat. Sitting, I barely noticed the chill rising from the damp sand, but instead letting the roar of the ocean hem me in. Across the early morning sky, golden fingers of sunlight lit up the scene, casting a rosy hue. I felt so powerless and insignificant amongst this vastness.

I longed for the comfort of my city apartment. My life was predictable there. Manageable. No surprises. But here.......so far little made sense.

"How long are you going to sit here feeling sorry for yourself, Annie?"

Startled, I lept to my feet. Tommy stood less than a metre away. All consumed, I had not heard nor seen him approach. He smiled broadly as the wind tossed his blond curls over his eyes. Annoyingly, I found the way he pushed the hair aside, tucking it behind his ears strangely alluring. Was I in fact grateful for his company right now?

"I was worried. How early did you come down here? The beach track is bloody treacherous in the dark."

He was worried about me?

My curious smile disappeared instantaneously as my eyes rested on the folded paper he had in his hand. Tommy had found Annabelle's letter.

I was such an idiot.

I'd carelessly had left it opened on the bed, fleeing to the beach a few hours earlier. Swallowing rapidly the burn of bile rose in my throat. Grimacing, I tried desperately to gauge his reactions. My blood was boiling. How dare he.

"What is that? In your hand?"

"I think you know Annie. Come on, let's go back to the house. We have a bit to talk about I think."

Tommy turned back towards the rocky track heading up the cliffs toward Brambly Estate. My knees collapsed from under me, and I fell heavily onto the sand.

What had I done? I am so bloody stupid sometimes.

Tommy was not only a stranger but an Anderson! The last person I would want to read Annabelle's letter. I felt the sting of angry tears. Was I madder at myself or him?

"That's private Tommy, obviously. You have no right. Was this all part of the plan? Did your family send you here to get more evidence from me? I know they are desperate to own Brambly Estate." I was yelling, crying, and rambling, I didn't care. I couldn't take this anymore and felt driven at this moment by my desire for vengeance.

"I hate you all, I hate this place. Get away from me Tommy…go!"

Tommy stared as he bent down and placed Annabelle's letter in front of me. As he attempted to pull me into a hug, I pushed him away.

"Leave me alone Tommy. Seriously, just go away. Go home. This is not your business."

Snatching my letter, I felt suddenly exhausted. I wanted to alone yet be comforted all in the same moment. Tommy sat firm, huddling even closer as I sobbed. I remained with my knees to my chest, my arms tightly circling them.

"Why did you take it, Tommy?"

I still refused to look at him, staring at the waves beyond.

"Sorry, Annie. I just freaked out a bit. Honestly, if this was addressed to me, I'd be losing my shit, too. I just wanted to find you and see if you were okay. I checked on you when I woke, and I saw a letter on your bed. Honestly Annie, I didn't realise at first it was from Annabelle. I thought maybe you had left the note for me, telling me where you were, or you had found your pa. I'm sorry, once I started reading it, I just couldn't believe my eyes. This is heavy shit. I've invaded your privacy. I'm really sorry, I'd be pissed too."

We sat in silence for the longest time. He seemed so genuine, and I felt myself becoming slightly less rigid. All the while Tommy continued to keep his grip firm over my shoulders. The sun was beginning to bite, its sting comforting too.

"I want to help Annie, that's the truth. I'm different from the Andersons, I promise.'"

Not knowing what to believe anymore, I stood suddenly, realising we were wasting precious time. The reality was, Pa was still out there somewhere. Someone had to know something. Tommy jumped up, remaining close. He looked at me so empathically, I had to look away.

"You can trust me, Annie."

Time would tell I suppose. The question was, was it a risk I was willing to take?

By mid-morning we were heading into town. As Tommy's old ute gained speed along the gravelled road, dust swirled in every direction.

What would an onlooker see I wondered, viewing us right now? A happy young couple, wild and free, embracing a summer of surf and adventure, not a care in the world apart from finding the best burgers for lunch or an uncrowded surf spot.

I wish.

Staring at the farmland beyond, I reflected on our earlier conversation. Tommy had taken the news of Annabelle returning all in his stride. There had been no point in me lying or being evasive. We were past that now. Instead, and maybe against my better judgment

I just put it all out there. Sitting in the kitchen, with a packet of chips between us on the table, I'd disclosed everything that had happened since I'd arrived.

Tommy seemed surprisingly wise and open to the spirit world, insisting it wasn't something to be feared or rebuked. He also made it very clear that just because my brain didn't want to believe the concept was real, it didn't mean that it wasn't. He challenged me to consider the possibilities. Could I?

His honesty was refreshing. I could see Tommy wasn't trying to please me, but instead provoke deeper thought. And at the same time, he made me feel completely validated. I'd opened up to him more in the last few hours than to any one boy ever, or my mum for that matter. Tommy was nothing like Caleb. Looking back, that arsehole had gaslighted me all along.

It felt good being able to be so open and honest with somebody. Still, I reminded myself of the need to be guarded. Tommy had listened so intently, before reaching over and pulling me into the biggest hug. He insisted we head into town to talk to his mum. Maybe she would know where to find Pa.

I wanted to trust him so badly. He seemed so gentle and assuring. If this was all a con, and this guy was a fake, I was going to feel like the biggest loser – again.

"Annie, earth to Annie. Where is your head at, hey? You seem a million miles away?"

I glanced over at him. How could I not be?

"Honestly Tommy. I'm confused and messed up over all of this. And don't take it personally, I'm wanting to trust you but it's hard, you know?"

Tommy nodded, keeping his eyes on the road ahead. We were nearly in town.

"I get it and I don't blame you, Annie. So, here's how I see it. You have two choices. I'm offering to help. Take it or leave it. My mum and I have known your pa for a long time. He is the closest thing to a grandfather I have. I'm worried about him, too. Whether you want to work with or against me, I'm going to keep looking until I find him. Mum loved your nan so much, and despite their age difference and forbidden friendship, their bond was tight, so I'm told. I only met her once or twice before she passed. And, if I'm putting it out there Annie, I'm pretty sure I've got a bit of a crush on you."

Was he for real? There was something about Tommy. I was undeniably drawn to him too. But this was real life, not a fairy tale.

As if on cue, the Ute stopped at the only set of traffic lights in town. People were everywhere. Laughter, voices, crowds of onlookers enjoying the free street music. Families eating ice-creams, groups with towels and surfboards heading to the water. Bravely I stopped picking at my fingernails and looked across at Tommy. He burst out laughing.

"Annie, you don't have to look so horrified. I'm not that bad! Maybe too honest, sorry. I, it's just that, well, I've never met a girl like you before. I am a little intense sometimes and tend to blurt out my feelings before I think.

My laugh turned to a snigger. Oh please, did he think I was born yesterday? He had to be playing me. Tommy was gorgeous, every girl's holiday dream. Surely, he was aware of that.

"What? What is so funny?'

"Tommy, come on! As if you haven't had a million girlfriends! I find it a little far-fetched to think I'm something new to you. I know your type, small town, no care, no responsibility, full cruisy surfer life."

Tommy abruptly pulled the car over to the side of the road. His relaxed demeanour vanished, instead his jaw clenched as he took in a deep breath. Tommy looked frustrated and almost hurt as he shook his head. I'd said too much. Why would I do that? Bloody hell, I'd morphed into a verbal monster in the last few days.

"Judge away Annie. You, the privileged one, hey. The big-city rich chick who knows it all, right? If you're so certain you know everything about me, it's best we go our separate ways from here. Forget we ever met."

Inwardly I cursed myself. This was why I'd kept my opinions to myself my whole life, avoiding this type of awkward moment was what I did best. I had no idea what to say next. I reached inside my pocket for the safety of my lighter, only to realise I'd left it in my room. Now I felt completely out of my depth.

Did Tommy want me to get out?

My own annoyance and mixed emotions began bubbling to the surface, and all at once I was firing back.

"My mum might be rich and successful Tommy, but that doesn't mean I'm privileged in the ways I personally value. I'm lonely, I don't trust people and I am near invisible when it comes to my mum. Long story short, she can't stand me. I'm nothing but a disappointment to her. But she is all I have.'

Tommy stared ahead. He was impossible to read right now. What was with my oversharing? He is going to think I am an idiot. Please earth, swallow me.

"Listen Annie. We both need to chill a bit. So far, I can see you are smart and funny. Kind of fiery though, sassy."

Tommy brushed his finger across my cheek before poking at my leg grinning. Somehow these small actions seemed to defuse me.

"You are far from invisible, trust me. What I like the most, is you have no idea how beautiful on the inside you are. There's a lot of depth and honesty to you and it's refreshing.

I wrinkled my nose as my smile wavered. I needed time to digest all this. But Tommy kept going.

"And most of all, you love your pa. So do we. I don't know exactly why, but I am intrigued by you… Sorry, I should have kept my trap shut. But Annie, don't judge what you don't know, right? Maybe my story is a little different from what you have assumed."

The sinking feeling in my stomach was interrupted by ramped butterflies surging internally. This guy was getting more interesting by the minute, not that I was about to admit it. Oh man, I was such a bitch. The space between us felt far too small. Every part of me wanted to run. Unable to meet Tommy's eyes, the manifestation of dread had kicked in.

"Shit Tommy, I am really sorry. That was too harsh of me. You've been so cool. Me, not so much. I don't have much experience in this department, and it's in my nature not to trust people. I'm far too sceptical. Also, I'm not used to compliments, so I kind of get defensive. My bad."

An abrupt knock on the Ute window interrupted our heated moment. A rush of relief swept over me, as it provided a timely distraction from the intensity between us. It was the police. The officers gestured for Tommy to wind his window down, their glares intense. Instantly the mood changed again, and I couldn't quite figure out what was happening. The larger of the two men leaned right into the car window. His body odour so disgusting, I had to force myself not to react.

"Morning Tommy. Not up to no good here I'm hoping. You can't park here mate, it's a tow-away zone. But I think you already know that right? Tommy's rules hmm! Not on my watch mate. Remember Tommy, it's the summer holidays, my town is full of tourists. Let's keep out of trouble now, can we?"

I side eyed Tommy. His eyes ahead, his arms rigid on the steering wheel he made not a sound. I watched his jaw clench again and his knuckles whiten as they tightened their grip. What was with this policeman's tone? The officer turned his attention to me.

"Hello there Annie. Nice to see you back in town. I'm Senior Sergeant Ray Osbourne. Tommy is a friend of yours then I assume? Does your mother know you are spending time with this fella?"

I suddenly felt nervous and claustrophobic, yet at the same time protective of Tommy. Responding without giving away my apprehension, I smiled at the jerk.

"Actually yes, my mother gives me her full blessing, as does Jack. . Not that it is really any of your business I'm thinking. We are not doing anything wrong, in fact, maybe you can help us with something officer, we can't find.."

Abruptly, Tommy cut me off, talking over me too loudly and squeezing my knee with his fingers.

"Actually, it's all good Senior Sergeant Ray. I was having trouble finding the street we are looking for. But I've remembered my mum's instructions now, so thanks. We will be on our way if that's okay?"

He straightened up before looking across to the other smirking policeman. Again, he peered further through the open driver's window, this time making it obvious he was looking around the interior.

"Any substances we should be aware of in this vehicle Tommy? Anything that's not yours perhaps we should talk about?"

Tommy sighed before letting an agitated laugh escape.

"Not for quite a few years now Senior Sargent Roy, as I am sure you know. But if you would like us to step out while you check, be my guest."

Tommy held and matched their glares now. I got the feeling he had been in this exact situation many times before.

"Nope, you can be on your way now Tommy. Look after Annie, mate. Let us know if you should need us, young lady. We will be watching you, Tommy."

These men clearly had it in for my new friend. I couldn't help myself.

"Thanks, officers. Have a wonderful day. How lucky this small town is to have such dedicated law enforcement. I feel so much safer now."

My smile was as sickly sweet as my tone.

Tommy drove away slowly, just out of eyeshot he raised his finger.

"There are people here Annie who refuse to let go of my past. Doesn't matter how hard I try, I have come to realise."

Covering her mouth with her palm, Stella's eyes widened with distress on learning about Pa, confirming what I already suspected. This was completely out of character for him. She promised to come over to Brambly Estate as soon as her shift at the café finished.

As discreetly as we could, we asked around the small town in case anyone had an inkling as to where Pa could be. I even checked the hospital and medical centre. Nothing. We drove back to Brambly in deflated silence.

All I could think of was Pa, injured I surmised, and alone. I felt so helpless.

I begged the universe that Pa would greet us on arrival. Never had I wished for something so much. I had a million questions for Tommy. Clearly, there was more to his story than I had assumed. But could I trust myself to tame my rogue tongue of late? Too many years of repression, I mused.

I burst into tears as the reality of stillness at Brambly Estate stabbed at my heart. My inner voice was self-critical. I felt an imposter in this place.

Time seemed stilted, yet we were running out of it. Fear gripped me.

"Annabelle, are you there? Annabelle?"

The wind had picked up today and my unsteady scream seemed to swirl around me.

Tommy had joined me on the veranda. "She is right Annabelle. It would be a really good time to show yourself."

As the tears of frustration streamed down my face, Tommy gently wiped them away before leaning in to kiss my cheek.

Startled, I stared up at him.

"Sorry, Annie. Inappropriate timing. You, well, you just looked so beautiful, like you could break into a million pieces."

I touched the place his lips had been, suddenly never wanting to wash my face again and risk losing this strange feeling. A smile formed through my tears.

"No, it's ok, it was....nice."

Tommy leaned in again, this time pressing his lips lightly against my own. He lingered longer than expected, smiling. I could taste his sweet scent and suddenly feeling lightheaded.

"We will find him, Annie. I promise."

I smiled back, not really knowing what to think. My head swirled in dizzy emotions. But I couldn't do this now, could I? There was too much going on and I didn't need any more complications.

"Hey, I'm heading out to the sheds to poke around and see if I can find anything okay? Text me if something turns up. Then I reckon in an hour or so, when the tide is really low, we should head back down to the beach. But wait for me. Okay?"

Sitting heavily, I nodded, slumping into the deck chair, not really hearing him. My lips still tingled. I pulled my phone from my back pocket. The screen was blank.

Stella's car roaring up the long driveway broke my scrambled thoughts only moments later. She pulled me into a tight hug before she had even turned the engine off or closed the driver's door. She smelt like a hot fryer, yet I let myself melt into her arms. I wish my mum would hug me like this. It seemed she'd never shared my need for human touch. Or maybe it was just me she didn't want it from.

"Any news, Annie?"

Stella looked concerned as she led me back to sit next to her in the shade.

"Nothing. It just doesn't make sense. All I can think about is him injured and wandering around somewhere. But, well, it almost looks like someone did this to him. I mean with his watch smashed, and his hat in the water and all…"

"He is a tough old bugger, Annie. Wherever he is, he will be putting up a good fight I know that much. I hate to think this is about the ownership of Brambly Estate but honestly, my gut says it is."

I stood, suddenly furious. Surely not.

"You mean Mabel? She wouldn't hurt Pa. Right? This is not fictitious, it's real life Stella. If you know something, please, I need you to tell me right now. In fact, I think I'd better call the police."

Stella defensively put her hands up, creating a barrier between us. Standing herself now, she backed away a little, looking hurt.

"Annie. Stop. Take a breath. I am not your enemy here."

"Really? No offence but do I really know that, Stella?"

I turned away from her, staring out toward the cliff line knowing I was being harsh.

"Fair enough Annie. I can't blame you for thinking like that. This feud, it's brought too much heartache over the years, I'm not going to lie. Honestly, Mabel is my mother, but I feel I don't really know her. She is filled with hate for Jack and has targeted him even more relentlessly over the last few years. He is the only one left standing in her way you see. I really don't know what she is capable of. She is consumed, obsessed and desperate to finally purchase Brambly Estate. You see, she is convinced the treasure is here, somewhere. Mum believes the Andersons deserve to lose it after Annabelle ruined her land for so long. The whole thing has made her quite insane over time......Then there is Tommy."

Spinning around I faced Stella.

"What about Tommy?"

Stella burst into tears, burying her head in her hands. All this I realised, was so much bigger than I'd realised.

"He is not my real son Annie. It's been so difficult for Tommy and me. Mabel is convinced he only came here to steal Jack's fortune."

Stella had my full attention now.

"When I first met Tommy, he had been arrested for stealing. I was delivering coffees to the police station across from the café. We do that every day. Be nice if they paid us once in a while, let me tell you. Anyway, there he was, all down and out, huddled in the corner of their holding cell. My heart simply skipped a beat that day. Here was this young boy, looking so defeated and alone, yet he managed a smile. Thinking he'd be starving, I grabbed him a burger and chips and took them straight back to him, much to the horror of the local coppers I might add."

Stella let out a hearty belly laugh, which bounced off the walls, dispelling some of the repression in the air.

"I didn't care one bit. It was like the lioness in me kicked in. Those that deserve love the least, are the ones that need it the most, I always say."

I nodded as I poured us a cup of tea. The kitchen seemed so alive with Stella in it, even despite the circumstances. I wondered how many times she had sat with Nan in this very room, maybe even with Annabelle. No wonder Nan had loved Stella so much.

"Long story short Annie. I had a soft spot for Tommy right from the start. Good old Senior Sergeant Roy was going to have him sent back to the city, send him to juvie again. I involved myself right from the start. Something in my gut told me it was right. Then as the story unfolded and Jack told me exactly what he had done for him, well I just knew. Took a lot of work to get that boy to trust me that's for sure. Tommy has a lot of emotional scars. I'm so proud looking at him now. He has fought some big demons to clean himself up and allow himself to trust us. He's a beautiful boy, an incredible human in fact, Annie."

I could hear the admiration and love in Stella as she spoke.

No wonder the cops had treated Tommy with such contempt earlier today. I'd assumed so much about him. Simple small-town surfer boy, I called him. OMG. I needed to grow up. And despite my judgemental attitude, he was still here, and offering me support no less. Still, I had my reservations, but it was smart to be a little protective of myself right now. Mum had taught me to trust last and assume the worst first. Not a great way to think really.

"So, he was a criminal then? What for exactly? How long ago was this, Stella?"

She smiled again, seemingly understanding patience was not my thing.

"I wouldn't call it that, Annie. Tommy has had to steal and break into places to stay alive really. Poor kid had lost both his parents in a fire when he was 13 and became a ward of the state not long after. He had had a gut full of foster homes and decided to leave Melbourne and start again in a small town, Brambly Cove to be precise. Nearly four years ago now."

Aghast, I looked away.

"I had no idea, Stella. He's said nothing about this to me."

"Tommy is a great young man. I know he'll tell you when the time is right, I promise. I just needed you to understand. He is the most loving, honest, and reliable kid. I officially became his guardian a couple of years ago. Honestly, he was a blessing to me from the start. I never was able to have a child of my own. Mabel would say that's because of the curse Annabelle put over our family. I don't believe that crap for a second. Mabel has hated Tommy since she first laid eyes on him. Tommy tried so many times, but she blocked his every attempt every time. She especially hates that Tommy has worked for Jack for the last few years and they have become so close."

I sat in stunned silence. Again, this was not something Tommy had really let on.

So, he wasn't a real Anderson. Interesting. Doubt was creeping in as my brain searched for both assurance and clarification. I knew nothing about him really. Obviously, Stella adored him, but he was also once a criminal....and I had just kissed him. What else had he lied about?

Awesome. Great choice Annie. So typical of me.

My pathetic inability to judge true character wins again...

As I wrestled to squash thoughts of Caleb, another thought hit me. Pa had trusted him from the start. Annabelle also made a point of telling me he was a good person. Stella clearly loved him enough to adopt him as her own. And truth be told, Tommy had been nothing but kind and supportive to me.

I wanted so badly to trust him. Should I be that brave?

The banging of the screen door jolted me into the present. Tommy was back to collect me as promised. Stella looked at me for the longest time, her features soft yet her pained look acknowledging our shared burden. Tommy was so lucky to have her. She stood, collecting our cups and leftover cake.

"I'll stay here Annie. Promise I'll let you know the minute I hear anything. Go with Tommy now. He will have a plan. You are safe with him, dear girl. I hope you guys find Jack. I simply love that man like my own father."

I hugged her fiercely before flying down the wide hall, nearly crashing into Tommy on the other side of the front door as I did. Part of me wished I had. At least that would have been another excuse for contact. Focus Annie. My emotions and thoughts had been so scattered and ever-changing since arriving here, not a personality trait I'd ever thought would apply to me.

Just then my hoodie beeped from across the veranda. Someone had left me a voicemail message. Fumbling to get my phone free from the front pocket my lighter fell onto the ground.

Retracting slightly, I cringed. I couldn't explain this now. Not ever really.

Tommy picked it up and handed it back to me without question, still smiling but with his eyebrows slightly raised. Intensely relieved, I got busy focusing on retrieving the message.

"It's from an anonymous number. Maybe my mum, man I hope so. She needs to get here soon I'm thinking."

Tommy nodded, standing so closely I could feel his warm breath on my neck.

"What, tell me, what's wrong Annie?"

Tommy gently turned my body to face him. Obviously, the shock on my face said it all. I felt the air leave my lungs. Instinctively I threw the phone away before I grabbed for him. Tommy held on tight. My legs felt like jelly.

The sound of my heartbeat thrashed in my ears. Stella came running to our aid, but I couldn't speak. She steadied me as Tommy retrieved the phone, replaying the message on speaker. I hugged my own body tightly. Suddenly unaware of my surroundings my vision blurred. Tommy replayed the message again and again, until putting my hands over my ears I begged him to stop.

We have Jack.

We will exchange him for the treasure.

All of it this time.

You have until midnight on Sunday.

Leave it in unmarked bags at the quarry.

Don't attempt to involve the police.

Or Jack will die.

Blindly I followed Tommy. We kept a steady pace heading toward the headland.

No point standing around he had said. Tommy was right, it was already Thursday, and that only gave us just over three days to find Pa, and the treasure, and somehow sort this mess out.

Stella had taken off to the Anderson Estate, giving me her word, she would do her best to talk to Mabel. Stella still seemed unsure Mabel had anything to do with it at all. My bet was absolutely she did.

Bitch.

The voice on my phone had been automated. Impossible to identify. There was no way of tracing the number other than going to the police station. That's if they would believe us at all. Clearly, Tommy hadn't wanted me to alert them to Pa's disappearance earlier in the car. But why?

My muscles felt so weak, forcing me to focus to even keep up with Tommy. The tightness in my chest was worsening. And as for Tommy, I could all but feel his seething anger as it leached from his core. Tommy cared deeply about Pa, there was no doubting this now.

"Hey Tommy, wait up a sec, could you."

I could barely catch my breath. Sitting on a fallen log alongside our track, I wiped beads of sweat from my face and neck. In an instant, Tommy was by my side. His look of concern replaced some of his hardened features. Placing his hand on my back, he offered me a reassuring smile.

"Try to take some deep breaths, Annie. You are as white as a sheet. Shock most likely. It will pass."

Tommy stood again pacing up and down. All the while, he kept a watchful eye on me and reminded me to breathe. He rubbed the back of his neck, cursing.

"When I find the person or people responsible for this, I swear to you Annie, it ain't going to be pretty. I don't care if they send me back to jail. It will be worth it."

"What's our plan then? Where are we going now?"

I stood, feeling a little more grounded. Tommy needed me to be strong. I got the feeling his tough disguise was merely an act. I knew all about facades after all.

"I figure we sweep the beach again and the cliff lines, maybe we missed something. Then, if nothing turns up, we go to the Anderson's. That's not going to be easy, but we don't have much choice. Security is tight there, and let's just say, I'm not a welcome visitor. Mabel has called the police on me on more than one occasion. Stupid old tart, I totally get it if you don't want to come with me, Annie."

I knew now wasn't the time to ask Tommy about his story. Instead, I reached out for his hand, squeezing it reassuringly.

"Where you go, I go. Lead us on then hey."

Tommy looked at me with renewed attention. Our connection was electric. Smiling and nodding he turned to walk on. Never once did he let go of my hand.

When we arrived at the edge of the headland, Tommy stopped. To my right, the same beach track we had been on only hours earlier came into view. Beyond that, was only the vastness of the open ocean. Coastal birds swirled and screeched, as the wind pressed in almost pulling us back. It was impossible not to think of Annabelle and what she had endured for her family.

My family.

Gazing across to my left, for the first time I noticed the small clump of well-established pine trees. Reaching tall, they huddled in unity, and almost seemed to peer over the edge of the cliffs. They looked out of place somehow.

"Have you been up there Annie, to Annabelle's tree house?"

With widening eyes, I shook my head, and biting my lip I turned away to try to understand my spinning thoughts. Surging from my core came a sense of betrayal.

For as long as I could remember I'd loved the painting along the staircase depicting this place. So many nights I'd imagined being there, seeing fairies and magical creatures. And for as long as I could remember my family had told me this place didn't exist. Annabelle had a wild imagination, too, they had said.

I barely heard Tommy beside me as he continued to talk. I fought to clear the lump in my throat. What else had they lied about?

"Captain Patrick built Annabelle a treehouse up in those pines. Ya Pa told me all about its history ages ago. I slept up there the first few nights after I came to Brambly Cove. That's where Jack first found me. We didn't know each other from a bar of soap, but he was kind to me from the very first moment. There I was, trespassing, angry and defensive. But do you know what the first thing he said to me was? You look like you could use a good feed and a shower mate.'

After a shallow sigh I smiled. Yep, that was Pa through and through. Tommy casually draped his arm over me.

"So, ya Pa told me, as the story goes, Patrick built the tree house for Annabelle so she could paint and sketch from up there, and all the while, watch for his ship to return. Apparently, after Patrick disappeared, never a day went by that Annabelle didn't climb up and search for him along the coastline. Rain, hail, or shine your Pa said."

Squashing down the ache, I forced myself to focus on the now. My admiration for Annabelle just kept growing, I had to see this place. I pulled Tommy toward the hidden treehouse.

"Let's go! Maybe Pa's there? Or Annabelle even? God knows we could use her help right now."

Tommy shrugged and started walking toward the pines. Eagerly I ventured closely behind him, a renewed energy had taken hold. The trek was slightly uphill from our current track, and deceivingly longer than I had first thought. We kept a fast pace for almost 10 minutes before coming to the clearing amongst the trees.

This was even better than the painting. Captivating me from the first second, I stood, completely mesmerised. Pa had refused to sell Annabelle's creations. He had told me as much just the other day. Now I understood why. I wondered how many other paintings reflected her special spots or memories.

Pine needles covered the ground, creating a thick cushioning around the trees. Tiny mushrooms and colourful wildflowers grew randomly. Daisies, there were so many daisies, I smiled thinking of Annabelle's letter.

The sun danced through the branches as a soft breeze whistled through the pines. Instantly I felt a sense of belonging; my emotions were on overdrive. I could feel Annabelle here for sure, and there was something else about this place, too, literally making the hairs on my arms stand upright. This land held a strange energy and magnetic pull that were unmistakable.

Closing my eyes, I inhaled the sea's scent. I listened for the wind to whisper its truth as my hair danced around me in the breeze. Significant secrets remained, and I knew it was no accident I was here.

"Well, this is it, Annie. Cool hey. That ladder over there on the tree closest to the headland, leads up to the wooden platform overlooking Brambly Cove. Okay, Ready to go back?"

Raising my eyebrows, I felt my jaw drop.

"What? Are you kidding? I can't go now! I've got to see up there for myself. I can't explain it, but I need to be here for a bit. I feel it in my gut, Tommy."

"But Pa is not here Annie, so we are wasting time."

I knew he was right yet couldn't seem to tear myself away from Annabelle's treehouse.

"I will catch you up on the beach Tommy. I promise. I'm fine now, I feel better. But I just need some time alone here. Sorry, I know it sounds weird, but I totally can feel it."

Tommy marched toward me. For a split second I flinched thinking perhaps he was going to drag me out of there. Instead, Tommy gently kissed me on the lips. This time I kissed him back, and a tingle of pleasure flooded my body. Entwining limbs I pressed into him, wanting the moment to last. Tommy pulled away gently.

"Then be careful Annie. Promise me? Ring me if you need. I will be right below you on the beach. "

He paused, his eyes locked with mine.

"Annabelle did say you were the chosen one right? Then at some point ya have to believe in ya self. You gotta own it. Who am I to argue with that!"

There was no malice or smart-arse tone in his comment. Just trust. It had been so long since I'd felt validated in my opinions, that I felt myself standing a little taller as the rush of relief took hold. All I could do was nod and smile.

I watched him go for the longest time, almost unable to tear my eyes away from the mysterious yet utterly gorgeous Tommy. He sure was full of surprises. And to add to that, his genuine concern for me was beautiful, almost too good to be true. Feeling a little defensive again, I was starting to think maybe Tommy wasn't the only one with a crush. These feelings had never been on my agenda.

Shaking away thoughts of Tommy, I twirled in anticipation, heading toward the laddered tree. I was buzzing without question, eager to see what lay above and beyond. Annabelle had cherished this place.

Loved and grieved here. Although impossible to see it through her eyes, I would do my best to try. I'd have to ask Pa all about it as soon as I get back.

Mid thought, I felt the heat rise from my toes. I gripped onto the ladder, steadying my dizzy head.

How could I have forgotten?

My breath restricted in my chest.

I couldn't ask Pa. He wasn't back at Brambly Estate.

What if I never saw him again?

Captain Patrick had vanished, then Annabelle, and now it was happening again.

But this time it was different. Worse.

This time the outcome was up to me.

The view was spectacular, bringing me a sense of calm. The entire cove unfolded before my eyes, followed by an endless horizon. Soon the sun would set once again.

That meant 24 hours since Pa had been gone.

We had two days left.

Time stilled, captivating my imagination, and giving me goosebumps. Annabelle had spent hours, days in this very spot. Retrieving her letter from my backpack, once again I let her words wash over my subconscious. Annabelle had only been two years older than me, so young and naive when writing it, yet also so brave. It made me smile knowing her desire to create love between Patrick and herself had been fulfilled.

Sadly, the reality was, that love had not been enough to protect Annabelle and Patrick.

Needing to get back to Tommy and our search for Pa, I texted him, letting him know I was on my way before descending the old ladder carefully. As I turned to leave this newfound haven, I froze.

Annabelle sat gracefully amongst the daisies at the base of the tree. She smiled up at me briefly before returning her focus to the flowers, picking one after another and looping them together.

"I loved this place, Annie. It was always where we would spend our final moments together before Patrick would sail abroad. And it was always here, where I'd see his ship finally returning. He would sail by Brambly Cove, before docking just around the headland in Welshpool. Patrick always said he could see me waiting up here from the deck of his ship, I knew he couldn't, but it made me feel so loved. Never did I miss even a day coming here after he disappeared in case there was an ounce of truth to it. I wanted to be the first thing he saw, upon finally returning to us."

Her voice was soft, but clearly her inner torment was still ever-present. Yet this afternoon her aura was strong. She looked completely alive and human like; only tiny speckles of orange light gave her away. Maybe it was this place, considering it was her most cherished connection to earth.

Annabelle reached toward the ground and began brushing away the thick carpeting of needles just beneath the old, laddered pine tree.

"Annabelle, I think Mabel might have something to do with Pa's disappearance."

Still, Annabelle seemingly disregarded me. On her knees now, she was getting quite rigorous in her task. What on earth was she doing?

I crouched beside her.

"Annabelle, did you hear me? Please, I need your help."

Looking up at me through the swirling dust she'd created unearthing the deep seeded groundings, Annabelle's face remained motionless. She was fading, seemingly recoiling from me.

"I need your help too, Annie. And yes dear, you are correct. Mabel has everything to do with this. And she is not alone in her venture. They are a dangerous force those women."

And just like that she was gone. Pressing my hands into my temple I wanted to scream, scrunching my eyes tightly shut instead.

This was impossible. Enough with the cryptic crap Annabelle. What women?

I sat heavily next to where Annabelle had been only moments ago; only her scent remained now. I closed my eyes again, forcing myself to calm down and get it together. Unconsciously, I moved my hands around the exposed fresh earth below.

"Ouch. Shit!"

Something rough had splintered my palm. My eyes flashed open as I paused to examine the cause of the sudden sting. Instantly my pulse increased. Wide-eyed, I scurried back, remaining crouched to get a better look.

Disbelief swept over me, and I dared not blink.

Staring down at the old wood, adorned with a heavily rusted lock and latch, it was unmistakable.

"Trust in your intuition Annie."

Annabelle's voice danced through the trees.

I smiled, shaking my head.

Annabelle had exposed a hidden trap door in the ground.

Leaping onto my knees, I frantically cleared the area further, all the while scanning my surrounds in the hope Annabelle would re appear.

Once again, a curious sea hawk circled before perching on a branch beside me. I wondered, was this the same bird that had followed me along the beach yesterday? The majestic creature eyed me suspiciously, seemingly as intrigued as I was with my find.

Should I text Tommy?

Common sense said yes, yet something was holding me back.

Did Pa know about this?

I had no doubt that behind these mysterious doors, were answers I desperately needed. Resting on my knees I listened. Looking around silently, suddenly I felt nervous that I would be exposed. I just wasn't ready to share my find. The wind rushed the pine trees bringing with it a damp salty air. The waves crashed below, the seas roar abruptly all-consuming. The hawk remained above me, floating with the wind, yet now fixated on something out at sea. I was convinced we were alone.

The door itself was no larger than a metre by metre, weathered from many years of exposure. I traced the two brass hinges with my fingers. They were cold to the touch. Lifting the rusted padlock, I was surprised at its weight. Pulling at it, the lock held firm, tightly fastened.

"Really Annabelle? You couldn't just unlock it for me? So annoying!"

I looked up again for my new friend. He eyed me curiously, before beginning to circle. Jolting at the sudden screech, then instinctively ducking in fright, I covered my head as the sea hawk swooped. My heart thumped wildly at the creature's close proximity. When I dared look up, I saw it had landed in a tree further into the small plantation.

Was it trying to scare me away? Warn me perhaps?

"She was my bird Annie, my companion for many years after Patrick disappeared. This clever creature saved my life. She is guiding you too. Trust her."

I spun around, still crouched on my knees.

"Annabelle?"

Once again Annabelle's voice echoed through the trees. The bird shrieked again, this time flapping its huge wingspan from its position on the low branch. Scrambling to my feet, I tentatively began walking toward her and the tree in which she perched. All the while we eyed each other.

Circling the wide trunk, I ran my hand along the aging façade. Noticing first a hollow in the trunk, then the rough initials of Patrick and Annabelle. I stood completely captivated for some moments before reaching up and tracing the carving with my fingers. Again, a sense of connectedness took hold.

Instantly smiling up at the heavens with gratitude, I knew what I'd find.

Without hesitation I reached into the small hollow in the trunk, cringing slightly at the thought of a creature attack in response to my invasion of its privacy. Instead, I was relieved when my fingers touched a cold, hard object.

My instinct had been right. *Twice in one day, not bad Annie.*

I sat directly under the tree, bewitched. Completely energised, I buzzed on the adrenaline racing through my veins. Squealing like a child on Christmas Day, I hugged my find to my chest. The three skeleton keys were rusted and almost twice the size of any I'd seen before.

A beep in my back pocket pulled me from my elation. Shit, how long had I been here? Tommy was checking in. I'd promised him I'd be right behind him. But I wasn't ready to leave this place, not even close. I had to know what was below the door. It was like a magnet.

Begrudgingly I got to my feet, my stance restless. Pacing I tapped my index finger to my lip. Every part of me wanted to stay. Rip the door open and attempt to discover what was down there.

What if it held the answers as to where Pa was?

Letting out a slow breath I text Tommy back, letting him know I was on my way. The trapdoor would have to wait, Pa was still out there somewhere. I placed the keys in the front pocket of my backpack before doing my best to cover my find once again with loose pine needles and bracken. Satisfied with my work, I began heading back toward Tommy. My skin still tingled with the astonishment of my find.

As soon as I emerged from the covering of the trees, a blast of the late afternoon heat hit me. Despite being 6pm, the sun still had a sting, and the breeze was all but gone. Looking back, I searched for Annabelle's sea eagle, wondering about her connection with the bird, but it too had disappeared.

Meeting Tommy on the beach we agreed to spend the next couple of hours before dark searching the small caves along the rocky headlands. Dinner could wait.

"So, what did you think of the treehouse then Annie?"

Tommy kept a steady pace in front not looking back as he spoke. I was glad as I didn't want my excitement to give anything away.

"Amazing, totally surreal, I felt Annabelle there, and her sadness. I mean I really felt her Tommy. Annabelle's dreams and her hopes, her anguish and anger. It was real to me."

"I hope I get to meet her too, one day. You 're lucky she has trusted you with all this Annie. It's a privilege you know. Did you find anything interesting while you were there that might help us?"

I stopped mid stride.

A privilege.

Was it? I hadn't thought of it like that, too busy feeling the burden of it all I suppose. Typical Tommy to look on the bright side. Obviously, he had been through so much, yet he really did refuse to let it tarnish his outlook on life.

He turned back, smiling at me.

"Earth to Annie? Well, did you find anything?"

I swallowed hard, averting my eyes. I didn't want to lie, but I also wasn't ready to let my secret out. Not yet. I shifted awkwardly on the spot.

"Nah, but it was awesome to see. A sea hawk kept me company the whole time. Annabelle told me it was the same bird that had helped her on the beach. I definitely want to go back there, 100% when I get the chance. So, what's our plan now?"

I did my best to smile casually up at Tommy briefly before turning my attention to the ocean and praying he didn't see right through me.

Night had long since fallen, its stillness all too loud. Tommy had left a few hours back, promising to return bright and early with some food supplies and a new plan of attack. I wandered restlessly through the hallways, uneasy in my soul.

I knew Tommy wanted to head to the Andersons tomorrow, and even that thought made me nervous. But I couldn't let him go it alone. Stella had said Mabel had just laughed when asked about Jack's disappearance, animatingly stating an old woman like her could never have kidnapped Jack. Bullshit I say. Stella had said Mabel had then turned suddenly, like flicking a switch. She'd become furious at the accusation and Stella had been shown the door.

Guilty conscience maybe?

I could just imagine her reaction when Tommy and I showed up. That's if we even got through the well secured front gates, or past the two German Shepherd dogs Tommy had told me about. Last thing I wanted was to see Tommy back in trouble with the cops, and I had no doubt Mabel wouldn't hesitate to call them.

But surely it was time for me to involve the police? I get it, they were not Tommy's favourite people, but this was not a game. Tommy and Stella had warned me about Mabel's connections with all the right people. Apparently, she had much influence in this small town, as did her mother in her day.

Scary if that meant the police, too.

Hesitantly I asked Tommy if he could bring me back a torch. I hated that I had lied to him as to why. But it was a half-truth, however, as I did need one in the house at night, relying on candles was hard work.

Brambly Estate was eerie tonight. Annabelle was nowhere to be seen. I wished she would come back. I'd sat for ages on the landing of the grand staircase looking at her artwork in the candlelight. Annabelle's depictions of beaches, landscapes, birdlife, and Chinese artefacts all seemed to dance and flicker in my candle's faint glow. There was one, however, which drew me.

Annabelle and Patrick's tree house.

How long ago had she painted it? If it was up on the wall, then obviously mum and gran knew about it. So why was it never mentioned to me?

Her art was all created in soft pastels. She had painted speckled sunlight flowing through the trees and rays of golden light reaching toward the base of the ladder. A vine covered in small white flowers twirled up the trunk of the tree and its branches were entwined in the treehouse floor. Ornate seaside daisies carpeted the ground below, soft pinks, white and purple flowers, all with rich yellow centres. I smiled, thinking of the joy they must have brought Annabelle.

Joy, then absolute despair.

I wish Tommy was here tonight. I'd insisted he go, of course, not wanting to be a burden, yet now I felt myself wondering what it would have been like if he had stayed. I unconsciously smiled at the thought of him, of the electric shock I'd felt earlier today when he had sat close, and our knees touched. Even in such a short time of knowing each other, we had shared so many secrets, hopes and fears. I'd never done that before.

As I walked outside to the front porch, I flicked my lighter on and off. What would Tommy think if he knew? Crumpling onto a deck chair I pulled my arms and legs into my core. Would he still have a crush on me then? Doubt it.

I dialled my mum, only half listening as I assumed it would go to voice mail, and nearly dropping my phone when I heard her chirpy hello break through the night's silence.

"Mum! OMG hi! I'm so glad I've caught you. I've been trying to reach you for days. You all good?"

"Hello my Annie! Yes, all good here sweetheart. Syria is an eye opener that's for sure. I'm busy busy, but that's what I do best, right. I've had an amazing opportunity come about. An exclusive interview with one of the women on the frontline of this civil war. Annie, can you believe it! This is a huge offer, a game changer, and it will be amazing for my career, of course. I'm absolutely ecstatic as you can imagine. I simply can't miss this one. My people are setting it up as we speak, but I just need to be patient as it could take a couple of weeks to meet with her."

I listened distantly as I moved my phone down into my lap.

My heart continued sinking as she chatted on, oblivious to my responses or not. Mum as usual was in her own world. A world in which I simply didn't exist. My defeatist thoughts began dominating again, I was worthless to her.

"Mum"

I interrupted her mid-sentence.

"Did you hear that, Annie? The actual Minister of Defence has agreed to give me an exclusive statement."

"MUM! I need you to stop talking!"

I almost screamed into the phone. Silence met me on the other end.

"Mum, I need to tell you something. Can you please just listen to me for a minute."

"Annie, what on earth is wrong, hun? I was listening. I just thought you would be excited for me. God Annie, you don't need to yell at me."

I stood and began pacing.

Mum was not going to like what I had to say. But I knew it was time.

"Mum, I know you love me, and I love you. But you have no idea what I am going through right now. Actually, you have no idea what I have been through over the last year, but that's for another time. You are always so caught up in yourself, it is like I don't exist."

"Annie! That is no way to talk to me, I give you everything a teen could want. You live a wonderful life, and it's because of all the hard work I put in. Growing up I never had half of what you have. I think.."

Closing my eyes I took in a long breath, forcing my bouncing knee to still. The pre-programming in my brain was screaming at me to stop, to hang up the phone, make peace, but I wouldn't, not now. Things had changed, I was changing.

I'd spent enough time being invisible.

"MUM…STOP."

I kicked at the stone pillar. My voice was shaking, and heat flushed through my body. I forced another deep breath.

"Mum. Can you please just listen, don't speak, just listen."

Silence. Tightening my fists, I was determined to say my truth. Feeling lightheaded I sat and focused on what I needed her to hear.

"Mum, I know what I am about to say will seem weird, but it's the truth, I promise. Pa is being held captive. I got a text message saying if I hand over the treasure he will live. But I don't know where the treasure is mum! Brambly Estate is in ruins, Pa is dead broke, and time is running out. I know this sounds even more ridiculous but…… Annabelle is here. I have seen her. She needs my help, which will in turn save Brambly Estate. Annabelle says I am the chosen one. Tommy and Stella are trying to help me, but it's not good here. I need you mum. I'm scared and…"

Roaring laughter stopped me mid-sentence. My eyes bulged and I felt the heat rising to flush over my face.

"Oh Annie. You sound completely off your dial! Totally unstable chick! Are you joking around with me? Have you been drinking? Or smoking weed? Mind you, I think it's good to let your hair down a little, you are so awfully reserved most of the time. And who is Tommy? I hope you took my advice and got yourself a holiday romance. I like the sound of that…"

She shrieked with laughter again.

I couldn't do this. Not tonight, not ever. I was done with her.

For the first time in as long as I could remember, I felt almost worthwhile, like maybe I had a purpose. I was beginning to think maybe I was okay.

Time away from mum had shown me just how toxic she was.

Disconnecting our call, I switched my phone off.

Tears flowed freely now as I slumped down onto the front step. I began to shrivel internally, equal to each time I'd been dismissed by her.

Angrily I flicked on my lighter, watching as the flame came to life. An owl hooted somewhere in the darkness beyond. The ocean roared and for the briefest moment I wondered if drowning was as peaceful as they say.

Was I angry at mum, or myself?

Starting with my wrist I counted. Lasting till the count of 9 before the heat became too intense. Then I moved to burn the palm of my hand. Swirling the flame in a small circle I was almost oblivious to the pain and the smell of my skin burning.

"Round and round the garden, chasing teddy bears….one step, two steps burn me over there."

Angry hot tears continued to stream down my face as I spat the words into the night.

The flame circled again and again, scorching my skin. I watched almost in a trance like state.

It was addictive the way its intense pain brought me focus. In a moment like this, nothing else clouded my mind.

Who was I kidding, I knew it. As if she would listen. I'm so stupid.

I was in control of the hurt again now, and self-mutilation was the only thing I could count on. Burn pain was my friend, my constant other when the world tossed me aside.

When Mum rejected me.

I relished the familiar numbness as it washed over. For a short time, it would take my reality away.

This was the part I lived for.

I hadn't thought this through.

Too late now.

I'd needed to escape the internal dialogue. Block the voice of my mum, and her belittling words.

I felt like being reckless. Who would really care, should something happen to me anyway?

Not mum, that's for sure.

It was 4.17am.

Stars sprinkled the vivid sky, and the salted balmy air was near still. The moon loomed large, its yellow glow offering my only light.

Beyond me, the waves crashed and roared, seemingly more deafening than I'd ever heard the ocean before. The pine trees appeared somehow menacing tonight. Before me stood Annabelle's tree house.

Had she come here at night?

Down on all fours, I felt the earth's slight dampness. Moving quickly, I cleared the pine needles and loose ground hiding the old door.

My phone light was all I had. Stupid to have come here really, but I just couldn't have stayed at Brambly Estate another second. This place had drawn Annabelle many times, and tonight it had beckoned me, too.

My wrist and palm were excruciating, but I knew how to block that out. I had gone too far this time, leaving my skin swollen and blistered. At least I knew I could still feel.

I grabbed at the decrepit padlock. The first key I tried was the wrong shape, but the second slipped straight into the lock as if it had only just been released yesterday, smoothly turning, and clicking open with ease.

Yes! Finally, something was going my way.

Jumping to my feet I pulled at the old door. It was stuck tight. Taking a firmer grip on the aged metal handle again, I yanked. Nothing. Moving my hands around each side of the old wood, I felt for any sign of movement, tugging, and attempting to jam my fingers underneath.

With frustration setting in, I sighed. Catching my breath for a minute, I forced myself to think. Be rational Annie. You can do this, I willed, shaking my head silently and letting out an agitated laugh.

Nothing was rational about coming out here alone, in the middle of the night, with the sole purpose of heading underground.

I was filled with a mixture of excitement and trepidation knowing without question whatever was underneath me was of great importance. Annabelle had all but told me so.

Startled, I froze, a loud crack came from the bushes somewhere beyond. Last thing I needed was to get caught. Staying low to the ground I switched off my phone light, slowly edging my body toward the now consistent noise.

Something was coming toward me swiftly, snapping bracken underfoot as it moved. I could just make out the looming figure in the tree line, as my eyes battled to adjust to the shadows. There was nowhere for me to hide now. I braced.

Realizing I was holding my breath, I let out a silent sigh of relief as a huge deer entered my small clearing. It was so beautiful, seemingly unaware of my presence it began grazing on the sparse foliage. I'd never seen a deer in the wild before, but this beast was near the size of a small horse. I dared not move a muscle.

Suddenly noticing me and stomping its hooves, the deer backed away slightly at my intrusion. Together, frozen in the moment, the deer eyeballed me as I crouched. Time skewed, I flinched at its every move, not knowing what would happen next. The deer flared its nostrils before making a long soft grunting sound, raising its head slightly. Moving in closer still, it sniffed at my backpack. Should I run? Was I in danger? Its eyes were a rich onyx, and its light brown fur glistened with sweat. Had I not been so nervous at this moment, I would have been mesmerised by the closeness of this majestic creature.

Slowly the deer began to move away, not leaving entirely but continuing to graze further on toward the cliff line. Closing my eyes, I let my head fall back, relieved the moment had ended peacefully.

Re focused, I began moving my way around the edges of the trap-door, determined to get it open this time. On the left side I was able to slide my hand under a little further. Bracing, I used all my force to pull, and little by little the old door began to move.

Instantly a musty, earthy smell hit me, the rising air noticeably cooler and damper than my surroundings. I listened intently for signs of life but apart from the distant trickling of water somewhere down below, the tunnel was completely silent.

Peering inside, searching the blackness, my heart was beating wildly, nearly leaping from my chest. The space itself looked like a small mine shaft entry point. Perfectly square, rough wooden boards encased the structure. The only point of difference was an old ladder. Attached to the steeper wall, just below the door frame, flakes of rust disintegrated at my touch. Upon attempting to rattle it free, however, I could see it was still solid.

Just how far down did this tunnel go?

Had Patrick built this?

Did I dare climb down?

Then what?

I knew I should wait for Tommy, or Stella, or at least let them know I was here. That would be the smart thing to do. It was still dark, but as I stood to stretch and survey my surrounds one more time, I noticed the beginnings of a new day gracing the horizon. The deer was gone, I was completely alone.

Time was wasting as I procrastinated.

Never had I felt so brave, so alive, yet so utterly terrified.

Frowning, I narrowed my eyes, focusing on the tunnel. I grabbed my backpack and blocking any sensible thoughts or rational explanations as to why I shouldn't do this, I gingerly stepped onto the ladder, descending into the darkness.

It was impossible to hold my phone light and keep both hands on the ladder. A head torch would have been ideal. But I was here now and refused to stop. The ladder seemed secure enough. Deliberately travelling slowly, I gingerly placed each foot on the ring below, ensuring it was secure before continuing. Heavy bolts connected it to the rocky earth. Its metal was deathly cold to my touch, appeasing the sting of my burnt hand.

Metres below the surface now, I could feel the gentle flow of crisp air rising to greet me. This was a good sign, as it meant fresh air was moving through the tunnel. Somewhere beyond running water trickled faintly.

The smell was strong, dank, and mildewy, yet fresh and earthy all in one. Cobwebs were everywhere, dominating the small shaft. At least I knew I wasn't the only living creature down here. I wondered what else lived in this space.

Finally, my feet touched the earth once more. Looking above, I could see the faint glow of early morning and hear the greetings of the birds. I would have to be at least 10 metres down, I surmised. Retrieving my phone from my back pocket, I soon realised my torch light was not going to be enough. Its light, which seemed suddenly so insignificant in the vast space, bounced off the uneven rock walls, making it hard to decipher what was even real.

I knew tunnels like this one were not uncommon. Gold, coal and even lime had been sourced along this coastline for over 100 years. Breathing deeply, I noted that my fear had vanished. Replacing its impending doom was determination. I felt calm and purposeful, directly in control of this moment. I was completely intrigued as to why Annabelle had led me to her secret place.

Was this where the treasure was?

The shaft was only about 3 metres wide. Its old timber beams stabilised the structure and were placed every couple of metres along the side walls and roof. I only hoped it was still safe now. Nailed into the walls were metal candle holders with used candles. Finding my lighter, I went about creating a flame in the closest ones to get a better feel for the tunnel.

Running in two directions from the ladder, the mine shaft was in surprisingly good condition. One passage seemed to head out toward the sea, the other travelled inland. Tilting my head to the side, I squinted in both directions, totally absorbed in this moment of heightened curiosity.

Where to go first?

My thoughts scrambled again, returning without warning to my mum. She couldn't care less about me, nor Pa. I knew this for sure now, and the thought overwhelmed me with sadness. I'd lived in hope for so many years that I'd had it all wrong, that the stories in my mind were exaggerated. But her words today said it all, once again, she had gaslighted me. Absentmindedly I scratched at my scalded wrist, before shaking my head and pulling my shoulders back.

"I won't let you sabotage this for me, Isabelle. I'm done allowing you to steal my worth. People matter here. I matter, too, whether you can see it or not. I'm not going to run away like you did, mum."

My voice bounced off the walls, the raw malice in my tone even surprising me. Kicking at the stones I began to walk inland. I knew anger wouldn't help, yet it was hard to rein in. Normally I was good at detaching from mum, but I was finding that harder and harder to do since spending time at Brambly Estate. It was like I was discovering a different side to myself here.

If it were to be, then it's up to me.

I listened to Pa's voice in my head. He loved that saying. And he was right.

"I'm coming for you Pa."

Carefully I moved forward, lighting candles as I went. The uneven ground and loose rocks under foot, were making the journey hard to navigate. Grimacing I slashed at the cobwebs blocking my path stumbling and shielding my body as best I could.

Up ahead was some sort of table or box. Pausing I listened for any sign of movement, as I strained to see. Eagerly I lit more candles. Kneeling carefully before the small wine crate to get a closer look, I could instantly see it was a shrine for Patrick. Again, I felt the strong connection with my great great Grandma, and although hard to comprehend, the same instant internal response took hold.

A framed photo of Annabelle and Patrick took centre stage. Wiping the heavy dust away, I smiled at the happiness portrayed. Never did they envisage it would end like this. Unburnt candles stood tall on each side of the frame; I lit them.

Placed around the photo were Patrick's belongings. His pipe, ID papers and stopwatch, along with the diary Annabelle had written for him. Confused, I scrunched up my face, thinking back to the last time I'd seen them. I was absolutely sure they had been on Annabelle's side table only yesterday. I'd put them there myself. That meant she had been down here very recently.

Was she here now?

I flashed my torchlight in every direction, hoping to catch a glimpse of her.

"Annabelle. Hello? Are you here Annabelle? Please be here."

My echo was the only sound to follow.

Then I noticed a tiny Chinese bowl, partially hidden behind the photo frame. Were these Anabelle's wedding rings? Picking them up, I slipped them onto my finger without thinking. A sudden jolt of electricity ran through my body causing me to fall back, and almost hitting my head. The rocks below me were sharp, and pain ripped through my wrists.

Taking a deep breath, I attempted to stop my hand from shaking long enough to study the rings. Both gold bands, one was plain, the other had a large round carnelian stone in its centre. Nan had told me about this precious stone and its importance to Annabelle and her people. Its rich orange colour was unmistakable, even to a novice like me.

Suddenly I wondered if I'd disrespected Annabelle by trying on her rings and quickly attempted to remove them. A sheen of sweat formed on my cheeks, standing I flexed my fingers repeatedly, pacing the small space, all the while, they wouldn't budge. The rings were stuck.

"Stop fighting it, Annie."

I whirled around, searching for her.

"Annie, my rings are yours now. Keep them close, then you will always know the way forward."

Her voice swirled around the space, as the air became noticeably chilled. Suddenly I stood in complete darkness. The dim glow from the candles and my torch light had vanished.

Crawling amongst the rubble, I edged back toward the crate, knowing that was where I had placed my phone. Don't let it have gone flat, I willed. Sneezing, the strong smell of the vaporised candles and dust agitated my nose.

Never had I experienced such intense blackness, so dark I couldn't even see my hands in front of me. The shaft's stillness somehow seemed to intensify with the gloom. Again, yet further away this time, I noticed the distant trickling of water.

My fingers wrapped around my phone, and relieved it had charge, I switched the torch on again before re lighting the surrounding candles. Why had they all gone out anyway? The same thing had happened a few times at Brambly Estate when Annabelle had vanished.

Grabbing my backpack and checking the time, I decided to keep going. It was 5.15am. Each couple of metres I brought the candles to life on both sides of the tunnel, venturing on for what seemed like forever. Finally, I could go no further, the tunnel had ended, and I was faced with another ladder.

'Where on earth does this lead?"

My voice suddenly breaking the silence, seemed too loud for the space. I felt like my insides were almost vibrating with the energy and curiosity running through my veins. I was surprised to see it was now 5.52am.

Was I still under Brambly Estate's land?

Part of me wished I could have shared this with Tommy. I probably should have waited I surmised, testing the strength of this ladder before beginning to climb. Reaching the top, I was a little confused.

Instead of a door above me, this time I was faced with another small tunnel leading horizontal.

It was tight, I'd have to crawl, and there were no candles on the walls as far as I could make out. Considering my options, I stood entwined in the top of the rusted ladder. I began twirling Annabelle's rings.

I'd come this far, I needed to know what lay beyond, if anything at all. But this new tunnel was bloody small, it gave me the creeps. I knew I was stalling, and my arms were getting tense gripping onto the ladder.

I had to go for it. Pressing my lips together I moved up a step before crawling into the darkness. On hands and knees, I pressed on, cursing myself again I hadn't invested in a head torch. Cobwebs stuck across my face, constantly brushed them off with disgust.

Only a short distance ahead, maybe 4 metres the tunnel ended. But this time I wasn't faced with a dirt wall, instead, old lattice entwined with thick bracken. On the other side of this makeshift door the faintest tease of daylight greeted me. Smiling, I felt suddenly proud of myself.

"Not bad for a city girl, Mum."

I listened intently for any sign of life beyond my hiding hole. Cockatoos screeched above and a gusty wind seemed to be swirling outside. Pushing at the disguised lattice, initially it was hard to move. Eventually, the left side broke free, allowing me to poke my head out.

It was now or never.

Climbing out on all fours I scanned my surrounds, keeping low to the ground as I made sure I was alone. My exit point was hidden within large natural boulders, surrounded by an extensive native bush tree line. Unless you looked really hard, I could see this cave entrance would be easily missed.

Dusting myself off, I stood. The wind was fierce alright, the scent of eucalypts and dust swirled causing my eyes to water. The sun seemed extra bright after being in such darkness for so long.

Paddocks greeted me beyond, cows and sheep grazed contentedly. Distantly I could see a huge house and sheds. About 100 metres away, a farm gate separated me from the property beyond. Tentatively I crept closer, trying to make out the sign on the wire gate. Blinking, I couldn't believe my eyes.

Private property.

This land belongs to the Anderson Estate.

All trespassers will be prosecuted.

Mouth agape, I stared.

This was how she did it.

This was how Annabelle had burnt and poisoned their crops and cursed the Anderson's land without ever getting caught.

Arriving back at Brambly Estate, even from a distance I could tell Tommy was not happy. He stood, watching me approach, arms folded, a dark look dominating his usual relaxed demeanour.

"Finally! Where've you been Annie? Bloody hell, I've been stressed out of my brain!"

Perplexed, I stood in front of him, trying to get a read on what was going on. Had he found Pa?

Most of the time I wasn't used to being accountable to anyone really. Why should I answer to him anyway?

Truth or lie…should I tell him where I'd been? I tried to reach for him, but he moved away.

Pushing Pa's hat lower onto his head, he crossed his arms.

"Chill out Tommy, I just went for a walk to the tree house. I wanted to see if Annabelle or Pa were there. So what?'

"So what? I was worried is what! When you weren't inside, I went out there about an hour ago, and the beach, you were nowhere to be seen Annie. And we agreed to stay in contact on the phone. Hey and what's with the dirt and cobwebs all over you? Did you fall somewhere?"

He started pacing, running his hands through his hair. Oops, I hadn't thought to check my phone. Clearly, Tommy had not found the trap door I'd left wide open just beyond the tree house then. Inwardly I sighed with relief. Walking around him, I headed inside.

"Well, I'm back now, all good. I need a drink of water. You want one?"

Briefly smiling, in an attempt to appease, I struggled to meet his eyes. Hoping my airy tone would be enough to lighten his mood, I dared not look back. Dumping my backpack in the hallway, I headed straight for the kitchen. Coffee, the smell of a fresh brew had greeted me at the door, was exactly what I needed.

Doing a double take I froze, examining the kitchen from its doorway. That fluttery feeling returned in my stomach as fleeting elation took hold. Then just as quickly I was crushed with shame.

Tommy had done all this for me?

The table was set with a white tablecloth and a colourful bunch of flowers from the garden sat in the middle. A large blue platter held fruits, pastries, cheeses, dips, crackers and deli meats. A red love heart chocolate was next to a place setting with my name on it.

My hands instantly moved to cover my mouth. Blinking rapidly, I cursed myself silently for being so selfish. No one had ever done anything like this for me. Mortified I'd brushed Tommy off only moments before. Now I realised, I'd all but ruined his surprise, not to mention made him really worry. I'm such an idiot.

Tommy startled me, pulling me away from my humiliation as he gently ruffled my hair entering the kitchen. I hadn't heard him come in and his unexpected presence caused me to pause as my brain made its new connection. It was like I was on mute, standing here like an idiot. What on earth do I say now?

"I didn't know what you would like for breakfast Annie, but I thought it would be best if you ate properly before we went searching for your Pa today. Thought this might make you smile. I know you're feeling the stress."

I continued to stare downward like a stunned mullet as redness enveloped my face. After pouring us both a steaming mug of coffee, Tommy leaned back on the bench smiling at me. The gesture melted my heart. This guy was amazing. Me…not so much.

"Tommy I'm so sorry. I should have text you. I get caught up in my shit. My mum, she was so awful on the phone. She doesn't believe me. I told her everything and she acted like I was insane. Her laugh….it was so mean Tommy. But I know that's no excuse, I should have let you know. I'm…I'm so sorry…"

I hadn't realised my tears were so close to the surface, and without warning, they spilled down my filthy cheeks. Fleetingly I cringed at my appearance. Tommy must think I'm totally feral.

Instead, in a flash he'd crossed the room and embraced me in the biggest hug, kissing me on the forehead and removing some twigs and leaves from my hair. The twinkle in his eyes had returned and his brief grudge forgotten.

"You really need a shower, Annie. How'd ya get this filthy?"

I stood still as Tommy laughed and gently pulled some twigs from my hair.

"But after we eat okay, I'm starving, you must be, too. Let's pig out on this first, keep our strength up."

His amused grin said it all. I was forgiven. But I made a mental note not to let Tommy worry like this again. He really did care, and I was not going to take that for granted.

"This looks amazing Tommy, yep, I'm starving. Thanks so much for organising it. Honestly, I am sorry I worried you. It was selfish of me, I, well, I just got caught up in my own head. I didn't think things through."

"It's cool Annie, I get that, more than you know. I asked Stella to make some food for us at the café, and she came up with this! Pretty awesome hey!"

I nodded eagerly. More than awesome, it was the single most beautiful gesture anyone had ever done for me.

It was official, I was really into this guy. Not just his looks, his heart. Never had I met someone as thoughtful. Tommy was one of a kind that's for certain.

I was torn. Should I tell Tommy about the tunnel? I suppose there was no reason not to, but something was holding me back.

As I showered, I examined Annabelle's rings, watching the way the stone glimmered in the sunlight as the water splashed over them. To have been gifted these was such an honour, I'd cherish them always. Then looking beyond the rings to my damaged wrist and hand I wondered, did I really deserve them? My painful lesions were turning an angry red now. I'd been pretty rough on them in the last few hours. I'd better find some antiseptic when I dressed, in case infection kicked in.

That had to be the last time I pushed my burning so far.

As the water cascaded down my back, silently I pledged I would try.

But was I capable of keeping my promise this time?

Never had I envisaged I'd be the type to self-harm. Yet what did that even mean? Was there a 'type'? Obviously not. I wondered how many other people out there held close to their chest, similar secrets to mine.

This time I'd been senseless enough to burn where the scars could be seen. Idiot. I wasn't ready to be accountable to anyone for what I'd done. What I continued to do.

How could I ever even explain such an irrational act?

Truthfully, I hadn't cared at the time. My feelings of self-loathing had been more consuming than ever before, all due to Mum's phone call. The burn, like always, had been my saviour. Being in control of conflicting pain blocked out the world, and my stupid life.

Shaking my mood off, I hurriedly threw on my jean shorts and the long-sleeved white shirt mum had insisted I pack. Smiling into the mirror I shook my head as this was not something I normally would wear, but I liked the beachy effect it gave me, and secretly hoped Tommy would too.

Taking a little more time than I should have, I lightly applied some blusher, mascara and lip gloss. For the first time ever, I applied a little of the vanilla perfume Mum had gifted me on my last birthday. She had insisted I put it in my travel bag. Deciding to leave my hair loose and free to do its own thing today, its raven black shine draped over my shoulders.

Tommy was already waiting in his ute as I rushed outside. Music blared from the radio, drowning out the morning chorus of nature. Stopping briefly, taking in the sun and surroundings I almost felt a sense of calm, then just as quickly our reality hit. This was day three without Pa.

Tommy had jumped out of the driver's seat, half sliding over the bonnet to open the passenger door. He sure did make me smile, even when I was sad. Who even opened doors for girls these days? Tommy was one of a kind.

Greeting me with a wide grin, Tommy considered me for the longest time. Without thinking I reached up to kiss him, his lips felt soft and inviting. They tasted like lollies.

"You look beautiful today, Annie. Really gorgeous, and you smell delicious. This is the day! We are going to find Jack. I can feel it. You with me?"

Sliding over on the bench seat, I let Tommy's positive energy wash over me. Stretching my arms out in front before rolling my shoulders back, I found my breath coming a little easier. Carefully I tucked my hand further into the cuff of my shirt. The day was already too hot to wear a long sleeves, but I couldn't risk exposure. Not today. I spied the packet of open jelly babies on his seat and grabbed one grinning. No wonder he tasted so good.

"So, Annie, I figure, let's do it, drive over to the Andersons right now. My plan is to politely ask to come in and talk to Mabel. Then, if she goes into bitch mode about everything, we go to plan B."

My laughter went on a little too long, sudden nervousness taking hold.

"Which is?"

Tommy entwined his fingers with mine, vacantly staring ahead.

"I don't know yet Annie, I'm working on it. I'm so annoyed at myself, you know. I should have protected him."

Tommy removed his hand, crossing his arms protectively across his chest as he suddenly seemed zapped of the positivity I'd seen only moments before. A dark look came over his face, as he turned away from my stare.

"Hey, this is not on you, Tommy. Bloody hell, I was here too! The way I see it, we are in this together. I've got your back, you've got mine, okay?"

Silently I grappled.

And if this be true, shouldn't I tell Tommy?

He reached over and pulled me into a hug. *I need you Annie* the sudden gesture seemed to scream.

I knew I had to fess up.

"Tommy, there's another way."

Raising his eyebrows, he pulled back, with the cutest questioning look on his face. It melted me.

I took a deep breath, might as well dive right in.

"There's a tunnel. It leads into the back of the Anderson Estate. Annabelle showed me. I believe it was how she used to get into their property for years without being seen. I figure we can, too."

Tommy's eyes were like saucers. He shook his head, flicking his hands through his hair.

"And that's why you wanted the torch, right?"

I nodded. Tommy jumped out of the ute. Was he angry?

Rummaging around in the back he pulled out two huge torches, some rope, his backpack and some water.

"Lead the way then, girl!"

Tommy had been every bit amazed, as I was, on discovering the mine shaft. There was still so much of it left to explore, but today I'd lead him straight to the Andersons.

"You are one brave girl, Annie. Pa always said Annabelle was too. I'm impressed you did this all on your own. Should have told me, however. Would have been much safer ya know."

We stood staring at the trespassing sign on the Anderson's back gate.

"True, but it was nothing personal Tommy. Old habits die hard, you know. I'm fiercely independent."

"I get that girl, no stress. It's one of the things I love about you."

There was an awkward silence.

"I mean, like, that I like about you, oh shit, you know what I mean right?"

This was the first time I'd actually seen Tommy embarrassed. I broke out in laughter, giving him a shove.

"I get it! Chill out Tommy!"

I decided to change the subject.

"So, as far as I've seen, there are no cameras pointing toward Brambly Estate along the fence line dividing our properties or this back entrance. That's a win for us."

Tommy nodded.

"Good work girl!"

His animated tone and his spontaneous bear hug left me feeling on top of the world, just like every time he came near.

Jumping the gate, we stuck close to the tree lined fence, edging closer to the dwellings on the property. We agreed, should we see the dogs, no point in testing their friendliness, just jump over the fence and get the hell out of here.

In the lowline scrub, our last form of cover, we crouched about 20 metres away from the shedding. Beyond them was the Anderson's mansion. It was big alright. Clad in bluestone, it stood noble and proud.

Why on earth would Beth have wanted more than this? Or Mabel for that matter. I thought about Gran, who used to say greed is a bottomless pit which exhausts the person in an endless effort to satisfy the need without ever reaching satisfaction. Too true in this case alone!

Large fruit trees, green lawns and exquisite gardens filled the space between the shedding and the house. A cobble driveway ran down the centre to the sheds. To our left, a large stable, and to our right two more sheds. One was large, it was open and contained farm machinery. The other, much smaller, seemed old and forgotten, closed up and dark.

"So, what now?"

Tommy remained quiet.

"Tommy?"

"I'm thinking on it, just hang on."

He squeezed my hand. Then I remembered. Annabelle had said she was taken to the cellar of the property and held captive. My bet, Pa was there.

"Tommy, do you know the layout of the house? I think we should check out the cellar. Annabelle was kept there originally when Beth double crossed her, right at the beginning of this stupid feud."

I kept my voice low, and knew I had Tommy's full attention from the flicker in his eyes.

"How on earth do you know all this, Annie? And on that, what makes you think Annabelle used the tunnel to come here anyway?"

He looked so perplexed I had to stifle a laugh. Tommy's features softened.

"Actually, it don't matter, I trust ya on it all. Nothing would surprise me with the strange shit that's been going down here. Annabelle told ya right? The cellar is an awesome idea. Are you ready to move? We will stay low and head for the back of the stables. Ready?"

I didn't have time to think, as Tommy shot off sprinting across the open paddock. Blindly I followed, struggling to keep up.

The property seemed strangely still for mid-morning, something definitely felt off. The stables and machinery shed were both devoid of humans and animals. No dogs so far either, maybe they were inside the house with Mabel, if she was home at all. The only evidence which pointed to the house being occupied were the two white vans parked close to the home. Both had exactly the same black and gold signage splashed across their sides. 'Anderson Estate & Winery'.

I looked back across the paddocks, trying to imagine Annabelle appearing from the cave in the dead of night. Had she really been vengeful enough to destroy their crops?

"Annie. Concentrate! Let's do it. I can't see any sign of life, but we need to make this fast. Follow me okay. We'll go from tree to tree until we get to the shrubs surrounding the veranda. I'm pretty sure the cellar doors are around the back. Stay close, beautiful."

I nodded, my eyes following his hand gesturing toward the far-right side of the house. I was fidgeting, bouncing on the spot with antici-pation. I'd never dared do anything like this. But as aware as I was of the danger, my adrenaline was high, and I was completely committed.

I almost squealed upon making it to the old basement doors. They were so cool. Built into the old bluestone, stairs led below ground level to old wooden double doors. I pulled at Tommy to go, but he gestured for me to calm down and be patient. He was right, nerves were making me impatient. I watched him again scan our surround-ings, listening for even the faintest of sounds that might suggest we had been discovered.

Creeping closer, one step at a time, Tommy turned the handle gently after listening against the door for any signs of life inside. I tingled all over, my pounding heart drumming through my ears. I gripped the back of his T-shirt.

To our surprise, the door was unlocked and silently opened out toward us with ease. Surely if Pa had been in here, they would have locked him in? Tommy looked at me, shrugging his shoulders before turning back toward the dimly lit room and disappearing inside.

My chest suddenly tightened. I started after Tommy then stopped. Should I follow? My emotions were suddenly opposing. I was breaking the law, I wanted to run, but I also absolutely wanted to follow. I raced through the pros and cons seeking the rational information in my brain which was never going to come. I was struggling to focus on anything but the internal conflict.

This was not a game.

Jumping on the spot, I almost reeled back as Tommy appeared and grabbed my hand. *Come on,* he mouthed. *I got you, it's okay.* Reluctantly I followed. The room was vast, lit with softly glowing light, coming from lanterns in every direction.

An array of smells hit me straight away. Mixed in with the dampness was a sweet aroma from the jars of preserved foods along the far wall, and an astringent smell from the hundreds of bottles of wine lining the rooms façade. Both the walls and floor were bluestone and an old working bench stood tall in the middle of the room.

Old pipes lined the walls to my left, and in the far-right corner, a narrow set of stairs led up toward an old door, which had to be an entry to the house. Void of much light, and deathly quiet, we scanned the room.

"What now?"

I whispered, tugging at Tommy's sleeve.

"Pa's not here obviously. Can we go Tommy, something feels off."

"Hang on Annie. I'm just going to snoop around a bit. It's okay, we're alone. It's kind of cool right? I've only been on this property a few times, and never down here."

I wasn't so sure. Eyeing the exit, I wanted to flee. Second guessing this move, I suddenly needed this adventure to be over. Tommy moved around me silently. I seemed glued to the spot, hanging onto the old workbench as if it was the only thing keeping me from falling.

Abruptly I felt the overwhelming sensation someone or something was behind me, and all at once an intense blue glow filled the space between us and the only way out.

Spinning around I felt all the air leave my lungs.

Blocking the entrance was a woman. Her blue aura almost blinding, and her sudden laugh far too loud. She spread her arms wide in a welcoming gesture. Her white dress seemed to float just above the ground, moving as she spoke as if there were a breeze.

"Welcome Annie. I've been eagerly awaiting your arrival. We have so much to talk about, don't you think?"

Feeling exposed, my mind raced. My body heat was rising, as was my tightening chest. Vaguely I was aware of Tommy beside me, yet I was unable to tear my eyes away from this mysterious woman. Was she real?

Her smile was unmatched by the malice in her eyes. Her intense fevered stare chilled me to the bone. Clearing my throat, I dared speak.

"Who are you?"

My voice sounded weak, high pitched, and my tone uncertain.

The woman threw her head back, laughing again. A visible vein throbbed on her neck, as her jaw clenched. The blue mist surrounding her seemed to darken.

"Who am I? Oh, dear Annie."

Her inflection became scathing. She shook her head.

"Why, this is my home. And I've been waiting for you, for many years now, I must say. You look so much like her Annie. Just like Annabelle. She was my best friend once you know."

Swaying slightly, I blinked rapidly. Taking shaky breaths, I desperately tried to process what was happening. Tommy steadied me, securing his hand around my waist.

As impossible as I once thought it was, before us, smiling sweetly, was none other than the spirit of Beth Anderson.

Beth had insisted we sit, ushering us to the steps in the far corner of the room. Tommy and I waited and watched as she paced the small space. Her dress flowed behind her, almost cape like. Beth continually smoothed her hair, which was pulled tight into a low bun. The ornate Chinese hairclip, earrings and bangles she wore seemed completely out of place on her. Obviously, they had once belonged to my great great grandma.

"Ahh Annie. This takes me back. Back to the day I sat Annabelle on these very steps. Stupid woman. All she had to do was comply with my very simple instructions. We could have avoided all the years of angst between our families you know. Annabelle chose to be difficult. It was in her nature, you see. That bitch had been bred differently. I saw her true colours from the start. She honestly believed she was better than me, better than us all. Had she just listened, just followed my straightforward direction, life would have simply continued as it was meant to have done in Brambly Bay."

As she spoke, Beth almost spat her words at us. Tramping across the room, she appeared almost black now, but her eyes were surreal, glowing yellow. They radiated a fierce, uncompromising rage. Tommy remained silent, hanging onto me protectively. Pushing him gently aside, I stood. Oddly this woman didn't scare me, and the reality was, she was just a spirit. Beth, like Annabelle, was long since dead.

I needed to gain control. Every minute we were here, we were wasting time.

"Beth, your death has made you more delusional. But the reality is, you can't stop us from leaving now. I can walk straight through you if I want. We came here to look for my pa, but he's not here, so we are leaving. So get out of our way right now Beth!"

I'd impressed myself, sounding stronger than my wobbly legs felt. But reality was, I'd do anything to find my pa. I had more inner strength right now than I'd felt my whole life, and I was beginning to like the feeling.

Beth's appearance seemed to fade before our eyes, before rapidly gaining strength once more. I pulled Tommy up to stand beside me. As Beth moved closer toward us, I stood firm raising my chin and crossing my arms. She reached out and touched my face, I felt its electric jolt, causing me to take a few steps back.

"You are just as naïve as your great great grandmother, Annie. Annabelle is not as innocent as you think. She ruined me, for years and years that wench made sure I would never succeed here. She is evil Annie. Maybe I never could prove it, but I know it was her. That stupid curse of her caused us years of grief and ruin."

Beth was becoming manic, pulling at her own hair, and scratching at her neck. Her eyes were wild.

"Beth, do you know where Jack is? Is he on the property some-where? Tell me what you want, and I'll get it for you. All I need is the safe return of Pa."

"You know exactly what I want Annie. So did Annabelle. I deserved more. I deserved so much more in this life."

She was yelling now, staring at the ceiling, her arms stretched high.

"When Patrick rejected me, I was left with no choice. I would have been a far better mother to Charlotte than that witch. But Patrick insisted he loved Annabelle, so blinded he was by her exotic spell. She had the whole town fooled, but not me Annie. You know, Annabelle, risked her own daughter's life when she double-crossed me. But her precious treasure, always came first. It still does, can't you see? She's using you right now to do her dirty work for her, all because of the treasure. It's all she cares about. Not you, not me, not Jack. Don't remain blinded Annie."

I moved closer still to Beth, raising my voice.

"Shut up Beth. You are insane. Just a woman scorned, and a dead one at that. Now get out of my way. We're going to find Pa, and there is nothing you can do to stop us. You have no power Beth, none."

Beth reached toward me, attempting to slap me in the face. Her hand passed right through my body and with it I felt an intense chill. Abruptly, Beth fell to her knees, screeching.

Tommy stood wide eyed, looking like he was in shock. Gesturing to him, we began moving toward the open door and the daylight beyond. But immediately our escape was blocked.

"And what do we have here?"

A large, gruff looking man obstructed our exit. He held tightly onto a rifle. Frozen to the spot we met his cold stare. Tommy pushed in front of me, shielding me from the man. At the same moment, a spiteful laugh filled the room from behind. Instantly recognising it, I shook my head. Bloody hell, it was Mabel.

"Did you really think you could come here unnoticed, kids?"

Ushered back inside, we were forced to stand with our backs up against the wall. Another hefty man stood beside Mabel. He was also armed. Beth had vanished.

"I had half expected you two yesterday to be honest. Anyway, no harm done, better late than never. Only problem I have now is, who exactly is going to retrieve the remaining treasure for me. Hmm? I can't possibly let you go now, can I just."

For the first time, Tommy spoke.

"Mabel, please. I know you hate me, but this was all my idea coming here. So, I'm asking you to let Annie go. She's got nothing to do with this. You can turn me in to the cops, whatever, I won't say a thing. But please, let Annie go. And what about Mum? What would your own daughter think of what you are doing?"

Mabel looked from Tommy to me and back again. The men hovered. She smiled that same sickly smile I'd seen the very first time we'd met. She rubbed her hands together against her ample frame. Ornate rings glistened on her fingers. My bet was they once belonged to Annabelle.

"Sorry! That's not going to happen kids. Now, I will need some quiet time to think about what's next. My plan was really simple you see, and it still can be if you both are smart enough to cooperate."

Mabel cleared her throat, rearranging the neck ruffle and belt on her ugly yellow dress. She smelt of cheap perfume and too much hair spray.

"All I want is justice for my family. Payback for all the wrongs Annabelle put us through. How? It's so easy for you, just three straight-forward steps you will need to take from here. The choice is yours really. Firstly, I need to be provided with the treasure. All the treasure this time. Annabelle fooled me once, but that's not going to happen again. Next, I will pay a small amount for Brambly Estate and take ownership. And lastly, you and Jack must leave my town, never to return. Actually, come to think of it, you can vanish too, Tommy."

I burst out laughing.

Maybe it was shock. Or maybe it was her face caked in heavy makeup, or her lips stained an ugly red. Or perhaps it was the fact that this was not some movie, or thriller novel. This was real life.

Mabel couldn't just make these demands. We had laws, and she was threatening us.

Tommy poked me, his eyes begged me to stop. I couldn't.

"Mabel, you have got to be joking. This is all bullshit. You will never get away with it. I have contacts Mabel, and once they hear you are equally as insane as Beth was, you will be locked up yourself."

It was Mabel's turn to laugh. Her own demeanour swiftly turned dark and without warning she slapped me hard across the cheek. This one stung. The men grabbed at Tommy who was immediately moving in to protect me.

"Maybe Beth can't hit you, but I certainly can. You are a little spoilt bitch Annie, just like your mum was."

Tommy leapt to my defence again, wrestling to break free from the men. Almost yelling now.

"That's enough Mabel, how dare you. I'm ringing mum. She seems to be the only one that can handle you in this town."

Mabel let out a strange kind of cackle before spitting at Tommy. I was flawed at just how unstable she was presenting right now.

Had the feud made Mabel just as crazy as Beth had become? Maybe it just ran in the family.

"Go right ahead Tommy. You are the criminal in this town, let's not forget that fact. Everybody knows it. You are the one who broke in and entered my home today, then proceeded to assault and threaten me in your rampage… a defenceless old lady just minding her own business. Your attack on me and my home was completely unprovoked. I have these witnesses here to prove it."

The men nodded, still ensuring we remained pinned to the wall. Mabel sure had the power over these two jerks. She smiled and turned to head back up the stairs into her house. Despite her age, Mabel didn't look the least bit frail at this moment, her power trip seemingly energising her every step.

"Oh, and Annie. If by contacts you mean your celebrity mother, I made sure Isabelle fled Brambly Bay long ago. She will never return, trust me. Isabelle is no help to you now. And Tommy, Stella is not your mum, she is my daughter. Blood is thicker than water, boy. You will never be good enough to be an Anderson. You are nothing but low life scum."

My legs instantaneously turned to jelly, and suddenly I was feeling faint. What the hell was she talking about? Had my mum left Brambly Bay because of Mabel? Lost for words I stared as she slowly climbed the stairs.

"Men, you know where to put them. I need to rest and have time to think. And make sure you take their phones."

Without warning, guns were poked roughly into our backs, and the men pushed at us, forcing us to walk forward.

The Anderson family was nuts.

Within minutes we arrived at the smaller of the sheds in the far corner of the estate. I'd grabbed Tommy on the way, refusing to let him go. My body shook so much, I feared I would collapse. Tommy, however, seemed calm. He motioned to me that everything would be okay, while squeezing my hand. But I couldn't see it, I couldn't see past the worst possible outcome right now. Any confidence I'd felt earlier was shredded. I had honestly never felt this completely terrified.

As we were roughly shoved through the opening, hitting the dirt underfoot, I heard the heavy door being locked just as swiftly behind us. I searched for Tommy in the near darkness, desperate for my eyes to adjust to the little light we had.

"Breathe Annie. This is just temporary. We are okay and we can get out of here. Just let me get my bearings."

Tommy stood, pulling me up beside him. The space was small, with a single window boarded up from the outside.

"OMG Annie!"

I turned to see what had Tommy's attention from behind.

"Pa!"

I rushed over to the motionless figure, crumpled, face down in the corner. Kneeling beside him, I desperately searched for any sign of life.

"Pa, it's Annie. Can you hear me?"

He was clammy and lifeless, and in an instant, I was crying. Shaking him I screamed.

"Annie, stop, move. Let me check him out."

Tommy took over. Firstly, checking for a pulse, then sitting him more upright against the wall.

"He's alive Annie. Most likely had a hypo. Grab my backpack, I've got one of his glucose packs inside. It will bring him around."

What the hell was Tommy talking about? I was way out of my depth here.

Rummaging through the bag, I retrieved a small packet, holding it up for Tommy to see.

'Yep, that's it. Thanks."

Tommy ripped it open, before squeezing the thick liquid into Pa's mouth and tilting his head back.

"Come on old mate. Hey Jack? It's Tommy mate. Swallow for me hey."

Slowly Pa began to stir.

"It's working Tommy. OMG, you are a genius. What's wrong with him?"

Smiling grimly through my tears, I held on tightly to Pa's cold hand.

"Now the drink Annie, there is a little juice box in the bag. That will do the trick."

Soon Pa was lucid enough to sip and swallow the apple juice. Before my eyes he slowly seemed to be recovering. I didn't understand what had happened, but I sure was grateful Tommy had known what to do.

"Jack's a diabetic Annie. It's really dangerous for him when his sugar gets too low. He can have what's called a Hypo, and eventually he can pass out. Jack taught me early on how to help him should this happen. He really needs to be on regular insulin injections, but the stubborn old bugger says he can't afford it."

"Why wouldn't he tell me this?"

For the first time in my life, I actually felt annoyed with Pa. Tommy just shrugged.

"I just didn't want to worry you, love."

Pa sounded weak, but when he opened his eyes, he winked before squeezing my hand back.

"Too late for that Pa. Thank God, we found you."

"And you thought Brambly Cove was going to be boring, hey girl."

Pa looked across at Tommy.

"Thanks, mate, I owe you one."

As the day stretched on, being in captivity became less and less bearable. I was starving, thirsty too, but was equally as determined to save any food or water we had in our backpacks for Pa.

Not a sole had returned to the shed to further bargain with us. I'd have to assume we had been in here around 4 or 5 hours now, as the sun was beginning to set. We had no phones, not even a watch between us. Basically, we were sitting ducks and fear was beginning to set in. At least we had Pa, so to me, and I knew Tommy agreed, our mission had still been partly a success.

We had all taken turns in pacing, screaming profanities, and basically looking for ways to escape. Turned out, what had first looked like a rickety old shed, was pretty solid. So far, we'd failed at every attempt to break out.

Scoping this place out over the last few hours had made me wonder just how many others had the Andersons kept prisoner in here? It was clearly set up to be used as such, almost bare inside, windows and doors locked tight, nothing left behind that we could use to aid in escape or attack. The worst part was, I was busting for a pee.

Pa had little memory of his attackers, or how he had ended up in the shed. He could only recall going down to the beach to fish, had heard at least two voices behind him on the pier, then felt a terrible pain in the back of his head. After that, everything had gone black he'd said.

My bet? It was the same two thugs who had pinned us at gun point that had taken Pa down. Bastards.

When Tommy had handed over Pa's old hat, they'd hugged for the longest time. Clearly, their bond was tight, and their admiration for one another was deeply genuine. The more I spent time with these two, the more I realised I knew so little about my Pa and his life here. I felt ashamed. My memories of Brambly Cove and the people in it I realised, were mostly through the eyes of a child in the few times we had visited.

Pa pulled me back from my thoughts. The three of us, sat closely against the far wall of the shed now, facing the only door, ready should any one return. My body felt still and sore, I could only imagine how Pa felt, the blow to his head looked nasty but he had fobbed me off when I'd tried to look.

"So, miss Annie, what do you think we should do when we get out of here hey?"

I smiled at him. Always the optimist.

"Find Annabelle's treasure, pay out everything we owe for Brambly Estate and get on with living our best lives, Pa."

His laugh quickly turned into a chesty cough. I sat up alarmed but before I could say anything, he held up his hand to my face.

"I'm perfectly fine Annie. That sounds like a plan. You make it sound easy."

Tommy spoke without breaking his forward stare.

"What I don't get, actually, one of many things I don't understand, is why Annabelle just doesn't bloody tell us where the treasure is! What's with all the innuendo?"

"Who knows right!" I shook my head in equal frustration.

"Well, at least we got to meet the famous Beth finally. She was one crazy woman that's for sure, just like Annabelle explained."

Pa startled me with his hand suddenly gripping my arm.

"What do you mean Annie? You guys saw Beth's spirit too? When? She died not long after Annabelle disappeared you know."

"Yep, she was here alright Jack. We ran into her before Mabel. Do you think Annabelle knows Beth is around still?"

Tommy was facing us now as he spoke, still drawing lines in the dirt with his fingers.

"Who would have thought we would be sitting here, chatting about Beth and Annabelle like it was nothing much, or that it wasn't mind-blowingly abnormal and freaky weird! Take me back a couple of weeks and I would not have believed it."

Tommy chuckled.

"I bloody would have."

Pa piped up, getting more animated and coughing again as he spoke.

"Annabelle has been hassling me for weeks now. Suppose I should have assumed that Beth might return as well. She never was one to be outdone. She always was a real nasty piece of work."

"Mum said the same Jack. I wonder why spirits or ghosts or whatever they are appear on earth anyway?"

I thought back to what Stella had told me.

"Unfinished business I suppose."

The boys remained silent; I didn't need a response anyway. I knew the only way to get them out of our lives now was to resolve the problem.

And there was only one way to do that.

Find the treasure.

At some point I must have drifted into sleep, and dreamt I was home in Sydney. I woke, startled, stiff, sore. The rising damp from the earth had left me deathly cold. This couldn't be good for Pa. Within seconds the heaviness of my reality took hold as I adjusted to my environment. This tiny space remained so dark, it was near impossible to see anything at all.

How long had we been trapped in here? Judging by the blackness replacing the small shards of light we'd had earlier, it was well and truly night.

Jolting, I sat further upright. Someone or something was outside the door. I couldn't quite pinpoint what the sound was, but it was there. Quietly getting to my feet, I tiptoed over and strained to listen. Jack and Tommy remained asleep, resting closely together where we'd all been huddled against the far wall.

I could hear movement all right. Maybe Mabel or one of her thugs had finally had a moment of good conscience and decided it was time we go free. If not, surely they'd at least be bringing us some water, or even better, food. The intruder was moving around the shed, tampering with the window, then moving to the back wall before rattling on the door.

What on earth were they doing?

"Annie. Annie, can you hear me? Are you in there?"

I froze.

Surely not! I had to have heard that wrong. Maybe I'd become delusional over the last few hours. They say captivity does strange things to people. I attempted a deep slow breath.

"Annie, if you can hear me, give me a knock or a sign."

I swallowed hard. This could not be possible.

"Mum?"

"Oh, thank God. I knew it would be here or in the basement that old bitch would stash you. I'm here now, all is good. I'll get you out. I've had a stack of coffee and I'm amped and ready to roll. Is Pa in there, too?"

I silently stared at the back of the door, blinking profusely. Then turning to check on Pa and Tommy, I was relieved to see neither had stirred. I felt every muscle stiffening as my brain scrambled to keep up or even begin to process what was happening.

What the hell?

It was absurd, my celebrity mother should have been on the other side of the world right now.

Did I even want her here?

"Annie? Are you still there? Are you injured? Talk to me sweetheart."

How did I know this wasn't just another trick? Maybe ghosts could take on other's persona or something. Nothing would surprise me after coming to Brambly Bay.

"Is that really you mum? How do I know it's you?"

"Oh Annie, typical. Let's not make a drama of the how or why please. Let's just get you out of here. No time for melodrama if you want to get home, okay!"

A slight smile formed. Yep. It was Mum all right. I shook my head, absolutely baffled as to how that could be, but she was right, this was our opportunity to finally get out of here. I forced myself to focus.

"Mum, we have been in here for ages. I'm here with Pa and Tommy, Stella's son. Pa is pretty weak. Mabel has had him in here for days before we got to him. She is such a mole!"

"That we agree on Annie. I know all about Mabel! You have done well my girl. I knew you would. Now, I'm here to help. And Annie, for what it's worth, well... I'm sorry chick."

Right then and there I started to cry a sea of mixed emotions. Tears just kept coming. I stood in the darkness, hands covering my face, silently sobbing. Maybe it was the rush of relief that we were found, or maybe it was the fact Mum had seen me as worthy enough to come back for. Then again, my scrambled thoughts were still considering if I could trust her at all.

Tommy was suddenly by my side, pulling me into a hug.

"What's going on Annie? Are you alright?"

I smiled through my tears, nodding, then shrugging. Was I?

"Don't ask me how, but Mum is outside. She has come to get us out of here apparently."

He looked suddenly as dumb struck as I felt. All I could do was shrug my shoulders.

"Well, I'm not going to argue with that! I will get Jack ready to move then, hey."

I nodded, returning my attention to the door.

"Mum, tell me what I need to do."

"That's my girl. Now stand back a bit. I'm going to bust this darn lock open with my bolt cutters."

I'd never seen mum use a tool in her life and felt my eyebrows raising in amusement.

"I see my daughter has arrived."

Pa had joined me and was laughing, shaking his own head now and clapping.

"Hi Issy. Thanks for coming. I'd offer you a cuppa, but I'm fresh out in here unfortunately."

"Dad! Hi! I'm on this rescue thing, just give me a sec."

Again, I shrugged at Tommy, Pa winked at me, we all chuckled somewhat nervously.

"She is more than capable Annie, don't you worry about that. Pa turned his attention back to the door.

"Issy, just keep the noise down, there are security guards and dogs, not to mention Mabel. So be careful."

"I've checked everything out dad, and it's quiet as a mouse out here."

Before I knew it, there she was. Isabelle Robinson in the flesh. Grinning from ear to ear, Mum rushed to embrace me, then Pa and finally Tommy.

"Let's get out of here. You lot have some explaining to do, but by the look and smell of you all, a long shower should come first."

I stared as she spoke, swirling emotions rendering me unsteady. Part of me was ecstatic to see her, but an even bigger portion felt guarded and confused. She was dressed in a black jumper and jeans, and farm boots I'd never seen before. Her hair was pinned back beneath a cap.

Who was this version of Isabelle Robinson? Just a day ago I loathed her. Impulsively, I reached for the security of my lighter in my pocket.

"Okay, we all need to stay close, and make this fast. Let's aim to get out the same way we came in hey, Annie. Otherwise, the cameras will spot us for sure. Isabelle and Jack, we will show you guys the way."

Tommy sounded confident and just as eager as I was to get the hell out of here. Mum grabbed my arm gently, smirking as she pulled me forward.

"I know the way Annie. How do you think I got here."

Restless and unable to sleep, I was beyond expecting reason. If nothing else, I'd learned common sense didn't seem to apply within this town. Brambly Bay's crazy residing spirits were a law to their own.

How many other spirits roamed our earth?

I had wanted to resolve some things with Mum as soon as we'd arrived home, but stating she was tired, she promised we would talk in the morning. Disappointed, I felt the familiar feelings of rejection take hold at her dismissal but reminded myself, she had travelled a long way to be here for me, and I needed to be patient.

Brambly Estate was eerily still and cloaked in darkness. In a few hours, another new day would be greeting us. Surely it couldn't be more dramatic than the last few weeks. Bloody hell, I hoped not.

Creeping into Pa's room, I listened for his soft breath as he slept. I wish he'd let us take him to the hospital to get checked out.

"You can cart me to the hospital when I'm dead" he'd said. "I'm staying here with me shot gun, in case those bastards return to cause trouble."

He was a stubborn old bugger, there'd been little point arguing.

Tommy had gone home earlier, and I found myself missing him already. His hug had said it all, empowering me to be brave. When Tommy had whispered in my ear, I'd felt my skin tingle from head to toe.

You are amazing Annie. Remember who you are.

He was the amazing one. The way he'd saved Pa's life, I'll never forget. Descending the stairs silently, heading for the kitchen, I saw the flicker of light beyond. Was it Annabelle?

Mum sat with her back to me as I entered, emailing at a fast pace on her laptop. The screen's brightness seemed out of place in the dull surroundings. A small candle flickered in the middle of the table, another was placed near the sink. As soon as she saw me, she closed her device, smiling and pointing to the coffee pot on the stove.

"Do you want one, too? Couldn't sleep either, Annie?"

I smiled but hesitated, almost stumbling over which words to say. I felt suddenly awkward, not quite knowing who to be.

I was not the same girl anymore.

It felt as though I'd grown up so much in the few short weeks that I'd been at Brambly Bay. Despite not really having a choice, I liked who I was becoming. I was starting to accept that never were things going to be the same.

"Oh, while I think on it Annie, I've ordered 3 new mobile phones. They will be here first thing in the morning, I've had them delivered. One each for you and Tommy, and I will attempt to get Jack using one, too. We all need to be in close contact and I know Mabel took yours."

I was a little taken aback with her gesture.

"Thanks heaps Mum, that's really kind."

She gave me a fleeting smile before looking back down at her laptop.

"I'm not trying to be kind Annie, just smart. Clearly, we are dealing with some very unstable characters, and this town seems to have its own set of rules."

Awkwardly I sat on the plastic chair nearly tipping it over. A little of my coffee spilled across the floor. Jumping up I grabbed a cloth, putting all my attention into the clean up so I could avoid eye contact a little longer. Finally sitting, I stared into the steaming liquid almost jumping at the sound of mum's sudden high-pitched tone.

"OMG, Annie, where on earth did you get those rings? They were Annabelle's, I'd know the carnelian stone anywhere. Please tell me you didn't just help yourself? That would not be cool, Annie."

Flinching, I stared at her in disbelief. Was she actually accusing me of stealing? I felt my body go rigid. Squinting, I lowered my brow ready to defend. Instead, mum just kept talking like nothing was amiss.

"So, I bet I surprised you by coming here, right?"

Mum's big reporter smile was plastered across her face, yet tonight it looked out of place. Slowly standing I folded my arms across my chest. She looked tired. Without a full face of hair and makeup, Mum looked vulnerable, somewhat exposed.

"Yes, that's an understatement. What made you come here, Mum? Why the sudden change? Normally you just ignore me."

Unaware my suppressed hostilities were so close to the surface, I felt an angry heat spreading across my skin. Mum looked taken aback.

Typical I thought, she has no idea.

"Is that really what you think Annie? I ignore you?"

Deepening my tone, I glared at her.

"Who am I, Mum?"

She stood, taking her cup to the sink, pausing there with her back to me.

"What on earth are you talking about, Annie?"

"Answer me. Who do you think I am Mum? Tell me what you know about me."

There was a hard edge to my voice. I sat a little straighter as I watched Mum stiffen before turning to face me. For the first time I could feel the energy had shifted between us. She put her hands up the way she often did to stop me from speaking.

"I'm not sure what this is all about Annie, but I didn't come here to argue, that's for sure. I came because you needed me, and lucky I did, hmmm. I certainly don't think I need to stand here and listen to this."

Mum marched abruptly over to the table, grabbing her laptop, diary and phone. But I wasn't about to be silenced.

"Where are you going to run to this time, Mum?"

I stood, matching her defiant energy. Although she towered over me, tonight for the first time, I didn't feel as small.

"I beg your pardon! What on earth has got into you? You seem like a totally different person. Has that Tommy been a bad influence on you? I've heard lots about him you know."

I smiled but without any warmth. I'd rattled her all right, and it felt good.

"Was it easier for you when I was invisible? Well, I don't want to be that person anymore Mum. Pa and Tommy, even Stella make me feel worthwhile. And maybe I am. Annabelle understands me, too.'

Mum stared, mouth agape. I could see the hurt in her eyes for the first time.

"I didn't want to come here, Annie. I gave up a lot to travel halfway across the world. But I did it for you."

There was a quiver in her voice now, but she remained facing me, clinging to her belongings as if they were her shield.

"Maybe you shouldn't have, Mum. You clearly haven't cared for Pa, or Brambly Estate for a long time. And you sure as hell don't care about me. What was the lure, the smell of treasure? A good news story to boost your career? What is the famous Isabelle Robinson really doing back in her forgotten hometown."

I sounded like a bitch as my pent-up anger was leaching out. Yet as ugly as it was, I couldn't stop. Mum had backed up further, her scrutiny spoke volumes.

"Go home Mum, we're doing just fine without you. And just in case you are concerned I haven't stolen these rings, far from it. Annabelle gave them to me."

Turning to leave, I could see the shocked tears in her eyes. Pausing at the doorway, Isabelle looked back at me with a regard I'd never seen before. She went to say something but simply closed her mouth again before vanishing into the shadows.

I wasn't proud of how I'd behaved.

But I knew I wasn't sorry either.

I wanted Mum to hear my truth.

A heavy feeling swirled in my throat, making it almost impossible to swallow. I reached for my lighter and began to burn my thigh. Jamming my eyes shut, I relished the pain.

I wanted to be visible, but not like this.

The new day had dawned crisp and clear. I headed out for a walk to clear my head. Last night I'd been harsh, and it wasn't sitting right. Today I was determined to be more civil towards Mum. After all, she was here now, and if I wanted things to improve between us, then maybe I need to take the lead.

Tommy would be here mid-morning as planned and together we all needed to decide on our actions going forward.

I stood on the edge of the pine forest now, in awe of the moment. Breathing in the smell of damp wood, seeing the dew drops on the wildflowers, and feeling the salted air on my skin was breathtaking.

How had I not known I was missing this all my life?

Crepuscular rays. Pa had taught me all about them. He used to say when the sun's rays radiate from a singular point in the sky and stream through the gaps in the branches like this, it was God's fingers reaching down to tickle me.

Suddenly ripped from my moment, my smile faded. Abrupt voices filled the air, pulling me from my thoughts.

Where were they coming from?

As I cautiously approached the cluster of trees surrounding Annabelle's tree house, venomous voices echoed through the bracken. Pausing, I wondered, should I leave?

As if.

Instead, I crept up to a hidden spot behind a stump. Crouching low I listened, straining to see where in fact the heated debate was coming from. The sunlit air was separated by dark shadowed regions, making it near impossible to see clearly.

"How dare you, Annabelle!"

"It is you Isabelle, you who in fact should be acting with a little more remorse right now, don't you think? And it's Nainai to you, thank you very much."

Mum and Annabelle stood barely inches apart.

How had this come about? Had Mum connected with Annabelle's spirit before now?

Mum was gripping the ladder to the tree house. Was she trying to steady herself, I wondered? She ran the other hand through her hair before massaging her temple. Mum had taken a tongue lashing from me earlier, and now Annabelle was giving it to her as well. I kind of felt sorry for her. Annabelle stood tall and proud, hands on her hips. Barely moving she pinched her lips together and intensified her glare.

"You never should have fled. You betrayed our family, Isabelle. Did you think this would all just go away?"

"Are you for real, Annabelle? How could I possibly have believed you? It just didn't make rational sense. Not then, and not now. I did what I needed to, for Annie. To protect her."

"Are you daring to suggest I would ever hurt Annie? My great great granddaughter? She was the chosen one, and that fact still remains."

Mum threw her hands up in the air.

"Oh, enough with the *chosen one* bullshit, Annabelle. You just wanted to use me to get to the treasure. It was so obvious. And after the threats from Beth, well there was no way I was hanging around."

Annabelle stilled, completely focused on mum. Even from my hiding spot, I could tell she was instantly thrown.

"What are you talking about Isabelle?"

Her voice had softened. Mum shook her head, before sitting on the ground and burying her face in her hands. Annabelle crouched beside her. Attempting to touch Mum on the shoulder, Annabelle was abruptly shaken off. Mum turned further away from her.

"Tell me, Isabelle. What are you talking about? What did Beth do? Why did you not tell me back then?"

"What does it matter now anyway, Annabelle. I've done enough damage. My daughter hates me, and I can't blame her. I thought coming here was the right thing to do. I thought maybe, just maybe it was not too late for us. Clearly, I was mistaken. I will leave tonight, and I'm taking Annie with me. The sooner I can get us out of this screwed up town the better."

I shot to my feet, and without thinking began marching toward them.

"NO!"

Both women turned and stared at me. Mum leaped to her feet first.

"Annie, oh Annie, we need to talk, please. If you would just give me a chance to explain."

I held my hand up to her face. My look must have said it all as Mum closed her mouth and looked at the ground. Anabelle stood and walked closer to me. I ignored her.

"I'm not going anywhere, Mum. Neither are you. Not again.'

Annabelle went to speak, but one glare from me and she, too, put her hands up nodding as if she understood.

"I don't really know what the hell is going on, but it's time I did. So, let's just get it all out there. I want to know everything, from both of you. That I deserve."

I looked from one woman to another. Three generations, all of us connected by a history of torment and hate.

"Mum, we are not going back to Sydney right now. You left once, and in your mind, I am sure you had your reasons. But Pa needs you, he needs us. We are his family. Brambly Estate is our home. Treasure or no treasure, he deserves our support."

Annabelle was smiling, looking at me as though she admired my speech, her aura seemed to brighten. Mum was quietly crying, shaking her head.

"Annie, you don't understand."

"Then tell me Mum, I'm listening."

Mum sat again. I'd never seen her cry, not ever. Sitting beside her, for the first time I could ever remember, I reached out to place my hand on her back. Annabelle began to fade.

"I will return tonight, Annie. For it is then we must act. Time is running out, the new moon is coming, and should it pass, it will be too late."

With that, once again Annabelle vanished. Her yellow mist swirled up through the trees before it finally dispersed in the breeze. Mum watched, her eyes glassy and vacant.

Suddenly remembering one of my favourite pastimes as a kid, I began picking at the wildflowers and creating a daisy chain. I needed the distraction from this insanity.

"You used to do that when you were little. Do you remember Annie?"

Looking up, I smiled at her. Each teddy and doll I owned at Brambly Estate wore a crown of daisies on my visits. Those simple times I suddenly realised, were some of the best memories I have.

"Why did you leave here, Mum?"

"It's complicated Annie."

"I can see that. But it's too late to pretend I'm not involved now. Annabelle has told me it's up to me, all of it. I know all about the Chinese prophecy. How the hell am I meant to deal with that? I need you Mum. You owe me an explanation!"

Mum was nodding, staring at the ground, her tears becoming sob-like now. I intended to keep pushing her.

"I do Annie. I have always known about the prophecy. That's why I left before you were born."

"So, you became pregnant with me while you were still living here right? Just a blow in, a summer fling you said?"

Mum nodded, making swirling patterns in the pine needles and dirt. Her normally perfectly manicured nails were now chipped and broken. She still hadn't looked at me. She looked so ashamed. Never had I seen her like this.

"Then Annabelle told you something that made you want to leave? Right? What? What did she say?"

Mum hesitated, looking at the ground. I was intent on waiting this out.

"You've got to understand Annie. As much as I love you and wouldn't want it any other way, you were a big surprise. I was young, a bit mixed up. And well, when Annabelle returned as a spirit and told me all about how you were '*the*' baby, the family member she had been waiting for, the chosen one blah blah, well it kind of freaked me out. I thought she had lost her marbles. Never had she spoken like this before she disappeared. I mean she was secretive and weird at times, but not like this. Suddenly she was back, claiming she had died, but was not able to move onto the next world yet because of unresolved issues on earth. She insisted I kept our conversations private. Bloody hell, I was young Annie. It was a lot to try to get my head around. Still is honestly."

I tried to consider how Mum must have felt. It was impossible to imagine, and for the first time, I was beginning to see Mum in a very different light. There was more to her than I saw on television.

"So, you just left?"

"I'd never considered having a child before Annie. But as soon as I became pregnant, everything changed for me. Impossible to explain, but I wanted you more than anything. And that included keeping you safe."

"But Annabelle would never have hurt me mum. Surely you were not worried about that. She was your Nainai, you had lived with her your whole life. You knew Annabelle well."

"Annabelle never really let anyone close enough to really *know* her, Annie. I was so freaked out when she told me the whole story of her life. She showed me the letter she had written to you that first day as she sailed away from China, and the diaries she had written for Patrick. She shared how she had travelled through the mine shaft so often to destroy the Anderson Estate. But in the end, it was not her that finally sent me packing.'

I grabbed Mum's hand, forcing her to look at me.

"Then who?"

Mums face suddenly hardened. Clearing her throat before continuing, she fidgeted on the spot, twirling her hair repetitively.

"Beth. She cornered me one day shortly after my discussion with Annabelle. God, it was so awful, I will never forget it. That woman could be scary in her day, let me tell you."

Mum didn't have to tell me.

"Keep going Mum."

"I was in the supermarket, nauseous from morning sickness, still reeling from all Annabelle's recent revelations when Beth appeared, and boy did she get into my space big time. Somehow, most likely because this is a small town, she already knew I was pregnant. But congratulations weren't on her agenda that day let me tell you Annie. She threatened me, and you. And right or wrong, I believed her."

"Why? Over what?"

Mum was becoming more animated by the minute, and I was totally and completely fixated on this story.

"When Annabelle and Beth had been friends, Annabelle shared the letter she had written you on the boat. Beth knew from the start, all about you and the prophecy. She was well aware of what was predicted you would do, and in turn inherit. Beth was bat crazy, black with envy. She warned me then and there, that if I remained in Brambly Bay, or should I ever return, she would ensure you suffered a nasty accident, just as Patrick had."

I stood, almost reeling back. I couldn't believe what I was hearing. Mum hugged her arms closer to her chest.

"Shit Mum, that's horrible. I get why you took off."

"A strange thing happens when you become a mum, Annie. Even though you were yet to be born, you became an unexplainable force within. I loved you more than myself. Valued your life more than I could ever my own. So, the decision was made there and then. I would leave Brambly Bay."

I had no words, yet at the same time a million questions ran through my mind. All these years I had felt unloved, invisible. Yet she had done it all for me. Mum was not the woman I thought, well, not in the beginning anyway. She had been selfless back then, and she had been brave.

This woman, sitting beside me on the forest floor at this moment was seemingly a stranger. I'd never imagined Isabelle Robinson being capable of feeling insecure, yet right now, her mannerisms reflected just that. And if this was all true, why then has Mum acted the way she has all these years?

Fact was, Isabelle was distant, career driven, and absent emotionally. And as much as I wanted to forgive, it was going to be a battle.

Ambling back to Brambly Estate we walked in comfortable silence but despite the newly formed peace beginning to settle between us, my questions raged internally. Rounding the fruit trees separating the back lawn and paddocks, I stopped.

"What on earth is he doing, Annie?" Mum laughed.

Tommy ran toward us, waving his arms in the air. I smiled broadly, as my heart skipped a beat. He could be such a goof ball. As he came closer however, I grabbed at Mum unconsciously, as a wave of fear took hold. The anguish on his ashen face told me he wasn't joking around. Tommy began yelling, his voice shrill and shaky.

"Annie, hurry, it's Pa. It's bad. We can't wake him."

Was he crying? Images of what-could-be flashed through my mind.

Time seemed to slow down. I felt Mum push past me as she ran towards him. Stumbling, knowing I had to move, I just couldn't seem to budge. Frozen in the moment, I watched Mum sprint past Tommy, hardly acknowledging him as she continued toward the house.

I didn't understand. What could be so bad that Tommy couldn't handle? He'd been so confident yesterday with Pa. Tommy had known exactly what to do to help him. So why was he acting like this now? I replayed my movements this morning, cursing myself. I hadn't even checked in on Pa, assuming he needed the sleep. Had Mum?

Tommy reached my side and instantly braced himself on his knees. I reached for him, needing to connect by placing my hand on his back. I could feel him trembling through his raspy breaths. Tommy pulled me into a hug, his face was pale, eyes wide, his body clammy.

"Tommy, what's happening?"

Tommy held my hands as he spoke, almost whispering as he shook his head, tears streamed down his face.

"Mum and I came over about 20 min ago with breakfast for you all. I couldn't wake him, Annie. I tried, but I couldn't. He's so cold, I can just feel a faint pulse, but barely. He's at the bottom of the stairs. I think he must have fallen. God knows what injuries he has."

He was pulling me forward now. I didn't resist. Gripping his hand, we began to run. Everything seemed to blur. Images of Pa flashed before me and suddenly I felt as though I'd vomit.

Just inside the front door, there he lay, just as Tommy had described. A deep chill ran through my body, and as I looked around for Annabelle, I could smell her presence.

Mum crouched on one side of Pa's crumpled body. Stella was on the other. Clearly distraught, both women looked up at us as we burst through the door.

"The ambulance should be here any minute, Annie. He is still alive, but only just."

I fell onto my knees next to Mum, desperately trying to process what had unfolded too quickly. Despite wanting to flee, I couldn't take my eyes away. Pa's mouth drooped; a trickle of blood escaped his nose. Swelling and bruising were already forming around his left eye. He looked so small and frail.

"How long do you think he has been like this?"

I choked on my tears attempting to get the words out.

"Pa, Pa, it's Annie. Come on Pa. Please. Can you hear me?"

Tommy crouched behind me, letting me know he was there placing his hands on my shoulders. I could feel him sobbing.

"He's a fighter Annie, I know it."

Sirens, distant at first were becoming louder. I could only pray it was not too late. Tensely I reached for Pa's hand, which was partly tucked under his side. I wanted to squeeze it, just like he used to do to reassure me as a kid.

The first thing I noticed was how cold he felt, just like Tommy had said. But as I wiggled my fingers further into his fisted hand, I noticed he was holding something. Pulling the small piece of paper free, I unfolded the crinkled note.

In disbelief, my focus became solely on the words scrawled on the paper, barely registering the medical assistance arriving, let alone being pulled aside, I stared.

"May you live in interesting times, Jack."

My own voice was foreign, almost detached as I whispered the words. No one else had noticed, their steadfast attention on Jack and the paramedics. The room seemed to swirl and close in around me. I swallowed rapidly, trying to dispel the sudden thickness in my throat.

I knew exactly what this was.

The very same curse Annabelle had placed over Beth all those years ago.

Gasping for a breath, I sat bolt upright, sweating profusely as my heart thumped rapidly. Had I been having a nightmare? I couldn't remember. I'd been lucky to fall asleep at all, truth be told.

The old wind-up clock beside my bed read 3.12am

With shaking limbs, I struggled to light my candle and open the French doors. Welcoming the slight breeze, I stepped heavily out onto the balcony. Despite my exhaustion, my body remained agitated and tense with its overwhelming sense of dread.

Would Pa live through the night, into the future?

A blanket of stars covered the night sky, and the pale moon shone like a silvery claw. Apart from the distant crashing waves echoing from the blackened ocean, stillness presided.

The last 24 hours had been horrendous.

Pa remained in a coma in the Critical Care ward of the hospital in the neighbouring town of Wonthaggi. The doctors themselves were still unable to commit as to whether he would wake. His brain scan had revealed he'd had a stroke. No one could confirm if that had occurred before or after he had presumably fallen down the stairs.

Fallen or pushed?

I had my theory.

Pa's leg was broken, and his left lung punctured. It was a miracle Jack was even still breathing so the nurses had told us yesterday. A lesser man would not have survived. Jack Robinson was as tough as they came. This much I knew. But would that be enough? What I couldn't get past was the note. Where had Pa found it? Had someone been at Brambly Estate the morning of his accident and threatened him?

Was that 'someone' Beth or even Mabel?

In the chaos that had followed the accident, I still hadn't shared the note with anyone. It perplexed me no one had mentioned that I took it from Pa's hand. The whole thing was a blur however, shock had scattered us all from that moment on.

A stirring in the darkness below startled me. Leaning over the railing, I searched for the intrusion.

"Come down here Annie. I want to show you something.'

Annabelle had returned for the first time since Pa's fall. The way she looked up at me as if all this was perfectly normal, was agitating. But what choice did I have. Rushing downstairs, I moved through the house as quietly as I could.

Annabelle beckoned for me to follow without uttering another word. Did she even know Pa's situation?

"Where are we going, Annabelle? I need to stay close to the house, can't this wait till the morning?'

Ignoring me, Annabelle walked further into the night, striding through the garden towards the paddocks. Her pace was fast. Still feeling the weariness from lack of sleep and despair, I struggled to keep up.

Annabelle's aura was almost red tonight, different from how I'd seen her before. It reminded me of fire, with sparks and embers almost dancing around her frame. Her hair was loose, flowing down her back. Her bracelets jingled and her long gown made a swishing sound as she moved. Without question and despite my frustration, my great great grandmother was simply the most graceful woman I'd ever seen.

Just as abruptly, Annabelle stopped, turning to face me.

"All is not what it appears to be Annie."

No shit! I thought.

"Annabelle, you know about Pa's fall, right?"

Leaning against an old oak tree, Annabelle looked at me gravely, nodding. Making a prayer gesture with her hands, she whispered words I didn't understand.

"Was it Beth? Or Mabel? Somebody tried to scare him, he had a note in his hand, with the curse you supposably used on the Anderson's written on it."

Annabelle's hands fisted tightly, she closed her eyes, again uttering inaudible whispers.

"They are powerful words Annie. Not to be used by the unwise. History be my witness."

I drew breath and released before speaking, attempting to hide my agitation. She didn't try to deny she had put a curse over the Anderson family, which was interesting, but I needed to know more.

"Annabelle, I know you can't just come out and tell me where the jewels are. I get the whole prophecy thing but come on! It's pretty bloody desperate around here, you need to be a little more obvious, and more direct with me as to where I can find it. Please."

Her glow seemed to illuminate, almost sending sparks into the air around her.

"Annie, be patient. I understand it's frustrating, having to wait. Believe me, I do. But the prophecy was not something I wished upon myself either."

I nodded. Had I already ruined it? Her voice was stern.

"So, I shouldn't have taken Tommy to the tunnel then. Is that what you are saying? My intentions were to find Pa, not the treasure that day."

"There was a great purpose in that. You did the right thing, Annie. But when you find the treasure, and you will, it is imperative that you adhere to what must transpire. As you know, it is foretold that should another's eye fall upon it before yours, the treasure will never be seen."

Crossing my arms, I felt the rush of familiar unease. Excessively swallowing, I attempted to clear my throat. Again, feeling completely out of my depth, I was desperate for answers and needed reassurance.

"Annabelle, what if your ancestors were wrong? Maybe I'm not good enough or smart enough. I never asked for this, it's too much pressure. So far, I've stuffed up things pretty good."

My fears were escalating fast.

"Don't be ridiculous Annie. Hush. Your mind will believe your words. You must never speak of yourself in a negative way, as it is destructive for the soul my child."

'But Annabelle, I've messed up with Mum, Pa is really sick, I've gone and fallen for Tommy at the most selfish of times, and well there is other stuff about me…you just don't know.

Annabelle grabbed me, almost pushing me back against the tree.

'Quiet Annie. What did I just tell you, child."

Annabelle cupped my face, expressing both annoyance and empathy in her stare. I tried to pull back, but she held me firm.

"Isabelle did the best she could. But the years hardened her, messed with her head. She is a product of the walls she has so cleverly built around her, captive to her fears. Your mother's behaviour, was never your fault Annie. I know you have done the best you could, and in time you will see why she behaves as she does."

I was crying again. Annabelle moved her hands to my shoulders.

'As for Jack, that is up to fate now. Other spirits are at play. He is lucky to have you here Annie, but you must have faith. It is you, and only you, who can keep him alive."

Annabelle looked at me so intently, I found myself turning away. Then gently reaching for my hand, she turned it palm up.

Suddenly aware of what was coming, I fought to resist, yet Annabelle's grip was secure.

"But this, my beautiful Annie. This must stop. By punishing yourself you fail to see your true light."

Attempting to hide in the cloak of darkness the night provided, I felt the heat of embarrassment creep up my face. I couldn't not meet her eyes. Pulling away I hugged my hands protectively into my stomach.

Annabelle knew.

My deepest secret was no longer.

Slumped and still groggy from sleep, I knew I probably looked as dishevelled as I felt. Heavy with exhaustion, concentration on anything was near impossible.

Staring out the window of Mum's car, we sped toward the hospital. Pa remained in critical condition. The doctor had contacted Mum this morning saying he had attempted to communicate with the nurses briefly overnight. This was promising he had said.

Waking in my bed this morning, it just felt like any other morning as the sun streamed in though the French doors. Until I remembered. Then I felt kind of scattered,

and like I was hungover. Life was not that simple anymore.

Trust yourself Annie. Allow your mind to see, only then you will truly understand.

Annabelle had whispered that to me many times.

"What are you pondering on, Annie? You seem a million miles away, chick."

I gave a half-hearted shrug, exhaling loudly. How could I ever explain?

Facing Mum, I turned away from the dotted clouds scattered along the vivid blue sky. She looked tired, harsher lines had appeared around her eyes and mouth. Mum was certainly not as polished as normal. Strangely I found this comforting. Maybe she was in fact a regular human after all, just like the rest of us.

"Nothing much" I lied. Did I trust mum enough to share? I wanted to, but old habits take a while to change. I was so used to keeping my stuff close to my chest. Maybe I'd tell Tommy what I'd been through, then again maybe not.

"Are you worried about seeing Pa?"

Mum gave me a fleeting fake smile, patting my leg. Unconsciously I tensed.

"I really believe he will make a full recovery, Annie. Jack is as tough as they come, you know."

Did Mum really believe her own speech? Or was she just trying to polish the situation as usual and create a reality she could control. Irritated, and not sure why, I tipped my head back to look skyward. I couldn't be bothered even talking right now, truth be told, yet here I was, about to poke the bear.

"Beth tried to kill him. She was the one who pushed Pa down the stairs you know."

Unexpectantly Mum swerved, causing me to grab at the door in fright. Suddenly I was awake, my heart pounding rapidly. Swiftly regaining control, Mum took a long breath out before glaring at me. I could see the tension in her knuckles gripping the steering wheel, and the anger flash across her face.

"Enough Annie! Bloody hell. That sort of talk is not going to help anyone."

I shrugged but didn't look away, twirling Annabelle's rings in my fingers.

"Just stating a fact, Mum."

Mum threw her head back in laughter, a cynical almost ugly snigger. I saw red as I knew what was coming.

"Annie, I don't know what has gotten into you, but goodness child, that is certainly a far-fetched statement. You are coming up with some beauties. I really am trying my best here with you Annie, surely you can meet me halfway. Let's stick together in this, keep a level head, okay?"

It was my turn to laugh, after a sharp intake of breath. I felt the heat rising in my face.

"This is not about you Mum. I don't care what you think. You didn't believe me last time when I said Pa was missing, yet I was spot on, remember?"

I suddenly couldn't sit still, rubbing my tight forehead.

"Why just shut me down Mum? Can you listen to why? And I know you have seen far more in your time here than you are willing to admit, yet you are so quick to make me out to be the village idiot?"

I knew I should shut up, but I wasn't about to stop there. I couldn't. Something inside me had snapped.

"And you know what has 'gotten into me' so to speak, since coming to Brambly Bay?"

I didn't wait for her to answer. Mum continued to stare at the road ahead, speeding up.

"Self-belief, that's what. For the first time in my life, this place, and the people here, well they have shown me I matter. I can see I'm important to them, and it feels nice. That's what a family should be like Mum."

Her bottom lip began to quiver, then slow tears spilled. Still, she refused to look at me, remaining fixated on the road ahead. Finally, she cleared her throat and smoothed her hair.

"Believe it or not, I didn't realise you felt that way, Annie. So, let me get this straight. It's all my fault, right? I'm keen to hear this. So, what was it exactly that I never did for you? What haven't I given you growing up? I bet you can't even answer that, Annie."

She was angry now, but I didn't care. I laughed again in disbelief, yet just as quickly I found myself swallowing hard, fighting back my own tears. Reality was, Mum just didn't get it. She didn't get me.

"I thought when you came back to Brambly Estate that you finally understood. I hoped that maybe, just maybe you actually came back for me…. Mum, it is so simple. All I ever wanted was you. That's it, nothing more. Just for you to be my Mum, and for us to be a team. But you could never give me that, and as a result, my whole life I have felt basically invisible. You know what the saddest part for me is Mum? I feel the most unseen when you are near."

Pulling up to the curb, I hadn't noticed we had already arrived at the hospital. She still hadn't looked at me. Mum's face was set in stone, but I could see the glazed look in her eyes. Relief swept over me knowing I could escape the confinements of the car. I'd said too much and hurt her. But it was my truth. Hurting people hurt others, right? Deep down I knew this was no excuse.

Suddenly I felt awkward, fumbling with the zipper on my jacket. The air seemed so thick I found myself shallow breathing as I felt for the comfort of my lighter in my pocket. Finally, Mum looked at me, her eyes dark and heavy. She barely whispered as she spoke, her voice croaky.

"I think it's best you go on in and sit with Pa on your own for a while first Annie. I will be in soon, okay. I have a few work calls to make."

Nodding, I rushed to unbuckle and grab my backpack. I didn't need to be asked twice. With one foot already out the door, Mum suddenly grabbed at my hand.

"I'm trying Annie, I really am."

I sighed, studying my fingernails.

"Me too. I've had a steep learning curve since coming here, don't forget that. I never asked for any of this, yet here we are. But the difference between you and me? I don't intend to run away from my family like you did."

My words must have stung. I knew lashing out in anger wasn't going to help, but it just seemed to keep bubbling up, almost like it was beyond my control.

I pulled my hand roughly away from Mum's, slammed the door and stormed toward the hospital. Not once did I dare look back.

Pa's ashen skin seemed to concave around his face bones. As I reached up to cover my mouth, attempting to stifle a strangled sob, I realised I was shaking. This was just a shell of the man that had been by my side just a few days ago. Why had I not checked on him before I'd left the house that day? Maybe then he would be okay.

Frozen to the spot, I remained just inside the doorway to his hospital room, not really sure what to say or do. Pa seemed oblivious to my being here, not that I'd dared make a whisper since arriving. He was hooked up to so many different machines, all beeping and monitoring his vitals. Pa's skin looked so grey, almost translucent. But the sight that killed me the most, was his much-loved Akubra sitting on the bedside table. Tommy must have left it here for him. Briefly

I wondered how Tommy was doing. We hadn't text much since Pa's accident. I wasn't sure why.

"Hello lovely. How are you doing today? I'm Nurse Pam. Come on in and sit down love, he won't bite. Jack is doing really well, you know. We are taking great care of him here, sweetie. So don't you worry now."

Startled, I hadn't heard the matronly looking older woman bustle past me. I watched her as she began focusing on the chart at the end of Pa's bed.

"Hi." I turned my attention back to Pa, my voice sounding unsure and weak. I attempted to clear my throat to remove the thickness.

Suddenly Pam was beside me, placing her hand over my shoulders. I couldn't remember if this had been the same nurse I'd met when Pa had first arrived. It was all such a blur, despite it being only days ago. She was comforting and I almost wanted to hug her back.

"I know exactly what you're feeling sweetheart. It's rotten to see your Pa like this isn't it."

She rubbed my back as I stared at the ground.

"Just the hardest thing in the world. Take some deep breaths for me Annie. You're as white as the bed sheets lovely. I don't need you fainting on me now, and we sure as heck don't need any ghosts!"

She laughed as I started to cry. If she only knew, I thought.

"You know Annie, even though you might think Jack hasn't a clue you are here, my bet is, he does. I've worked with lots of semi-conscious patients in my time dear, and it's amazing the little miracles I've seen as a result of loved ones talking to the patient. I will leave you to it then. Just ring the buzzer if you need us, okay."

Struggling to find words as I choked back my emotions, nodding was the best I could do. Wiping my eyes, I desperately tried to get myself together. Pa needed me to be strong after all.

Hearing the door click softly behind me, I suddenly felt very alone and responsible. Pulling a chair up beside Pa's bed, I sat, taking some deep breaths in. Gingerly I reached out for his hand. Surprisingly it felt warm, I was flooded with relief. The other day, lying in at the base of the stairs he had been so cold.

"Hello Pa. It's Annie. I've just come to be with you for a while. Mum is here, too. She will be in soon."

I stared at him, desperate for a flicker of response. None came. The nurse had said talk to him, but what should I say. I'd babbled nervously. Maybe I needed to slow my words down.

"All is good at Brambly Estate, Pa. We are taking care of everything, so you don't need to worry… Annabelle has been teaching me about things. I'm trying my best to get my head around all this, you know, Brambly Estate. I miss you Pa. We all do. I miss our chats. Tommy misses you so much, too. He told me about when you guys first met."

I could hear myself rambling, continuing in a quick high-pitched tone. *Slow it down Annie.*

I paused, searching for any sign of life in Pa. I squeezed his hand.

"I love you, Pa. I'm sorry I wasn't there to protect you. I'm sorry I haven't visited more. Truth is, I feel more loved here, with you, than anywhere. I've been thinking about all the times we spent together when I was a kid."

Suddenly I felt it. He had squeezed back, I was sure.

I stood, keeping a firm grip and placing my other hand on his, too.

"Pa? Can you hear me? I'm here Pa. You are going to be okay. I'm going to take care of everything. I promise I will."

Nothing. Maybe I'd imagined it.

"Annie."

Despite his voice being barely recognisable, and less than a whisper, it had come. Nothing else but his mouth had moved. I leaned in closer still."

"Oh Pa! Yes, It's Annie. I'm here.

"The paintings. She told me to search in the paintings."

His voice was a little stronger this time and I could see movement behind his closed eyes as if he were desperately trying to open them.

"What paintings, Pa? Who told you? You mean Annabelle's paintings at Brambly Estate?"

No response.

As I searched his face, I heard the click of the door to the room being shut behind us. Without letting Pa's hand go, I glanced back briefly but no one was there.

Flinching suddenly an alarm began to sound furiously above Pa's bed. Frozen, as if rooted to the ground I stood, alone, still clinging to his hand for what seemed like an eternity. Why wasn't someone coming?

Relieved, Nurse Pam and another male nurse swept in, quickly shutting down the noise as they focused on the machines. I backed away a little.

"It's okay Annie. Seems Jack's heart rate has just gotten a little high. Happens from time to time dear. I might just stay here a bit longer to keep an eye on him and monitor his blood pressure. Did you notice any changes with Jack?"

With my mouth open about to answer, Mum appeared. Moving directly in front of me, she stood over Pa's bed.

"Is everything alright here?"

Nurse Pam took charge, nodding at mum. I was feeling a bit light-headed again, like my legs would buckle if I didn't sit. I shuffled back further into a corner chair.

"Hello Isabelle. Yes love, Jack's heart rate has spiked a little. I'm just monitoring him now. I think he has really enjoyed the company of your lovely daughter. It's a positive thing to see him responding to the outside stimulation."

Pam smiled at me. I longed for the same reassurance from mum, yet she didn't look back at me at all.

I had to get out. Backing away I was grateful no one seemed to notice, all busy with their own agendas. Silently I slipped out the door.

I was invisible once again.

Momentarily confused, I gripped onto the wall as I stepped out into the long hospital corridor. It was swirling.

How the hell do I get out of here?

Finally spying the exit sign, I bolted left. Everything was white and stark with a distinct smell of disinfectant. It was so oppressive I wanted to vomit.

As I rounded the corner, I was relieved to see the familiar hospital café, which meant the front doors were close. I froze mid stride, doing a double take. I was unable to believe my own eyes.

Mabel sat at one of the café tables, take away coffee in hand, talking intently into her phone. Furious at the mere sight of her, my need to escape was forgotten. I marched over intent on protecting Pa.

"What are you doing here, Mabel?"

My voice was loud, but I didn't care. Startled, she stopped talking and stared up at me as she disconnected the call.

"Oh, hello Annie. Nice to see you again."

"That's bullshit. Answer me, Mabel. Why are you here? We don't want you anywhere near us."

She smiled, gesturing for me to sit. I remained exactly where I was, hands on hips, appalled at the very sight of her. Mabel waved her hands up in the air, attempting to buffer my rage.

"Fair enough Annie. Perhaps we have miscommunicated in past meetings dear. We both have our reasons, right or wrong. But at the end of the day, I do care for Jack you know. I was just here to offer my support in any way I could. When I arrived you were with him, so I thought I'd wait."

My brain strained to process as a tense heat flushed through my veins. I knew I'd heard someone come into the room earlier when Pa had been attempting to speak to me.

Had Mabel heard our conversation? Surely not?

"Leave us alone Mabel. You have done enough damage for a lifetime. If we never saw you again it would be too soon. Jack is no friend of yours, you know it, we all know it."

She smirked up at me so calmly that ever fibre in my being heightened. I could see we had the attentions of onlookers in the café now, but I couldn't have cared.

"It's a free country, Annie. A public place. I'm doing nothing wrong by being here. Unlike you, as I'm sure you will recall. Remember last week? It was you wasn't it who broke in, assaulted and threatened me at Anderson Estate, my own home, hmm?"

I wanted to retaliate and had a million reasons why I should. Scattered images of me screaming, ranting, shaking her or pouring her coffee over her ugly head flashed internally.

But I shook my head, attempting to quash my beast. I was better than that.

Breathe Annie. Be smart.

"You really have no idea what I'm capable of, do you child?"

Mabel stood, knocking her coffee onto the floor. Staring hard, I matched her glare.

It was my time to smirk. I spat at her.

Suddenly I was being dragged away from behind. Already in such an elevated state, I venomously began to fight off whoever it was restraining me. But as I struggled, a familiar voice washed over me, and I felt the overwhelming rage begin to drain from my body.

"Let's go Annie, she is not worth it."

Tommy. He locked his eyes into mine, cupping my face. I threw myself into his arms, desperate for his comfort. Thank God he was here, again. Numbly I let him lead me outside, away from the scene I'd created. I dared not look back at all the onlookers. As we exited, I stumbled, blinded by the invasive sunlight. Covering my eyes, I felt completely disorientated. Falling heavily onto the grass, finally I began to cry.

The fight with my mum, seeing Pa so helpless and then Mabel. It was all too much. Tommy just held me tightly. I loved the way he just knew when I needed him close, but silent. I had nothing left to offer him right now anyway. I was so grateful for the ease between us, despite the chaos.

Finally, pulling my hair back from my face and sitting up a little straighter still on my knees, I looked around. The bustling movement and noise surrounding the hospital came back into focus.

Tommy remained laying back on the grass, eyes closed, beside me now like he had not a care in the world. His hand still rested on my knee. I bent down and kissed his lips. Without opening his eyes, he smiled.

Then, my gaze fixed on a figure just over the road from the hospital car park, gesturing to me, waving her arms.

"Annie, the paintings are in danger."

I stumbled to my feet, confused despite her words being as clear as day. Taking my eyes off Annabelle for a split second, I grabbed my backpack. To my dismay as I looked again, she was gone. Tommy had leapt up beside me, looking dazed.

"What? What's going on Annie?"

"We've got to go Tommy, right now. Something is wrong at Brambly Estate. Annabelle was just here."

Tommy nodded and pointed to the far corner of the carpark.

"Let's go then, my car is over there."

He grabbed my hand, and I squeezed it tightly. He'd become my lifeline; I didn't want to be alone in this anymore. Had Tommy already sensed that? Was that why he had come all the way here to find me today?

Jumping into his ute, despite the urgency, my heart felt full as I lay my hand on his shoulder.

Tommy's laughter broke my thoughts.

"What?"

He smiled across at me as we drove.

"I can't believe you spat at her. That's the funniest shit I've ever seen!"

I burst out laughing too. It was good to ease some tension.

Journeying home, I bravely relayed everything that had happened in the last 24 hours. It was exhausting. When would this madness stop? Tommy's expression as he drove, gave little of his thoughts away.

Did he believe me? I sure hoped he would.

Even if he didn't, I knew.

As we pulled up in the driveway at Brambly Estate, I was eager to get out, but Tommy stopped me, holding tightly onto my hand.

"Annie. Slow down. You are not going to help anything by rushing."

"Slow down? There has been enough of all that. Come on, let's go, we've got our strongest lead so far."

Still, he didn't let go. Tommy looked straight into my eyes, smiling warmly. Just for the briefest moment, I forgot I was heavy with the weight of the world. Leaning in closer still, he kissed me for the longest time. His touch lingered, first on my jaw then travelling down my neck. I was flooded with a warm tingling, absorbed by his closeness.

"I love everything about you, Annie Robinson. You've totally got this, girl."

Stunned, my lips formed a smile.

He loved me?

That was the second time he had said it, but this time was no accident. Yikes, how did I dare respond? Did I love him? Wasn't it all a bit soon?

Like he was reading my mind, Tommy chuckled.

"It is never too soon Annie, when you know, you just know. And the moment I saw you on the veranda, well, you had my heart. Even though you sassed my arse right off the property that day."

I traced his hand with my finger, daring not to look at him. No words seemed to come despite feeling completely captivated by this moment. Tommy, however, quickly changed the subject.

"But that stuff later okay. Come on, let's get to it then."

I adored Tommy right back. Was this more than an infatuation? As quickly as the thought came, I squashed it back down.

Later.

Jumping quickly from the ute, together we bound up the front stairs of Brambly Estate. I seemed to almost float with anticipation. But my elation ended so abruptly. I felt the sickening heat of panic rise from my toes, eventually sucking the breath from my lungs. Wide eyed and wordless we stared. Every painting that had hung from the walls above the grand staircase for as long as I could remember, was gone.

Speeding back down the dirt road toward town, a million possibilities raced through my brain. But the reality was, I already knew exactly the scenario.

Why had Tommy insisted we go into town first? We were wasting time.

Mabel had heard my conversation with Pa all right. My bet was I'd interrupted her on the phone to whomever it was she'd organised to do her dirty work and steal them from Brambly Estate this morning.

Sneaky bitch.

The nerve. Whatever the clues were on the paintings, I just had to pray she was too stupid to work them out. But what if she destroyed them out of spite?

"Tommy, can we just turn back, I do trust you, but shouldn't we be going straight to Mabel's? What is so important in town?"

I saw him hesitate and grip the wheel a little tighter.

"My gun."

I sat straighter as I spun around, deliberately facing my whole body toward him. Tommy didn't even flinch. Instead, just kept his eyes cast ahead as his ute barrelled along.

"Tommy no. No way. Stop the car."

Suddenly I wondered if I knew this guy at all.

Shaking his head, Tommy slowed, then stopped at the red lights in the main street of town.

"Tommy. No way we are doing this. OMG, think Tommy, the cops already have it in for you. Why give them the green light. This is not who we are Tommy."

He sighed deeply.

"We have no choice, Annie. You don't understand. The Andersons, they are evil. And I've had a gut full of it. Jack would want me to do this. He would encourage me to do what I needed to get the paintings back. I know it. I'm willing to do time in jail for him. It's the least I can do. Jack gave me my life back without ever once questioning my past."

Reaching for Tommy's leg, I gestured for him to pull over. I just needed to buy some time, talk some sense into him. Relieved when he did, I slowed my breath and prayed for the right words to talk him down. We sat silently for a few minutes. The busy streets bustled with holiday makers, all oblivious to the feud that had poisoned this small town for generations.

We held each other tightly.

"Maybe this *is* who I am Annie. I'm not like you. I've done some bad shit. Reality is, I'm not good enough for a girl like you. You are perfect Annie. I admire you so much."

He pulled away from me, crossing his arms and staring vacantly out into the street. I couldn't believe what I was hearing. Could he really be as insecure about being emotionally exposed as I was? His vulnerability in this moment was so unexpected, I found my own guard lowering. Reaching up, I tentatively pulled his face toward mine. Tommy didn't object.

"You are wrong about me Tommy. I totally have my secrets, and I'm terrified if you ever find out, you will run a mile. You are more than good enough, trust me. But now's not the time to get into our stuff, okay. We need to get to the paintings."

Instantly I could see he had reacted to my words, questioning what I'd meant. Tommy's eyes had softened and seemed to be searching my face for answers. I let out a relieved breath.

"Unless you told me we're through Annie, there is nothing about you that would make me want to be apart from you, ever. Maybe you are right, we all have our stuff, right?"

Nodding, I pulled his hands toward me kissing them, before placing them on my heart. The emotion between us electric.

"Tommy, please listen to me. Nothing good will come from using a weapon. I know these people are bad, but there's got be another way. Why do you even have a gun anyway?"

He sighed again.

"Let's just say this stupid feud has been a long one, Annie. Might shock you, but the truth is, your Pa gave it to me. He said he trusted me to only use it if I needed to protect someone I loved. He never divulged much but said there were some people in this town with bad intentions. Well, this is one of those times, right?"

I shook my head.

"We don't even know the paintings will be at the Anderson Estate anyway Tommy. Basically, we are on a wild goose chase really, but it's no good just sitting here."

Getting a little overwhelmed, I willed myself to keep it together.

"Maybe we should go through the tunnel to the Andersons, instead of storming through the front gate like vigilantes? Or talk to Stella. Surely, she would know what to do. Or at the very least distract Mabel while we searched the property. And the police are there for a reason you know, Tommy."

Tommy scoffed before revving the engine to life once more.

"Fine. You win Annie. Let's go back. But if it doesn't work your way, then we are doing it mine."

As he made a U turn toward Brambly Estate, a white flash in a side street caught my attention.

"Tommy stop! Over there! We need to go back. Can you turn around again, down that street we just passed. I'm sure that was the van from the Anderson Estate."

Tommy nodded, and without questioning, once again turned his Ute around and headed us toward the side street. Sure enough, there it was, the same white van we had seen on our last visit to Mabel. The signage read, 'Anderson Estate & Winery' clear as day. Parking just a little further down on the same side, Tommy shut the engine down. We searched the street for any signs of the men.

"So, what now?"

I smiled broadly. Strangely I felt full of confidence again. Must be the adrenaline.

"We check it out! You never know Tommy, maybe this is our lucky day. I would put money on the fact Mabel phoned one of her thugs. The same bastards that caught us and threw us in with Pa in the shed, and she had them grab the paintings knowing we were still at the hospital. With the tight time frame, I'm thinking the paintings could easily still be in that van."

Tommy grinned, suddenly getting very animated.

"And maybe the dumb arse has stopped in town for supplies or is even having a quick drink at the pub. It's just on the corner, there see!"

I followed Tommy's hand as he pointed behind us.

"Well, let's check it out then, Annie. But discreetly, hey!"

I threw my head back laughing. Suddenly our body language had completely changed, the air between us energised.

"And what is that supposed to mean Mr?"

Tommy was smiling from ear to ear now, the twinkle had returned to his blue eyes.

"Oh, I think you know. For someone so tiny, you are certainly mighty when you want to be. You were causing quite a scene if I recall at the hospital before I wrestled you out of there."

I burst out laughing. Yep. I couldn't argue with that. In fact, I quite liked the feeling to be honest.

Every move we made right now counted.

We'd sat in the car for the next 10minutes or so, watching the comings and goings of the street. Despite it just being off the main drag, it was pretty quiet. The street itself had a mix of small business along it, and residential homes. To our left was a laundromat, tyre mechanic and some sort of computer supplies place. All had little movement this afternoon which was good. They also didn't have security cameras that would see us on this side of the street. Over the road a number of old houses seemed almost vacant. Another bonus. The street itself was lined with huge pine trees, car spots were dotted in between. The trees would provide us with cover.

Tommy and I agreed on what would happen next. It was pointless involving the police, how could be possibly explain anyway. I would keep lookout. Tommy would attempt to break in, if in fact he could see anything through the windows. If the paintings were inside, he would back his car up to the van, we would then load up and get the hell out of there. Sounded simple enough.

Just as we were about to execute, the worst possible thing happened. Well nearly. A police car rolled up beside us, no siren, but lights flashing. What were the odds! Of course, it was Senior Sergeant Roy!

Tommy swore under his breath before smiling and giving a small wave. Senior Sergeant Roy gestured for him to wind his window down.

"Well look who we have here. Hello again Tommy. Hello Annie. What brings you to town today may I ask?"

Tommy hesitated, and as I seemed to be on a roll today, I swiftly took charge.

"Hello officers. Nice to see you again. We are on our way home from the hospital if you must know. You can check if you like. We have been to see my Pa. I'm sure you heard about his accident. Now we are picking up some supplies before heading back to Brambly Estate. Is that okay with you, because last time I checked, it was not an offence." Roy stepped out of his car, strode around, and bent down into Tommy's open window.

"Is that so?

"Yes, that's right" Tommy finally spoke.

"Well then, why have you been sitting in your car for over 15 minutes now? I saw you pull into the street after doing a u turn Tommy."

I just couldn't help myself. This was harassment. Jerking my head sharply toward him, I refused to break eye contact.

"Actually Senior Sergeant Roy, we were discussing the status of our relationship if you must know, got a little caught up in some saucy details….again, not a crime. I hate to be rude, but it's totally none of your business considering we were doing nothing remotely wrong."

He stood now, almost seeming a little taken aback. He looked back at his colleague who had remained in the police car. I could tell Tommy was fighting to stifle a laugh as he continued to stare at the steering wheel.

"No need to get a tone about you, Annie. I was just doing my duty, ensuring no one was loitering, doing drugs or that kind of thing. Tommy has a history you know, so I like to keep a close eye on him. For the safety and wellbeing of the town, of course."

This jerk was such an arsehole! I breathed deeply trying to rein myself in, yet my deportation of sarcasm seemed to speak louder than my words.

"Thanks for that Senior Sergeant. Did you know I'm studying law at present back in Sydney? I'm particularly interested in discrimination of character, false harassment, that sort of thing. I'd love to come into the station and chat with you on the topic some time. A man of your ranking and all. You do seem extremely experienced in this area."

It was a little white lie, but I didn't care one bit.

I felt the heat rise from Tommy. He glanced sideways at me as if to tell me to stop poking the bear. Maybe I should. Senior Sergeant Roy stood straighter, clearing his throat. Suddenly, as if it was divine intervention, his car radio began alerting him to another incident across town, and he paused to listen.

"All right then, I will be watching you two. But right now, I've got a more pressing issue to attend."

With that he marched back to his squad car, and with sirens blazing, sped off.

In stunned silence we stared at one another before bursting into laughter.

"Shit Annie, that was a gutsy move."

I shrugged.

"He's a bully, Tommy. You know that right? And I won't sit here watching him do that to you. I care about you too much.'

Tommy smiled, breathing out and shaking his head at the same time.

"You are so amazing. Come on, we've wasted enough of the day on that dick head. Let's get this happening."

Squeezing my hand one last time, Tommy jumped out and wasted no time heading for the van. My stomach fluttered as I followed suit to take up my agreed position.

With my senses on high alert, standing half hidden behind one of the big old pines, I scanned every possible angle of the street. I knew we had a very valid reason for breaking the law right now. I also knew, should we get caught, we'd be arrested. OMG Mum would just love that!

The bravery and enthusiasm I'd felt in the safety of Tommy's ute, had vanished. Instead, here I was fidgeting on the spot, bouncing on my toes, and biting my lip a little too hard.

Tommy, however, seemed so cool and collected. It looked to me like he had seemingly transformed into another mode entirely. He moved quickly and confidently, checking for open doors and trying to see beyond the dark tint of the windows. As our eyes met, he offered me a reassuring nod.

I was holding my breath, transfixed as Tommy swiftly and almost soundlessly used a hammer and screwdriver to manoeuvre the lock on the back sliding door, just enough, it seemed, to get it open.

It all happened so fast. Blinking rapidly, I searched the street for movement. I had no idea breaking into a car could be this easy. Clearly, Tommy had done this before, yet I felt nothing but admiration for him right now. Scanning the narrow street once more, I forced myself to breathe out before re focusing on the crime scene.

I didn't need to see inside the van.

Tommy's instant reaction as he slid the door open said it all. Briefly he gave me a thumbs up. His smile was huge, but I just felt instant steaming rage.

That bitch. My assumptions had been correct.

Mabel had stolen all our paintings all right, and it was time to get them back.

We'd sat on the hard wooden floor for the longest time, devouring chips, coke and far too many lollies in our attempt for a breakthrough. Standing restlessly, I stretched and yawned before pulling Tommy to his feet.

Scattered around us were Annabelle's paintings, leaning against the walls in the front room. Hours had passed, yet we were no closer to finding any answers hidden within them. I was running out of patience. Somehow, I'd imagined it would have been easier than this. Tommy's frustration was written all over his face. The whole thing just felt like another dead end, and right now I was over it.

"Let's get out of here for a while Tommy. I can't stare at these a minute longer. And I'm ruminating about the deadline for repossession. We've only got two more days! And are you sure we shouldn't go to the police about these being stolen? Oh man, there's so much happening in my head, it feels like it's going to explode. Maybe we go to Annabelle's tree house?"

He nodded, snuggling into my body as I rubbed at my temples. Tommy knew just how to calm me. I loved it when he kissed my neck so softly; it gave me goosebumps every time.

"Breathe girl, we've got this."

Moving in closer to his touch, I wanted nothing more than to get lost in his distraction.

Or maybe we could just stay here?

Shaking my head, I forced myself to get it together.

"Yep, good idea, fresh air's the go. It'll give us new perspective maybe. I can tell you one thing though, this time we lock up here before we go!"

Creating some subtle distance between us to clear my head a little, I smiled back at Tommy as I grabbed my backpack and headed for the kitchen.

Did he know the effect he had on me?

"I'll grab us some snacks." My voice sounded more rushed and higher pitched than intended.

By late afternoon, there we were. Annabelle's treehouse felt just as amazing as the last time I'd been here. We lay on our backs, hands entwined, eyes closed, absorbing the sweet scent of pine. The dappled afternoon sun warmed our skin as it danced through the leaves, and the roar of the ocean felt almost dreamlike. I was more relaxed than I had been in days. So different to my tension this morning.

I wondered how often Annabelle and Patrick had done just this. I could feel her presence so strongly today. Tommy sat up, but feeling content, I stretched completely out, just needing to linger in this blissful moment a little longer. I knew we needed to get back soon, but not just yet.

The birds sang out in the forest. As we had walked earlier, a sea hawk had tracked us, following behind for some time, yet I couldn't hear it now. Could it possibly have been the same one?

"Hey Annie?"

Tommy pulled me back from the lull of light sleep. I smiled yet didn't open my eyes, as he reached again for my hand.

"Is this what you meant when you said I'd run a mile if I knew?"

I froze.

No.

Oh, bloody hell.

How was I this stupid. I shot up, jumping to my feet so quickly, dizziness forced me to grab onto the railing. My jacket remained on the ground near Tommy.

We both looked over at it simultaneously. Shit, having felt so secure, I didn't think when I took it off. Cursing myself for being so careless, I turned toward the horizon, wishing the ocean would swallow me up. I couldn't meet his eyes.

What was he thinking?

Did he hate me?

"Really Annie? Don't do that."

Tommy's voice was soft. I wanted to run. Embarrassment surged through my body; I felt completely exposed. My scars began to itch. Glancing around, I desperately scanned for an escape. Tommy moved toward the ladder.

"You're not going anywhere right now, Annie. We need to talk about this. You are safe with me babe."

Maybe I'd mis read the situation? There was still a slight possibility he hadn't seen my burns. Tommy might have been referring to something completely different.

Yeah, right Annie.

"Annie. Look at me. It's okay, I promise. Please, come back over here and sit with me."

I hesitated and felt my stomach drop with the manifestation of dread. Covering my face with my hands, I just stood there like an idiot. Then Tommy was beside me, hugging me tight. I was so ashamed right now, my body rigid. Tommy pulled me down, crossed legged we faced each other. I still hadn't looked at him. I couldn't.

"Breathe Annie. There are plenty of worse things, trust me."

Tommy lifted my chin to meet his eyes. Taken aback, I noticed he had tears in them.

"I…I'm sorry Tommy. You must think I'm pathetic. I didn't want you to ever find out. I wanted to stop….but it's been hard."

"I won't ever tell Annie. But you've got to let me help."

Did I need help? I was in control of burning. Right?

"I started ages ago. The more invisible in my life I felt, the more the burning became my friend, my solace. It's hard to explain."

Tommy smiled, his face flushed. His tears weren't of disappointment, but concern.

"Actually, it's not that hard to understand, well not for me anyway. I self-harmed for ages Annie, just in a different way. No judgement here at all. We all have our reasons. It just kills me to think you felt so alone that you turned to burning."

Now he really had my attention, and I felt some of my inner turmoil dissolve.

Tommy understood?

I felt myself wanting to talk about it. Truth be told, I had for the longest time. Unexpectantly, I felt the release of tension and looked heavenward with an overwhelming feeling of gratitude.

"It's how I've learnt to cope I suppose. Mum has spent years barely noticing me. I tried so many times to connect with her. But I just couldn't. I just wasn't important enough. Not worth the effort, I suppose. I'm just not the type of person she likes. It made me kind of shrink inside, you know? And sometimes on the dark days, I felt so numb it was scary. I needed to know I still was here on earth, I needed to feel something. When I burn, she can't control the hurt, I do."

As I reached up to wipe Tommy's tears away, he held on tightly to my hands, gently inspecting them.

"Annie, there are so many scars on your beautiful skin. We gotta find another way for you to vent, okay. I want to be your person. The one who can take your pain away."

I nodded, but deep down I wondered, did I even want to stop. It was an addictive feeling. Strangely, it empowered me, as irrational as my own thoughts sounded.

"I used to pop pills, drugs, alcohol whatever I could get my hands on really. Same reason as you Annie, to numb the pain. Or sometimes when I was numb myself, I did it just to feel alive. So I totally get your drift. I think I wanted someone to find me, notice that I needed help. Eventually someone did care, and I stopped."

I smiled.

"Pa, right?"

"Yep."

No wonder Tommy and I had connected. Tommy was wise, had been through so much. I knew he wasn't judging me one bit.

"Listen, I love you, Annie. And I'm here for you. I want to help you work on stopping this. But I get it, in your time, okay? Maybe from now on, if you feel like burning, find me, and I will distract you from your thoughts…deal?"

I nodded. Secretly I was not sure if I would.

Time would tell.

Opening the front door, I felt different. Again, I'd experienced a personal shift. This roller coaster was exhausting, I'd done more growing and learning here at Brambly Bay than it seemed in my whole life. Much of it good, but other experiences had damaged me, no question about that. My time here would colour my views on life forever, that was for certain.

I knew in my gut I needed to be kinder to Mum. I was a better person than I'd shown lately. I, of all people, should know the effects our words can have. Shuddering slightly, as I stood frozen in the doorway reflecting. I was ashamed of the bitch I'd been, shocking even myself truth be told, with the nasty words I'd spat at her. Tommy had made such a great point earlier. He'd said he was sure she behaved the way she did because of her own life experiences, her fears and regrets, and not necessarily because she didn't love me. I'd never really looked at it that way. But in my defence, I'd never known the truth about Brambly Bay either.

Tommy and I had parted at the treehouse. Only for a short time he had promised, yet part of me had been relieved. A lot had happened, and I needed to process the ramifications of my exposure. Tommy wanted to head onto the beach to check on Pa's boat and the nets he had dangling from the jetty.

I breathed in the comfort of the silence. Mum was still at the hospital most likely, which bought me some time. The paintings seemed to stare back at me, daring me to discover their secrets. Sitting in the middle of the room, I sighed. The wind had picked up outside and rattled the windows. The waft of old coals stirred as the breeze travelled down through the fireplace. I wondered how long it had been since the warmth of an open fire had brought life to this room. Munching on my jam toast, and sipping sugary tea, I looked from one painting to the other, willing my brain to discover something of use.

Nothing.

Annabelle sure was a talented artist. Her portrayal of landscapes was so realistic, and portraits of family members back in China exquisite in their details. I wondered, had she painted these from memory, or used photos. That was something I needed to ask her for sure. Had Annabelle been able to communicate with her family after arriving in Australia?

Crawling closer, I gently touched the paintings. Was there a pattern to them? A similar marking maybe? This was getting frustrating.

Focus Annie. I was wasting time.

Cursing under my breath, I scrunched up my face then released it again, attempting to regain control. Jumping to my feet I paced.

Think Annie.

Eyes closed, I roughly massaged my temples, forcing some deep breaths.

I am running out of time.

Suddenly the slamming of the front door jolted me back into reality. Someone was here. Maybe Tommy or Mum?

As I headed into the entrance hall, I froze.

"Oh, well hello there, Annie. The door was open. I did call out but assumed no one was home."

Mr Stanton, the weasel from the bank. Briefly, a wave of hot panic rushed through my body. Was our time up? So much had happened, had I lost track of days? I shook the thoughts away, clearing my throat. He wasn't going to see my fear.

"So, what, you just decided to let yourself in then?"

Mr Stanton shuffled awkwardly on the spot, clearly not missing the malice in my tone.

"Well, you see Annie, I just wanted to touch base with your mother. She said I could find her here. Is she in? Now that Jack in out of action for a while, the responsibilities of Brambly Estate fall on her you see, as next of kin. Despite Jack's unfortunate accident, decisions still need to be made regarding the sale, and as I'm sure you know, it is of an urgent nature."

Was this vulture for real? I walked closer to him, raising my chin and glaring.

"Get out Mr Stanton."

He stood firm, matching my stare and smirking slightly.

"You can ignore it all you like Annie, but fact of the matter is simple. Whether your mother signs or not, whether Jack recovers or he doesn't, come Wednesday at 5pm, which is just 48 hours away now, unless full payment is received, Brambly Estate will be forcibly repossessed. It's the law."

My head was swirling. I'd never felt so protective of anything in my life.

"Get out!"

I stepped closer to him.

"No problem, Annie, but be sure to give this paperwork to your mother. From recent conversations we've had, I gather she is far more accommodating to the idea of selling than you lot are. Finally, a Robinson who is intelligent enough to see sense has been refreshing, I must say.

Mr Stanton dropped the envelope of paperwork at my feet before turning and walking out. I remained frozen to the spot and suddenly nauseous.

What the hell was he talking about?

The breath had seemingly left my lungs, my mind raced trying to rationalise what I'd just heard. With trembling hands, I scooped up the thick envelope.

Had Mum betrayed us?

Was this the real reason she had returned, to sell Brambly estate?

I honestly didn't know. Mum only let me see such a small part of her, she absolutely could have agreed to this. Ripping the envelope open, I frantically searched for an answer. There it was, plain as day. Although it was not yet signed, the documents were correspondence regarding Isabelle Robinsons agreed price of sale for Brambly Estate.

Letting the papers slip to the floor, I fell to my knees and began to scream.

Angry tears spilled as rage took hold.

I hated her. Never would I forgive her. This was too much.

I took my lighter and set the documents alight. Throwing them into the fireplace I spat at them for good measure.

Annabelle
Brambly Estate Cliff Tops 1986
Mortality

Shifting uncomfortably in the small ledge, a deep weakness was setting in. Jagged rocks had torn at my flesh. I knew my reality, and I'd offer it no resistance. The wound running down my neck was too big, too deep; it had a force of its own.

My gaze focused in and out, as a strange peace took hold. Perhaps it was a state of surrendering. Death was near.

I'd survived so much in my 85 years, yet this time my fate would prove different.

The ocean crashed below, all-encompassing in its deafening roar. The familiar sea air brought comfort, almost as if it was hemming me in.

I'd not fight, my energy was no more. All was in place. I'd done the best I could. Soon Patrick would come and take me, and together, finally, we would be again.

There was so much blood. Pressing on the wound made little difference now. Only moments before, walking along my favourite cliff line, I'd been careless. The same stroll I'd taken every day for as long as I cared to remember. Only this time, I wouldn't be returning home to my beloved Brambly Estate.

My sea hawk. She had flown so close, hovering above me, screeching. Perhaps she had been trying to warn me? I'd sensed however, she was calling to me. I'd reached out, just a little too far over the rocky edge, then toppled to my near demise.

Would my family find me? Maybe, but they would not make it in time to save me now.

Using the little energy I still possessed, I strained to see my surroundings. I'd landed partially down the face of the steep cliffs. Mostly hidden from view now on a small ledge, my crumpled body lay shattered amongst rock shrubs. I couldn't see the top nor where the vast beach lay below.

I was hidden. Alone in my journey towards death.

My mind swirled with the breeze. I ached to see my Patrick again and the thought was bringing me comfort. I had roamed this earth for 59 long years without him. Yet regret was also encompassing. I had longed to live just long enough to see the birth of my great great granddaughter Annie, the chosen one. I had faith in the prophecy, but now I would have to be content to watch her journey from the heavens.

So much time had passed, yet so quickly. Would I have chosen this life? Maybe, yet maybe not. However, my years with Patrick were the most precious and heart filled any woman could dream to have. My family was my world.

Sadness engulfed me, and time seemed to slow. I reflected on the time and energy wasted on hatred, on a senseless feud driven by greed and animosity. On Beth. Right now, I knew with certainty, it was not death I feared. My dread lay in the fact Beth would remain living. Who would stop her once I departed this earth? I knew Beth would stop at nothing to make Brambly Estate and its treasures her own.

I never thought myself possible of the many malicious acts I'd planned and executed, nor the curse I'd placed over Beth. But I would do it all again because it was for love and the protection of my family.

Beth deserved to rot in hell. She was nothing but pure evil.

As I began to drift in and out of consciousness, I welcomed the fogginess, as it dulled some of the pain encapsulating my broken body.

Had I done enough? Would my family be safe? Had I made the Qing Dynasty and my people proud? I surely hoped so. I had protected their heirlooms for 85 years now. That was my purpose after all.

My mind swirled back and forward through time, and as a heaviness pressed in, I could no longer open my eyes. Aware my hand was slipping away from the gaping wound on my neck, I let it go. The blood was soaking my clothes now. I was so cold. Soon I would be free. Momentarily my mind fixated on Isabelle. I had intended to speak to her, to try to prepare her for what was coming.

Too late. My resolution was near.

"Hello my beautiful wife."

Patrick. He was here. I couldn't open my eyes, but somehow, I could see him. As handsome was ever, Patrick knelt before me, reaching for my hands.

"Patrick, my love. I have waited so long."

My voice felt distant and unfamiliar.

"Yes, my dear. Are you ready to go?"

Patrick scooped me up, kissing my forehead tenderly just as he always had. Finally, the peace I longed for, permeated through my being. The heaviness was gone, a warmth spread through my entire body. I felt like I was floating. Yes, I was ready. Nothing would make me happier than being with my beloved Patrick again.

This time it would be forever.

Brambly Estate 2017
Annie
Vengeance

This was between Mum and me.

I wasn't about to concern anyone else with the potential contract of sale for Brambly Estate until I confronted Mum.

Face to face I'd take on the force that was Isabelle Robinson.

I'd text Mum asking when she would be home. She bluntly replied, 'in an hour'. That meant any minute now. I'd paced the house ever since, trying to tame my anger.

Tommy had returned a while back, then left for the evening. He would call me later. I'd been straight forward with him when I'd said I needed some time tonight with Mum to sort a few things out. I just didn't tell him exactly what.

Tommy wanted me to promise him that no matter how bad things got between Mum and me, I'd reach out to him first before burning. I was brutally honest, telling him that was a hard promise to make, especially now. But I gave him my word I would try.

Sitting on the veranda steps, amid the perfume of the summer blooms, the evening brought a slight breeze. Through the light of a near full moon I watched the shadows of the trees dance upon the wooden post and rail fence which surrounded Brambly Estate.

It'd be a near perfect scene had I not been so absorbed by shame.

I'd succumbed to its all-powerful call once again.

The aftermath was all consuming. Constant throbbing agony in my calf causing me to sweat. The warm night air seemed to magnify the pain beneath my tracksuit pants. They stuck uncomfortably to my wounds, but I dare not risk exposure and put my shorts back on now.

As much as I didn't want to, I would be honest with Tommy. Truth was, I had tried to resist, but an addiction was just that.

Abruptly Mum's car sped up the driveway. Coming to a halt only metres from me, she jumped out, grinned up at me and raised the pizza in hand. I let out a long slow breath, rubbing the back of my neck. Quivering, my muscles seemed twitchy and agitated. Mum stopped directly in front me still smiling.

"Truce? We could both use a break tonight, hey Annie."

Was that even possible?

I nodded weakly, following her inside. The smell of the pizza suddenly reminded me how hungry I was, and suddenly weary, too. We all had to eat right. The rest could come later.

Don't cop out on this Annie.

Sitting heavily opposite her on the tiny kitchen table tonight, it saddened me that I knew my Mum even less well than I'd thought. In fact, I really was struggling to work out who she was at all right now.

For a few days there, I'd wanted to believe we'd broken down some barriers, that maybe, just maybe, she was interested in changing things between us. Obviously, Mum had been through a lot, too. I see that now. It helped me understand a little more as to why she was so protective of her true self. From what I could ascertain, Mum had basically built the façade of a celebrity to disguise her pain.

So, was it too late for us?

The contract of sale from Mr Stanton seemed to suggest it was. There were some things impossible for me to forgive. Mum knows this is not what Pa wants, nor Annabelle, that should be enough. I needed to escape my head.

"How's Pa? Any changes?"

"Please don't speak with your mouth full, Annie. We don't do that remember."

I glared at her. I thought she wanted a truce.

Take a breath Annie.

"He is making small progress the doctors believe. It's still very difficult to say whether he'll make a full recovery, or whether he will be permanently impaired. That's if he lives at all to be honest with you Annie."

Suddenly the food stuck in my throat, and I gulped down some water. The reality of Pa not making it was all too confronting, and I simply refused to entertain the thought.

"He will make it. I know he will."

Mum sighed, put down her pizza and took a large mouthful of wine. She refilled her glass before looking at me intently.

"Annie, we need to be realistic here. The extent of his injuries is yet to be determined. He is old and frail, and the longer he lays in that bed, the more chance of other factors like pneumonia come into play. Especially considering he has a punctured lung. We must be prepared for all outcomes. Also, I have my career to consider. I can't be here forever you know, and neither can you."

I stood, claustrophobic. Her presence felt toxic like she poisoned the air. Jamming my eyes shut, I gripped the table. Ringing in my ears made my scattered thoughts harder to follow. I couldn't believe what I'd just heard. It was always about her.

Then a moment of clarity.

Why hadn't I seen it before?

I needed to call the shots from here. Isabelle Robinson was incapable. She was clearly devoid of emotion, so why had I expected anything different? Opening my eyes I frowned, seeing mum clearly for the first time, was, in one sense like a relief. The wounded child before me, trapped in an adult's body, was simply doing all she knew how to do. Run.

I sat back down, but this time sitting straighter, my shoulders back and chin raised.

"Mum. Can I talk, and you just hear me out? Please?"

Mum put her hands up in the air.

"Be my guest Annie. I'd like to hear your take on things, really, I would."

I chose to ignore the sarcasm.

"Mum. I know we have very limited time, well 48 hours to be exact, before the bank will foreclose on Brambly Estate. I also know, you have organised to sell. I had a visit from Mr Stanton earlier. He was delivering the contract."

Mum's face reddened. As she poured more wine into her glass, her hands were shaking.

"But Mum. I also know, that's not how this is going to end. I can save Brambly Estate. It is my birth right. I, too, have fought against the crazy notion that there is a prophecy, that I'm the chosen one, that spirits are at play here, and that there even is treasure to be found at all. The whole thing is bloody nuts! So, Mum, I totally resonate with why you are scared. I also understand why you had to leave and want to flee again now. It's out of your control, and for you, that feels terrifying. But Mum, for the first time in my life, I feel like I am *in* control. I am choosing to trust Annabelle, and myself."

I waited, holding my breath for the tirade that would follow and bracing for the sarcastic barrage of put downs about to shower me hard. Instead, Mum burst into tears. I sat for the longest time, not quite knowing what to do next. Finally, in a weakened voice I'd never heard before, she spoke.

"I am nothing compared to you Annie. Nothing. I don't know how on earth I got so lucky to have a daughter as strong and intelligent. Nothing phases you. I'm so proud of you, believe it or not."

I felt my eyes narrow in confusion and flinched when Mum reached for my hand.

"I have failed you, Annie. But that was never my intention. I thought that if I could just show you, and the world, how successful and important I was, that I was in control of my destiny, then maybe you would never know the truth about me."

I stiffened as Mum grasped my hand tighter and appeared almost desperate for my approval now.

"Mum, what are you talking about? What truth about you?"

Releasing my hand, mum stood and gingerly made her way to the sink. Wine glass in hand she shook and heaved as she cried, bracing against the bench.

"Annie. I had the chance to stay in Brambly Bay. Maybe I should have after what Annabelle revealed. Yet I ran. I was terrified. I still am. I didn't want you nor me to be in danger. And I sure as hell didn't want you to see me as the pathetic coward I am. So, I tried to create a woman, a mother, you could be proud of. I wanted us to forget about Brambly Estate, so we could make our own destiny. We would be safe and secure in our better life in Sydney."

I walked over to Mum and turned her around to face me. The power had completely shifted between us. Finally, I understood.

"Instead, I've just made you hate me, Annie. And I don't blame you one bit."

Mum let out a huge sigh before sliding down onto the floor. Burying herself into her knees, she covered her face. I sat down beside her, and for the first time in as long as I could remember, I took the initiative to hug her tightly.

"Well Mum, we all do the best we can in a situation, right. I believe you did the best you could. That's the great thing about life. We can all get a second chance to do better. I can, you can. Okay?"

I wasn't sure she was hearing me through her sobs, but I continued anyway as I was on a roll after all, and it felt good.

"But this is what's going to happen next Mum. I have 48 hours to save and secure Brambly Estate. I will do that, and then we will make it a home again for Pa. That is what both he and Annabelle want, and so do I. I'm asking you not to stand in my way, not to sign any contract of sale until we have absolutely no choice. Can I have your word?"

Mum finally looked up at me, her eyes reflecting those of a bewildered child. She nodded, reaching over, and hugging me like she never had.

The embrace was what I had longed for my entire life.

I felt strong, completely capable as I held her. We had a long way to go, but for the first time I could see forgiveness was possible.

Then, from across the room, in the dusty shadows of the evening, I saw Annabelle. She simply smiled at me, gratified, which empowered me further.

I hoped to God, these feelings would last.

Mum had retired early, and Brambly Estate sure felt lonely tonight. I missed Mr Mittens. He'd be the perfect companion right now.

Maybe I should have taken Tommy up on his offer to come back over and hang out, but once again, something had held me back. I wondered what he and Stella had gotten up to tonight. Tommy said he was keeping her up with all the latest. Stella was such a lovely woman, as soon as I could, I'd go visit her. Annabelle had taught me to trust my intuition. Maybe the silence tonight was just what I needed. Tommy was one gorgeous distraction, that was for sure. Even just the thought of him made my stomach flip.

It was 1.10am.

I should go to bed I suppose. I sat on a single pillow in the middle of the front room, I'd dragged it downstairs, along with as many candles as I could muster earlier. Surprisingly the light was pretty good. All around me were the paintings. I'd shown Mum them earlier and caught her up to speed with everything I knew and had discovered.

Together we had stared at them for the longest time. I'd rambled on, somewhat nervously as I had told her all about seeing Mabel at the hospital, then Annabelle, then breaking into the van to get our property back. I was still not sure what her reaction would be.

Mum had smiled, then laughed for ages, almost hysterically at one point when I told her about spitting on Mabel. Not that I was overly proud of that. Moments like that, sitting and chatting like earlier tonight I'd longed for. Just to feel heard, let alone affirmed by Mum was incredible. I hoped it wasn't the last time.

The words seemed so foreign coming from her mouth, yet Mum had appeared so legitimate when telling me how amazing and brave she thought I was. She'd then apologised again for failing to tell me before, promising she would learn to be better. It's what I deserved she said.

I hope she was genuine.

That was a few hours, a large packet of Dorito chips and 2 coffees ago now. Staring vacantly into one painting then another, I buzzed, Mum's words still dancing through my head. I know self-love needs to come first, and I shouldn't rely on the validation of others to see my worth blah blah, but at the end of the day, she was my Mum, and despite how much I had wanted to hate her, I had always wanted her unconditional love more.

It felt so good.

Still, I knew I could never tell her I self-harmed. Ever.

Rolling onto my back, I stretched and stared up at the chandelier on the high ceiling. The candlelight flickered off the golden stones and crystal beading. I wondered where Annabelle had sourced such a beautiful piece. Why had I never thought to ask Nan? Maybe I'd ask Annabelle next time I saw her.

Bending my head all the way back, I looked upside down at the paintings. The Forbidden City came into view. Upside down it looked almost like a golden monster, towering over all the smaller dwellings. I'm glad Tommy couldn't see me now, I mused. Too much caffeine was making me a little wacky.

But suddenly, just as I was about to move on to the next painting, my eyes fixated on one of the small buildings in the far-left corner of the city of Beijing. Rolling over onto my stomach, I crawled closer. Yep, no mistake, it looked exactly like my birthmark.

"Ha! That's weird" Touching the outline of the small hut looking image, I looked down at my own birthmark.

On all fours I crawled quickly to the next painting, a little further to my right. Annabelle's treehouse scene.

No way! OMG!

I blinked rapidly. My heart skipped a beat then began to thump just as fast. There, again barely noticeable in the far-left corner of the painting, in amongst the waves and whitewash of the sea, was the same little image as my birthmark.

I started to get excited. Surely that was no coincidence.

I began moving faster, crawling from one painting to the next. When I looked hard enough, each painting revealed the same tiny picture.

How did I miss this before?

All of them had been placed on the left-hand side, bottom corner of the paintings. My birthmark was just above my left ankle. As were Mum's, Nan's, and Annabelle's.

But what the hell did that mean?

The symbol was placed in all 18 paintings. I sat further upright. Come to think of it, so was the symbol at the base of the letter Annabelle wrote to me in 1920. Except that one had a second symbol beside it.

Whatever this symbol represented was the key to finding the treasure. It had to be.

I was close now I could feel it. Letting myself get carried away, without care about the noise I began jumping up and down, pumping my fists in the air. I knew I was onto something big. I felt capable of anything in this minute.

"Thank you, Annabelle. Thank you!"

I had to go find the letter, confirm what I already knew. Suddenly, again without warning the candles flickered out, as a chill swept through the room. I stood, instantly motionless, waiting, knowing her voice would come.

"Focus Annie. There are more days behind you than before you now. It is death or glory from this moment."

穀倉

Annabelle's letter in hand, I stared. It didn't matter how many times I read it in its entirety, I doubted full comprehension would ever come. Today, however, my focus was on the symbols. The first was new to me, but not the second, I'd been branded by it from birth.

How had I been as stupid as to not question this before?

Had Mum?

All this time, every minute I'd been alive, the answer to a problem I'd not known existed had been marked on me. Clever.

Now all I had to do was try to figure out what on earth it meant. The annoying thing was, Annabelle would know for sure. Had I been in Sydney, I could have scanned and googled the image on my laptop. Pa didn't have any type of computer, let alone Wi Fi here, so that was out of the question. My new smartphone's very slow data seemed to be my only hope right now. Great!

Sitting cross legged in the candlelight of the front room once again, my phone read 2.28am. I wasn't interested in sleep. I googled the Chinese symbol for house, home, temple, dwelling, shed, hut, even tree house…all were slightly different to the one staring up at me from Annabelle's letter seemingly screaming to be discovered.

I shook my head glancing across at the paintings. Even in the dull light, the little symbol was so clear in each one now.

Your eye does not see until your mind opens to possibilities.

Annabelle had said this so often.

Think Annie.

Laying back for a moment, I jammed my eyes shut, attempting to travel through my mind the way Annabelle had insisted I must.

How did I even do this? Truth be told I had no clue.

Within stillness we find wisdom.

That made me think of Mum. She simply couldn't stand being still. It was like she feared what it would reveal.

I breathed in deeper. A strong scent of incense filled the room, with it came clarity I'd never experienced before. This sense of being untouchable and having a mind over body mindset was new to me, yet really empowering.

I twirled Annabelle's rings. Images began racing through my mind. I let them just float, noticing what was appearing rather than trying to figure it all out for the moment.

I saw the Forbidden City, Patrick's ship, then Brambly Estate. Images of Pa with Nan, Tommy, Beth and Mabel, swirled like a windstorm. Then mum, fleeing to Sydney, alone and frightened. Next came Annabelle. Her image causing me to draw a sharp breath. There was so much blood. Clearly injured she lay somewhere on a rocky ledge. It was near dark. Was this her death?

Then came a younger Annabelle, crawling toward the driftwood, starving and near death after weeks at sea. Yet still she had fought for her family. Men came for her, dragging her from the beach.

Next, another vision of Annabelle came. Her workshop was lit with lanterns, and she worked amongst the many candles and bottles of incense she had created. Humming contently, filling orders from the locals, Annabelle looked happy and peaceful. But unlike the first time I'd witnessed this scene, now she was surrounded in exquisite pieces of jewellery, heirlooms of the Qing Dynasty.

Without warning, Brambly Estate raced through my mind. Suddenly seemingly soaring like a bird, I flew over every inch of the property, swooping over the dwellings. There was Annabelle, standing so unsure in the driveway, hugging her body tightly, almost shivering. Patrick, stood proudly on the steps of Brambly Estate

The answers lie below.

Suddenly I saw the sea hawk circling again and again above the barn. Screeching and diving, before flying high again, only to return and repeat the pattern.

Abruptly flickering my eyes open, I sat bolt upright and felt my chest expand.

'THE BARN!'

Scrambling to grab my phone I frantically typed in Chinese symbol for barn into the google search. Covering my face, I begged the Internet to load. Seemingly taking forever, I leant in watching the circle go round and round, crossing and uncrossing my legs, agitated and hopeful all in the same breath.

This had to be it. I begged the universe it was.

Squeezing my eyes shut, I repeated opening one, then the other, until the moment they locked on the source of relief.

There it was.

The very same image.

A match, a perfect match to my birthmark, the paintings and the letter.

"The treasure is in the barn!"

Standing, I squealed with joy and relief, jumping up and down on the spot. This just had to be it. The treasure has been under my nose the whole time. Far out, how had Pa never found it? Then again, I thought, all along it had been waiting for me.

Dialling Tommy's number, I paced.

Thank you, Annabelle, thank you.

"Annie, hi, are you okay? What's wrong? Is it Jack?

Tommy sounded sleepy and confused.

'Tommy, everything is better than fine. Sorry to wake you, but Tommy, GUESS WHAT! OMG Tommy, you are not going to believe what I've found."

I could hear Tommy sighing and chuckling with relief.

"Well? Don't keep me in suspense, girl?"

I smiled, wishing he was here to hug right now. I had no doubt he would be soon.

"I've done it Tommy. I know where the treasure is!"

Light had barely begun gracing the land around us. The sunrise appeared held up by the treetops as the birds had begun dancing from branch to branch, chirping and greeting the new day.

We stood somewhat perplexed, yet totally wired and excited all in one. What lay beyond the entrance of the open barn doors seemingly was daunting.

Tommy casually draped his arm over my shoulders. I'd not slept nor showered but was happily munching my way through an egg and bacon roll and sipping the strong coffee Tommy had been thoughtful enough to bring.

"I just don't get it Annie. There is not much in there to be honest. You and I have searched every inch, so has Jack over the years. Just a couple of work benches, heaps of old paint tins, some ladders and feed buckets. We barely used this shed."

"Yet the treasure is here, I know it."

I smiled up at him. Feeling confident was a nice way to be for a change. Tommy took another enormous bite of his breakfast.

"Then that's good enough for me Annie!....So, what now?"

Shrugging, I laughed.

"I was hoping you would tell me."

Tommy burst out laughing, too.

"You're the chosen one, I'm just here to relax and enjoy the view."

I smacked Tommy lightly on the back of his head.

"I hope you meant *me* that you were looking at?"

"Well that all depends on whether you have a shower or not, really".

Tommy cracked himself up.

I pretended to look horrified, with mock sadness. But truth be told, I couldn't argue, I must look a sight. The ease between us was like nothing I'd ever experienced.

"Nah, I'm still just as crazy about ya with the bed head and all. You always look gorgeous in my eyes Annie."

I did feel beautiful around him. I nearly blurted out that I loved him, instead shoving the last part of my roll into my mouth, I managed to swallow the words. That would come.

Hearing the wire door slam we turned back toward the house. Mum was bounding down the stairs, gaping when she saw us. She looked down at her watch then back at us grinning but obviously perplexed."

"What on earth are two teens doing up at the crack of dawn?"

We smiled, walking back toward her.

"I've got a really positive lead on things. Today is the day we get Brambly Estate secured forever."

Mum pulled me into a hug I wasn't expecting, and after bracing initially, I let myself fall into her embrace. She smelt so good. When Mum pulled away, I could see the tension in her eyes.

"I hope so Annie, I really do. I know this much, if anyone can save us, it's you. The hospital has phoned, they need me in there asap apparently to discuss some issues with Jack."

I felt Tommy stiffen beside me and reached for his hand.

"Meaning what do you think Mum? Is that bad?"

She shrugged. "Best I get in there and see hey. It will be okay kids. It's good they are keeping us in the loop. Will you guys be right here to hold down the fort?"

Nodding, my mind raced. There wasn't much else to say, our faces reflecting the fear of the unknown.

My unstoppable mission had suddenly become even more important.

Tommy and I searched the barn again, leaving nothing unchecked. Every single corner, every box, tin, hay bag, even the tractor sitting in the middle of the space. Tommy had told me the old rig had been broken and unused for as long as he could remember, and they always used the more modern tractor in the other shed.

Jack had wanted to get rid of it ages ago, sell it for parts, but when he had told Annabelle, apparently she had become quite animated about the whole thing. Annabelle had made Jack promise never to get rid of it and always leave it in this very barn. Typical Jack, such a man of his word. Tommy had told me, even after all these years and as broke as he obviously was, he'd kept his promise. Even though she never told him why!

Sitting up in the old tractor seat now, I was starting to feel a tiny bit deflated. Tommy leaned against the bench.

"Could there be a fake ceiling or walls or something in here, you think Tommy?"

He burst out laughing.

"Oh babe, unless they're invisible, I am pretty sure all we are looking at is tin and weatherboards right now."

I laughed too, I knew as much, but I was pulling at straws, looking for anything that could keep my hope alive. Slumping forward, I lay my head on the tractors steering wheel. I was spiralling, discouragement causing my energy and enthusiasm to wane.

Why was this so hard?

A silver fleck in the ground caught my attention. I strained to spy through the rusted holes that dominated the tractor's base. The more I looked, the more metal I saw mixed in with the dirt and hay underneath.

The answers you need lie below.

"Hey Tommy, what is the barn floor made of?"

Tommy chuckled again and I could see him out of the corner of my eye shaking his head. Barely moving, he stood, arms folded, staring vacantly outside toward the main house.

"I think you've had an adrenaline crash or something Annie. It's clay, just dirt, been like that for years.

"Nope…..not under here it's not!"

Turning now, Tommy looked from where he stood, bending down and squinting.

"Oh that. It's just an old sump oil tray. See it has edges? It would have been used in the day to collect engine oil, you know, if the tractor was getting some maintenance done on it or leaking. Something like that. I know Jack could never get her going, not that he seemed very interested in trying."

Hopping down, I knelt beside it to get a closer look. The old, rusted tray had long since dried up, yet the odour was still strong.

"Actually, let's pull it out hey. I'll check if this old girl is still leaking oil. I'd like to fix her up one day soon. Be a godsend to have a second tractor up and running around here."

Shrugging, I leant in under the front wheel, wrinkling my nose before cringing away.

"It stinks under there."

Tommy laughed, crouching beside me.

"Just pull it out ya princess, it won't kill ya!"

Rolling my eyes, I went in for a second time. Swiftly I grabbed at the edge of the tray, giving it a good yank. It didn't budge.

"Are you actually trying?"

"It won't move, smart arse." I kept trying, with both hands now, determined to do it myself.

"Move over, let the man with the muscles have a crack."

He ruffled my hair, laughing. I flicked him away in jest.

Tommy shimmied further underneath, moving the mud and muck aside roughly. The old sump oil tray was quite large, around a metre in length and width.

"What the hell?"

"What?"

"It's bloody bolted to the floor! But that doesn't make sense because the floor is clay."

Tommy sat back up beside me, rubbing his forehead, then raising his eyebrows.

"So, I'm tipping that's not standard practice then?" Absentmindedly I touched the tingling sensation at the base of my neck.

Tommy shook his head, locking eyes with mine.

"Nope, sump oil trays are removable. That's the whole point."

"And if it was bolted into the ground, then you'd think we would be able to get it out, right?

He nodded again.

"Annie, this doesn't make one bit of sense."

All the hairs stood up on my arms as I grabbed at Tommy to pull him up.

"What if it's not clay under there? It makes sense if there is something underneath that was hidden."

Tommy stood looking at me, then the tractor.

"Wait here, I'll be back."

Without another word he shot off toward the back sheds. I let a deep breath escape, willing myself not to get false hope that this in fact could be something huge.

Within minutes he was back, walking at a fast pace showing me the shifter in his hand. His eyes sparkled as he winked at me before shimmying under the tractor again.

"Let's see what's going on under here hey."

I moved in beside him, feeling a lightness in my chest and fully energized.

"Can I do anything to help?"

Tommy grimaced, swearing under his breath as he tried to get movement from the bolt. Shifting slightly, he tried a different angle.

"Bloody hell, its rusted solid all right. The corrosion from the salt air won't be helping either." Tommy pulled back a little, sitting up on his knees wiping small beads of sweat from his forehead. A beaked chorus of birds shrieked, already the morning heat was becoming oppressive with the little breeze.

"You got this, I know you have." I squeezed Tommy's hand as he headed back under to make another attempt. Just as quickly he retracted, sitting up beside me again.

"Might need a kiss for good luck, I'm thinking."

Throwing my head back in laughter, I reached in kissing him passionately, taking in his sweet scent. Our eyes locked as Tommy cupped my face, before grazing my neck with his finger.

"Hmm, that's just too damn distracting girl."

"Well, get on with it then Mr!"

Tommy saluted in jest, before jumping back into action. I couldn't resist smacking him on the butt.

Time seemed to slow, even the birds surrounding us had ceased calling. Crossing and uncrossing my legs I bit at my lip, watching Tommy struggle and wrestle with the shifter. Then, without warning, the bolt snapped clean off, surprising us both.

"One down hey!" Instantly Tommy moved to the second bolt. This one snapping away quickly. He smiled back at me as I clapped silently, nodding my encouragement. Shimmying further underneath, Tommy cleared away more dirt and small bracket before getting to work on the two remaining bolts.

"Bloody hell, you are right!"

My heart began to pump harder. Suddenly I was on full alert, feeling like my breath was temporarily bottled up in my chest.

"OMG Annie, look! This bit under here is metal all right. In fact, I think it might be a door."

Suddenly I knew with certainty. This was our moment.

Covering my mouth with my hands, I dared not to imagine what this could mean.

Reality hit me like a ton of bricks. It wasn't about the tractor being sentimental to Annabelle at all. She had wanted it kept here to ensure whatever was underneath, was never ever discovered.

Until now.

The wires in the tractor engine had been deliberately cut, most likely plenty of years ago now and my bet, by Annabelle. Tommy jumped into action, excited by his mission to fix the old girl. Soon the red tractor was coughing and spluttering, eventually resembling the sound of a working engine.

I couldn't have loved Tommy more at this minute. He was covered in grease and dirt and goodness knows what else, yet he was buzzing and just as excited as me. Gently he edged the tractor forward, revealing the small metal trap door we had hoped for. It was similar in size to the mine shaft near Annabelle's tree house.

"Man, she liked her underground getaways, hey!"

I nodded, yep that was for certain.

"This must be the room Patrick set up for Annabelle. He designed it so that she could continue with her creative talents and feel a little like home. It was hard for Annabelle to adjust to Australia at first. She made incense, oils, and candles for the community you know."

"OMG, that I do know! Another reason Mabel hated her. She is still banging on about it to this day. Apparently, Beth tried her luck creating and selling lavender candles and soaps, yet it never took off, but the town women just couldn't get enough of Annabelle's exotic scents apparently."

The plot thickens again, I thought.

Tommy was off the tractor in a flash, helping me clear away the thick dirt the years had layered over the floor. Standing together we inspected our find. Tommy used a shovel, then crowbar attempting to open the metal lid, but it simply wouldn't budge. Large bolts were securing it in each corner.

Clearly frustrated, I watched Tommy begin to pace, eyeballing the lid in deep thought. Hands on hips he moved to each side, nudging the metal with his foot for any sign of movement.

"We'll have to use the tractor to open her Annie. Can you drive it? I will keep the lid secure from behind, keep her steady. It's really heavy and awkward too, best I do it."

A little taken aback, I looked from the tractor to Tommy.

"Maybe I can, I don't know. You'll have to give me a crash course in driving this thing though."

Tommy talked me through the basics. Something that was clearly so second nature to him, seemed far from simple in my mind. But I was determined to remain positive, hoping my face didn't give my reluctance away.

I'd never even driven a car let alone a beast like this! Luckily Tommy's instructions were clear, when I could feel the clutch engage, I just needed to rev the shit out of it and go forward. I'd feel it in the engine when it released, he said.

I really didn't want to stuff this up, by anything could happen here. I watched as Tommy backed the tractor up, attaching a heavy chain from the back of it and looping it around the metal handle on the lid.

"All right gorgeous girl, up ya jump. You got this. You are the brilliant and multi-talented Annie Robinson, remember!"

My nervous laugh barely eased any my tension, I forced a deep breath. Last thing I wanted was to look like an incompetent idiot, but when it came to tractors, that was almost a given. Instead, I nodded with all the enthusiasm I could muster.

"Ok, Annie, you ready? Left foot on the clutch and put the stick into first gear. Go girl go!"

I smiled looking across at Tommy.

"Perfect. Next, pull down the throttle behind the steering wheel, that's your revs, and slowly release your foot from the clutch. Ready, go."

I stalled, jolting forward abruptly, I felt the chain jar behind me.

"No stress Annie, you can do this. Let's go, we're going to try again."

This time I was better. Tommy was right, I could feel it when the engine engaged. Pulling the throttle down, the tractor moved steadily forward this time. Slowly I kept it moving. The resistance behind me was causing the back wheels to spin, and almost lifted the front wheels off the ground. It was freaking me out.

"Ok stop Annie. Shut her down. You did it girl, bloody legend."

Spinning around I could see Tommy standing beside the open hole. The metal grate was still chained to the tractor.

Leaping into the air, I punched the sky before jumping into Tommy's arms.

"Not bad for a city girl, hey!"

Tommy kissed me on each cheek, then my forehead before picking me up and spinning me around. I was on top of the world.

"You are far, far more than a city girl Annie. Don't you forget it."

I looked up at his gorgeous, filthy face. Feeling the pulse in my throat, I closed my eyes to savour the experience.

"Tommy….I love you." My voice cracked with emotion.

Again, he spun me around.

"Then stay with me forever, Annie. Together we can move mountains I reckon."

"Let's get down there Annie, I'm busting to see what all the fuss is about. Here, I've got some powerful torches, matches, and rope in my backpack."

I burst out laughing, raising my eyebrows.

"You just happen to have all that stuff in your Ute, right?"

"After all that's been going on around here, I wasn't going to come unprepared for anything."

Tommy smiled broadly as he got down on his hands and knees, inspecting the thin ladder disappearing into the darkness below. I crouched beside him, noting the mixed smell of damp earth and incense wafting up through the shaft. It looked like a long way down.

"I have to do this alone Tommy."

He froze, then his attention shifted to me. I couldn't tell whether he was hurt, disappointed, or just concerned. Maybe all three. We were only centimetres apart, and I swear I could hear his heart beating. Maybe it was mine. Last thing I wanted was to go down there by myself, truth be told, but the reality was, I had no choice. I curled my fingers reassuringly over his, squeezing his hand.

"It's not that I don't want you with me Tommy, of course I do, it's what the prophecy states, remember? Annabelle made it abundantly clear to me. If, and when I find the treasure, I must do it alone or the fortunes will not come to pass."

Tommy seemed to process what I was saying, yet still didn't speak. He looked away and intensely down into the shaft again, shining his torch around the opening.

"I don't know Annie. What if it's not safe? What if you get injured, or frightened, or worse…. What if Annabelle's body is down there and you freak out?"

Smiling gently, I reached over and ruffled his hair before giving him a long kiss on his lips. Tommy was so sweet under that tough muscly exterior.

"We both know I've got to do this right? And after everything I've been through so far, I feel confident Tommy, I can do this. I just know it. We are so close to finding Annabelle's treasure, that's the bit that's freaking me out, not going down there alone. Imagine, in just minutes I could be standing in front of a fortune in jewellery…. then, well it's all over Tommy, finally."

Tommy hugged me for the longest time. His body language seemed off, so different than I'd ever seen it before. He seemed somehow unsure, almost desperate.

"Not over Annie, just the start really, right?"

Was I missing something?

"Tommy, what's wrong?"

Hesitating, finally he met my eyes, but only after I literally forced him.

"It's nothing, don't stress. Go on, get going hey, that's what we are here for right, to find the treasure."

Maybe it had only been a short time that Tommy and I had been together. But our connection was intense, and it was real. I was pretty sure I knew exactly what he was thinking. I reached over and cupped his face, kissing him on the nose, his cheeks, then passionately on his mouth. When I pulled away just a little, I could see the fire in his eyes.

"Tommy, just so you know, I don't plan to go anywhere in the future that doesn't include you, if that's what you are worried about. I'm afraid you are stuck with me Mr."

His smile said it all, completely melting my heart. I could feel his relief. Who would have thought? I meant every word, and this we would absolutely talk about later.

I stood, pulling Tommy up beside me. It was time. Grabbing his backpack, he helped me to get it on. One of the torches I put inside my jacket, knowing I'd need it as soon as I touched the ground.

"Just yell Annie, okay. I will be right here; I won't go anywhere for as long as it takes. Just yell. And don't do anything dangerous. And if there are tunnels, don't get lost. And watch your head, in case, you know. Keep sharp, look around everywhere first, maybe even for snakes or spiders, you never know.

With one hand I gently covered his rambling mouth, the other I placed on his chest.

"Tommy, stop, all will be good. Remember, this is all in my destiny, just part of the plan foretold hundreds of years ago. I've got this."

In that courageous moment I really believed, I'd never felt so sure. Still, at the last minute I reached into my pocket to check, yes, my lighter was there. Just for security I told myself.

Grinning up at Tommy and winking, I descended into darkness. Just like the ladder in the mine shaft, this one felt cold, almost damp to my touch. Gingerly I placed one foot lower than the other, each time ensuring my next step was secure before proceeding. Strangely I began to feel a little claustrophobic. Annoyed at myself for needing the reassurance, I called back to Tommy.

Get it together Annie bloody hell.

"Hey, Tommy, can you hear me?"

I could see him instantly poke his head over the entrance in turn blocking some of the light.

"Sure can, all good down there hun?"

"Yep, nothing to see yet, just felt a little nervous all of a sudden."

"So would I Annie. Hey maybe if you get your bearings a little, it might help. Turn your torch on and look around for a minute."

Fumbling in my jacket for my torch, I gripped tightly onto the ladder with my other hand. Soon the strong light flooded my surrounds. Although the tunnel was thin, barely wider than a manhole entrance, it was reassuring to see I was nearly halfway down. Beyond that was still hard to make out.

"I'm going to keep going, thanks Tommy, I'm okay now."

"I'm right here Annie, always."

Smiling, I already couldn't wait to be back in his arms again.

Further I descended until finally my feet hit the uneven ground. Pressing my hands into my stomach I took a relieved breath. Flicking my torch on again, I was instantly overwhelmed and unexpectantly tears welled in my eyes.

I am with you Annabelle; I can feel you here.

Slowly moving my torch around the surprisingly sizeable space, I smiled, noting that this room was exactly how I'd seen it in my dream. Cobwebs thickly covered every surface now, yet even at a glance it was obvious time had simply stood still. It was like Annabelle had one day just up and left, intending to return, yet never had.

Had that been the case? Could she have still climbed down here in old age?

Long tables lined the side walls, and a large shelving unit covered the entire back wall. It was so huge. Its own attached ladder slid from end to end.

How had Patrick managed to get this stuff down here?

The shelves themselves caused me to stare in awe. It was almost like I was looking at a scene from Harry Potter. Each level was filled with potions and tonics, and bottles of all sizes and shapes. My imagination was on overdrive as were my senses with the intensity of smell.

Surely Annabelle wasn't a witch, right?

The tables were neatly organised. Each with their own wooden stool underneath. One had a stack of large leather-bound books at the end and some sort of purchase order book beside that.

I pulled a stool out to sit. A long-since dried-up ink pot remained open, its pen resting on the paper. I recognised Annabelle's scrawly writing, tracing it lightly with my finger. The paper felt so cold. She'd written product numbers, names, dates, and even delivery times, filling the double page. Unfortunately, most was near impossible to read now as dampness and time had blurred and faded the ink.

One of the dates I could just make out, however, was April 1996. The year Annabelle had disappeared. Had these orders ever been filled and delivered?

An ornate teapot and fine China cup sat beside the books, along with a single plate. Picking up the cup I tried to imagine Annabelle eating and drinking as she worked, lost in her dreams I hoped.

I turned my attention to the opposite table, sliding off the stool.

This one was filled, and I mean every square inch, with candles. Some big, some small, slight variations in colours, but mostly white. As I scanned the walls for lanterns, eager to get some proper light happening, I could see exquisite oriental artwork covering much of them. It truly was how I imagined the inside of the Forbidden City. I hoped in some small way, this had brought Annabelle comfort. Patrick had wanted it that way for her.

As I suspected, lanterns were placed everywhere. Bolted in at head height to the walls. Some had half-used candles, others completely burnt out. Reaching into my pocket for my lighter, relief swept over me as I clasped it tightly. Obviously, Tommy had packed matches, but as always, my lighter was my source of comfort.

As I brought the candles to life, instantly a warm and surprisingly bright glow filled the space. Within minutes, Annabelle's scent wafted through the room, her candles making me feel as if she were too. No wonder they were so popular. The town folk wouldn't ever have smelt anything like them was my bet.

Spinning around slowly I took it all in, imagining Annabelle spending hour upon hour down here. Had Patrick joined her often?

Walking back over to the tunnel entrance in the corner, I shouted back up to Tommy.

"Hey Tommy, can you still hear me?"

My voice echoed.

"Hey Annie, yep sure can. All good? Any treasure yet?"

His voice sounded distant but clear. I could hear his light heart-edness, obviously relieved I'd made contact.

"Not yet, but I'm working on it, sunshine. I will check back in 10 minutes, okay?"

"Got it Annie, I'll be here."

Ok, let's do this Annie. Time to focus.

High on adrenaline, I thought about my family. The sacrifices Annabelle had made for us. The endless possibilities Mum and I had in our futures, then my mind stopped with Pa. Would all this be for nothing if he didn't make it? Then what?

As my chest constricted, I felt a little woozy, the pressure suddenly a little overwhelming.

No. Annabelle believed in me.

I believe in me.

Shaking off the doubt, I threw my shoulders back in defiance.

"Okay, let's do this, where are you treasure, I ain't got all day."

I began to search. Starting methodically at the base of the stairs, I felt along every inch of the clay walls. It sure was chilly down here. Removing each wall hanging gingerly, I searched behind them as well as within their frames. Climbing the bookcase ladder, I slowly and delicately moved each bottle and explored all possible hiding places, including above the bookshelf.

Nothing, except lots of dust and spider webs. I sneezed and felt the dust constrict a little in my chest. Suddenly I remembered I hadn't checked in with Tommy. How long had it been? More than 10min-utes I'm sure. Quickly climbing back down the ladder, I strode over to the manhole.

"Sorry Tommy, I got caught up. All is good, I'm still looking okay, nothing yet down here."

I waited, yet no response came.

"Tommy? Can you hear me?"

Again nothing. That's weird I thought.

"Tommy, hey! I'm still down here remember. You all good up there?"

Apart from the echo of my voice, my only greeting was the silence that followed.

A strange feeling washed over me, and despite the cold and dampness of my surroundings, a sweat broke out on my brow. I could still see the faint light of day above, yet no human movement at all.

He said he would wait.

Was something wrong?

What the hell?

Should I go up?

I paced the room, muttering under my breath. It was all starting to feel a little claustrophobic down here. Fists tight, my fingernails were biting into my palms.

"Get it together idiot, everything is fine."

He is not Caleb. Tommy won't betray me.

My mind felt scattered, tormented. Why was I even thinking about this random shit now.

And what happens when I leave Brambly Bay after all this is sorted. Then what? Would Tommy follow me to Sydney? Did I even want to go back there now? He said he wanted us to be together, but things change, people change.

"Oh, shut the hell up. Focus." I cursed myself louder this time, kicking at the dusty floor and gripping my head.

These ruminations weren't helping anything. I'd been here many times.

Flinching, a foreign noise above caught my attention. An internal coldness enveloped me, causing my skin to tingle and my throat to constrict.

That's it, I'm going back up.

Within minutes I was standing in the barn, glancing around looking for answers. As I registered a noise beyond, a shot of adrenaline pumped through my veins. Moving against the wall, I tentatively peered out. Shit, it was a car, and not one I recognised coming up the driveway. Not good! We couldn't be exposed now, not at this crucial point.

Where the hell is Tommy?

Half throwing a tarp over the shaft entrance, I rushed to close the barn doors. Realising that was impossible with the tractor still parked halfway out into the driveway, I grabbed a fistful of my hair, wanting to lash out and scream.

Moving the tractor now was not an option. The red sedan was getting closer by the second, heading up toward the house. Best I could do was get away from the barn and get rid of whoever this was, and fast.

Then, from the corner of my eye I saw Tommy. He bolted toward the front of Brambly Estate, skidding to a stop at the same time as the car turned off its engine. Breathing heavily, he clenched and unclenched his fists. Briefly he turned back toward the barn. Locking eyes, he gestured firmly for me to stay put. Nodding, I ducked out of sight, but I was ready to pounce if need be.

The sun reflected off the windscreen, making it impossible to see who the two frames inside were.

A man stepped out of the driver's seat first. Mr Stanton was well dressed in a polished grey suit, his face plastered with a fake smile. Instantly an ill feeling formed deep in my gut. Without speaking, he nodded in Tommy's direction, before moving around the front of the car to help his passenger out.

Mabel.

No. Surely this can't be happening.

Mabel smiled broadly, just as all the air left my lungs. Tommy crossed his arms, broadening his stance. Was his confidence real?

"Tommy, where are the girls please?"

I strained to hear, leaning in as closely as I dared without risking exposure. Mabel was straight to the point, Tommy fidgeted on the spot.

"Hello Tommy, I'm Mr Stanton, manager of Brambly Bay's finest bank. I need to see Isabelle urgently. Is she here son?"

Tommy looked from one to the other. I could taste the bile in my throat.

Come on Tommy, you got this, don't let them rattle you.

"They're not here. So, I'm going to ask you nicely, just once, to leave. You need to get out of here right now."

Tommy sounded solid.

Mabel laughed, a wicked cackle. Could she sense his fear? Time seemed to slow as they eyeballed each other.

"Tommy, we all know it's actually none of your business son. You may have fooled good old Jack into thinking you were worth keeping around, but it's just you and me now boy, and I know the truth. You are scum. Jack will be dead anyway within days, so I've heard. So again, I will ask you, where are the girls?"

All rational thinking left me in that moment. The vein in my neck was pulsing rapidly as an uncomfortable heat flushed through my body.

Should I help Tommy? But what if they saw me leaving from the barn?

Tommy's rage was imminent. He burst toward Mabel. I stood gripping the wall, daring not to breathe as tunnel vision set in. All I could see were her beady little eyes glaring back at him.

Suddenly he was being intercepted.

"Boy! Hey! Stop. What the hell are you doing?"

Mr Stanton had moved into his space and was attempting to push Tommy back with his hands on his shoulders.

Bad move.

Tommy pushed him aside roughly without a second thought. I could feel Tommy's anger and it was far greater than his ability to calm down right now, its force too great to tame. Mr Standon hit the gravel hard. Tommy seemed oblivious, continuing straight for Mabel.

I began to run toward them, stopping abruptly and ducking behind a tree as I detected more movement from behind the car.

"Hey! What the hell is going on here! Tommy. Stop!!!"

It was Mum. Oh, thank God! I don't know where she came from, but it sure was a relief. Running frantically up from behind Mr Stanton's car, she waved her hands. Tommy braced as Mum boldly came in between them. Pressing her hands against Tommy's chest, her eyes darted between the three. Her stare was challenging and full of judgement.

"Would someone please explain just what is going on here?"

Mabel spoke first. She remained pinned up against the car, still close enough for Tommy to do some damage, but Mum eyeballed him, continuing to restrain the situation.

"This boy! This feral human was about to assault me, kill me I believe. The rage I saw in him, it's animalistic. Wait till I tell my daughter, and the police. That will be the end of you, Tommy. The end I say."

Isabelle grabbed his arm tightly, squeezing it reassuringly. He stumbled back a step, and for the first time in minutes appeared to breathe a little deeper. Mum took charge in an instant.

"Oh, shut the hell up Mabel, you stupid cow. Both of you, get back into your car and get the hell off our property."

A slow smile formed on my lips.

Mr Stanton took a step closer, and Tommy stepped forward again to protect Mum. Quickly raising his hands as a peace gesture, Mr Stanton attempted an awkward smile.

"If I may Isabelle. We were simply here to retrieve the contract of sale I believe you were agreeing to. If you have signed, just hand it over and we will be on our way. Remember you only have 24 hours left, so we might as well start getting some of the legalities underway hmmm."

Tommy stared at Isabelle. Moving slightly away from her, he opened his mouth to speak, instead remained quiet. I knew exactly what he was thinking.

Was Isabelle intending to betray us all along?

"Just wait a minute Mr Stanton. When my daughter and I discussed your offer, I realised I had made an error in even entertaining the thought. Mabel will be the last person on earth I will ever sign Brambly Estate over to. That you have my word on."

Isabelle looked at Tommy, nodding before continuing.

"We will be at your bank by 5pm tomorrow with all the funds we need to secure our property, forever. My daughter Annie has the situation well in hand. Just like Annabelle foretold she would."

For the first time Tommy smiled. I cheered silently, watching mum stand a little taller. Mabel's mouth gaped, and she turned a deep shade of purple. Mr Stanton simply stood, the colour draining from his face. This was the best viewing I'd witnessed for ages. Mum simply rocked!

"So, I will ask you one last time, before I arrange for my lawyers to put in place a restraining order against you both. Leave this property immediately."

Tommy's smile turned back into a glare as he looked from one to the other. Mr Stanton turned and walked back to his car. Mabel's eyes bored through Mum, and with a shaking hand she pointed.

"This is not over, you know."

Mum grinned, linking arms with Tommy.

"I was hoping you would say that, Mabel."

As their car sped back down the driveway, Isabelle turned to Tommy embracing him in the biggest hug. I rushed toward them, satisfied the barn was safe for now.

"Bloody hell, I'm glad I got here when I did. Well done, Tommy, you really are one amazing young man. I deeply regret underestimating both you and Annie. I hope we can put it behind us?"

Tommy grinned as they turned to watch the car speed away.

"Of course!"

"Hey, where is Annie anyway, is she okay?"

Hugging Mum from behind I squeezed her tightly.

"I'm more than okay Mum. It's a long story. Come on, we will show you."

Enough with the pity party, Annie.

I'd been back down in Annabelle's underground room for nearly an hour now.

Sitting on one of the stools, I was frustrated. Why was this all so hard? I'd really believed in myself this time.

All the clues lead to the here and now.

Every square inch of this room I'd searched. Not only with my eyes, but I'd physically either moved, patted down, shook or felt every surface, every candle, every bottle. There was nothing else in here. The roof, the walls, the floor, the table legs. Absolutely everything.

And what had I found?

Nothing. Nothing. Nothing.

Tapping my fingers on the cold wooden surface I fumed. I felt like screaming, storming out of this stupid room and never returning. Or smashing everything in sight. Instead, I pounded my fists against the tabletop, jolting some of the candles and watching them topple over.

Surely this was a cruel joke. I was ready to quit. Mum and Tommy were above, keeping a close eye on things. Everyone was counting on me. I laid my head down on the table.

Where the hell are you, Annabelle.

An all-consuming anger was bubbling, even my skin felt hot.

I can do this. I can.

Twirling Annabelle's rings with my finger, I forced myself up, taking in a deep breath and making a desperate attempt to shake off my mood. I had to give it another shot.

Just one more time.

The smell of the candles and oils had intensified, the aroma was making my nose almost burn. It was agitating.

Maybe it was the lack of fresh air down here?

Again, I searched through each section of the room, trying to look with fresh eyes and a positive mindset. Lastly, I pulled the large heavy cases of spare candles out from under the tables for a second time. Annabelle sure had made a lot of these. Oh well, I guess we'll never run out, I suppose.

The four chests were equally as full as the long table above. These candles were darker in colour, maybe because they had been kept in the chests for so long. I smelt them, noticing their scent was also not as strong. Maybe they were a failed batch.

Methodically I pulled out each and every candle. Then, as I had earlier, I checked the cases for a false bottom or hidden compartments. I already knew what I'd find, but I did it anyway willing myself to be vigilant. As I felt along the rim of the last chest, my finger pricked on something sharp.

"Ouch, shit." Pulling my hand away and inspecting it in the light I could see a deep cut, most likely from an old nail. Its sting was intense, as was the instant pulsing of blood. Shaking, I wrapped my finger in part of my jacket to stop the bleeding. Picking up one of the candles and staring at it, furious, defeated tears filled my eyes.

I was done, finally letting myself go, I began screaming. The almost primal sound filled every crevice, spooked the shadows, and echoed as it bounced off the damp walls. I didn't care who heard.

"Annie, what's going on? You okay?"

Tommy's voice echoed down.

"Annie, I'm coming down? What's wrong?"

"No Mum, stay up there. I'm just pissed off. I need a minute. I'm fine."

Throwing the brittle candle in rage, it shattered into a million pieces against the wall. I wanted to ruin them all. Stupid bloody candles, who cares.

"Too hard Annabelle. This is impossible. There's nothing here!"

I yelled at her at the top of my lungs. My breathing was noisy and my voice shaky.

I'd failed. I'd let my entire family down.

Reaching for my lighter, I decided to burn the open wound on my finger. I deserved it. I hated myself right now. Who was I kidding. Why had I believed I could do this?

Then something caught my eye. Amongst the pieces of broken wax and the dirt of the floor something sparkled. Was I delusional? Scrambling to my knees, I strained to get a closer look.

What is that?

Reaching up on the bench I grabbed my torch. Shining the light directly ahead of me, I crawled closer.

I froze. Blinking rapidly, I did a double take. With a small intake of breath, I fell to my knees reaching for the tiny object amongst the pieces of wax. Holding it up to the light I saw the most beautifully detailed ring I'd ever seen. I felt lightheaded, disorientated, shocked. Forcing myself to focus, I looked back toward the ground. Amongst the smashed up wax was another, and another, and another.

Screaming, squealing, shouting and hollering, I jumped up and down on the spot, hugging the jewellery close to my chest.

"I can't believe it. I've done it. Finally."

"Annie, what's happening down there?"

"I'm onto something Mum, just hang tight up there, I'll let you know in a minute."

I needed to do this myself.

Rushing back over to the chest I pulled one candle out after another, breaking them apart. Bangles, rings, necklaces, hair clips, single stones and diamonds. And that was just within the first few minutes.

The treasure was hidden in the candles all along.

"The answer is in the light. Annabelle that's what you had said right! Oh, thank you Annabelle, thank you."

Crying, I sat in awe amongst the dirt and rubble, surrounded by broken wax and exquisite treasure. Silently I took in the moment. Talk about a roller coaster of emotions.

Suddenly a bright blue light swept through the room. Annabelle had finally appeared. Wrapping me up in her arms without a word, she wept. Her touch was gentle, yet electric. Finally, she pulled away and I saw the relief in her eyes and elation in her smile.

"Annie, you have achieved what no other ever could have. You have done us proud. Our legacy remains safe dear one. And this is just the beginning for you. Brambly Estate is safe forever. There is plenty more down here, be sure of that. Secure it all dear child and be sure to live out your best lives. That is all I ever wanted for you all. Today I can finally leave. I have awaited this moment for so long. Joining my darling Patrick in the spirit world, my soul can be at rest. So, this is goodbye dear Annie, and thank you."

I grabbed at Annabelle's hands, but she seemed to slip through them. This couldn't be it. I still had so much more to say to Annabelle. So many things I needed to ask her. I wasn't ready for her to leave. Not now, maybe not ever.

"Annabelle, wait…please. Please don't leave me now. I need you. We all need you."

I could see her aura fading. She looked at me and smiled, with sadness in her eyes now, too.

"You have everything you need inside you Annie; I just came so you could see."

I reached for Annabelle, desperate not to let her go.

"Annabelle, it is you I need to thank. We all do. You believed in me and taught me to believe in myself. You never gave up on our family, and I promise you, neither will I. I will make you proud Annabelle, ensure your legacy always lives on at Brambly Estate. I know what is important now. And I will never forget you."

Annabelle moved toward me once again, touching my face, sending a powerful jolt through my body.

"Dear girl. Remember, I am within you, Annie. I will always be here with you. We are one spirit. You will see me and feel me, wherever you go from here. You will know the way, just be brave enough to travel on the path least taken, for there lies your true destiny."

And just like that, as rapidly as I blinked my tears away, she was gone.

I fell to my knees, totally overcome with emotion, grief and excitement all in one. The candlelight disappeared once again, and I awaited the chill that would soon surround me in the darkness.

But no longer did I feel alone. Aware for the first time of my inner power, I drew on its strength. The future was in my hands.

The Family
Brambly Estate 2018
The future

"What ya pondering in that pretty little head of yours?"

Tommy's eyes sparkled today. He launched up the veranda steps, pirouetting before sitting beside me and draping his arm over my shoulders. Our knees touched.

"I feel like my insides are vibrating, I'm that bloody keen to see ya Pa."

I couldn't have said it better myself.

Reggy attempted to bound up the stairs too, instead tripping and face planting before sliding back down with a whimper.

"Aww come on little mate." I reached down to scoop up the tiny ball of fluff. I already loved this kelpie pup more than life itself. Grateful, Reggy licked me profusely before wiggling to be set free again. Within seconds he was wrestling with the laces on Tommy's boots.

"We got some work to do with this farm pup I recon." Tommy laughed and I smiled at them both with a heart that felt full. Neither of us had ever had a pup before. Mr Mitton's was not a fan as yet, but not for lack of trying on Reggy's behalf. They'll be friends eventually, I'm sure.

"I think he is perfect just the way he is. I hope Pa likes him. I think Reggy will be the perfect incentive for Pa to keep active."

Tommy reached in for a kiss. He still made me weak at the knees with the briefest of touch.

"I'll tell what perfect is… being here with you."

Tommy leapt up, jumping down the stairs.

"But I'm going to head down to the gate with Reggy. You want to come for a wander? I can't sit still to be honest."

I smiled at them both, equally as bouncy in front of me.

"Nah I'm happy here for a sec. Mum text earlier saying they were leaving the hospital, so they should be back soon."

We had all waited so long for this moment.

As Tommy and Reggy headed toward the front of Brambly Estate, I let myself really breathe. The road had not always been smooth, nor will our path forward be, but worthwhile journeys never were. I was determined to keep working on the bits of myself that are still not great.

Self-love takes time, so I'm learning. Everyone has parts of them they hide. Everyone has been damaged at some point. But no longer did I use mine as an excuse.

I have one shot at this life after all. Beyond that? Well, we will wait and see.

I missed Annabelle. Never once had she returned after I'd discovered the treasure and we'd said our farewells. Yet I found myself looking for her each day, just in case.

Every time a chill was in the air I wondered, was it her?

Closing my eyes, I listened as the landscape sang her sweet nostalgic hues, a lullaby I'd come to cherish. I'd aways love Sydney and planned to road trip back often to see my friends, but this was my home. Today, more than ever I felt certain.

In the end, it had been an easy decision to move back to Brambly Bay, one Mum and I had made on equal terms. Mum could still do whatever travel she needed for her job, her location made no difference really, and the town itself had been buzzing with the return of their favourite celebrity. Me, well things were going okay. The local school was pretty cool, and I only had a month left till Year 12 exams.

Tommy and I were solid. We were strong together. I loved every minute we got to hang out. He was more than just my boyfriend; he was my best friend too. We complimented each other in ways I never thought possible. It was working out well having contracted him as the full-time yard hand and property maintenance guy here. Mum had made a good call there.

Sitting here, letting the sun's rays hug my body with its golden arms, I believed without question, what had begun as a wild and confronting ride returning here to Brambly Estate, now seemed to be turning into a life I never knew I wanted, nor needed in fact.

All seemed near perfect, for the first time ever. Did I dare to imagine it could be?

I knew better than that.

Tommy's animated voice broke my thoughts. Bounding up the driveway, carrying Reggy now, he beckoned for me to come.

"They're here!"

As I stood, biting my lip, a fluttery feeling in my stomach took hold. Clumsily I headed towards them.

Holding Tommy's hand tightly, we watched as Mum helped Pa from the car. I could see he didn't want a fuss. Wearing his Akubra hat and trusty checkered shirt, he suddenly beamed as he stood gingerly, taking in his home.

His rehab had been a long one, but not once in the nine months had he wavered. Jack maintained he was coming home to Brambly Estate to live out his days and fish. I believed he would do just that.

Leaning against the car, walking stick in hand, tears streamed down Pa's face, but his smile told the real story. Without warning an uncontrollable sob escaped my own lips. I felt a little lightheaded.

"Gday Jack!"

Suddenly bounding forward, Tommy pulled me with him.

"Kids! Bloody great to be back here, let me tell ya. I can't believe this is the same Brambly Estate. You guys have worked ya butts off so I can see. She's alive and kicking again all right. Bloody hell, I'm so proud of ya'll. Annabelle will be watching us smiling up there somewhere too."

I hugged him gently. He felt so weak and frail, but I knew time here would help him to get strong again. Tommy hugged him next, not letting Jack go as he spoke.

"Yep, all is good here, Jack. Well, it is now that you're back. I've been keeping an eye on things, just as you told me to. We have missed you mate." Tommy's voice was shaky with emotion, I dared not look at him, as I thought I might cry myself.

"And who's this little tacka?"

"This is Reggy Pa, your new farm dog." As if on cue, Reggy barked, bouncing on the spot, shaking his head until he almost fell over. Hearing everyone's laughter eased the knots in my stomach. I began to relax a little.

We stood united, quietly taking in all Brambly Estate had to offer in this moment. I could feel the energy of spring, finally, the shedding of winter had come. New blooms and bulbs were sprouting, the sun with a greater warmth and today's breeze a scent of sweetness once more.

Confused, I squinted a little harder through the rays of sun masking my view. No one was back inside as far as I knew, but I was sure I'd just seen movement from the balcony. Maybe I'd just left the French doors open and now the wind was dancing with the curtains.

Then I saw a distinct figure, blackness surrounding it like a vaporous mist. Instantly wrapping my arms around my body, I pulled away from Tommy. The sound of my heartbeat thrashed incessantly in my ears, I jammed my eyes closed in denial, desperate to ignore what I already knew deep inside.

"Welcome home, dear Jack,"

A theatrical voice boomed down at us, instantly drawing everyone's attention. Time stood still. I watched as the looming figure stretched her arms high in the air, as if in a warm greeting, before moving closer to the edge of the railing.

The elation I'd felt only moments earlier faded. I could feel mum's eyes on me questioningly. Tommy was pulling at my sleeve, but I dared not break eye contact. It was Pa who spoke first.

"Who is that, Annie? I can't quite make her out with the sun in me face and all?"

I grabbed Pa's arm, not quite knowing what to say. He shuffled slightly forward, looking confused, his hand shading his eyes to get a better view.

I looked across at Tommy, with fists clenched, he began shaking his head. Mum had backed away ever so slightly, her lips trembling. Both wore the same haunted expression clearly reflecting their comprehension of the now.

Again, the figure spoke, this time, her recognisable tone distinctly vile.

"Dear Jack, may you live in interesting times my friend. May you all live in interesting times. I will be here to ensure you do."

The vengeance in her speech was unmistakable. The intensity of her yellow eyes, pierced through my core. Yet I looked her right between the eyes, refusing still to break contact.

The black mist surrounding her was expanding and her body became clearer, bigger and more menacing as the minutes passed. I stepped closer, creating an invisible shield between her and my family. Jaw clenched, I crossed my arms rebelliously.

I could feel Annabelle. She was here, her unbreakable spirit surging through me now. As my fear dispersed, I felt my courage rising. Defiance flickered in my eyes.

Annabelle had been right. We were one, together an unbreakable force.

A knowing smile formed on my lips.

No, this is not over.

"Annie, please tell me. What's happening? Who is up there, can you see?"

Pa shuffled up beside me, his voice shaky and confused. I stood taller still, answering him in muted dissent.

"It's only Beth."

Acknowledgements

The journey forward when writing a book is always a long bumpy ride, filled with many emotions. But it's a task I love, and I hope to spend the rest of my life writing. It gives me such purpose and ignites a passion within like nothing else.

I live with a Panic and Anxiety Disorder and have done so since my nervous breakdown in 2019. Determined to be well again, I began to dabble in writing. This was something I'd wanted to do forever, but never quite gave myself the opportunity. Life gets busy right? Kids, career, and all that's in between.

As part of my wellness journey, I was encouraged by doctors and specialists to find a creative outlet to balance my mind. For me, writing became just that, and I credit the craft for my healing. I would encourage you all to find that special something that brings you into a space of mindfulness and hems you into a moment in time where nothing else matters. It's when I'm being creative, I feel alive. I feel present and powerful, and anxiety cannot take hold.

'*Where the Driftwood meets the Sand*' is my 5th publication, and I feel my best write to date. You'd think it would get easier right? In fact, the opposite for me is true, as my personal expectations of my writing elevate with each book. I love a challenge and I love learning. Achieving improvement in my craft motivates me entirely.

This novel took a little longer than my others, nearly two years to execute as the death of my father-in-law changed our lives forever. Doug Wilson was a huge part of my writing journey and the first person I would like to acknowledge. Doug was the most knowledgeable human I've ever known. Each time I was researching or gathering information I'd ask him, and sure enough, he gave me the answers

I needed. The last thing Doug ever said to me was to keep writing. Well, I'm doing just that Doug and I hope this book makes you proud.

I'd also like to thank my amazing family. Particularly Joan Rademaker and Jill Wilson for the many read throughs, advice, and edits. I know I go on and on about characters, get random plot ideas at the least ideal times and am always sneaking off to my studio to write. Your encouragement and belief in me is everything.

To world renowned Australian artist and all-round great human, Alan Borg. (@alanborgdriftwoodart) Thank you so very much for allowing me to use one of your many incredible driftwood sculpture designs. Your beautiful 'Ocean Goddess' captivated me from the first moment I saw her, and never did I imagine you would say yes, I could feature her on my cover. I look forward to more collaborations.

To my cover designer Latte Goldstein. Thank you for your exceptional work. Your expertise and creative flair are greatly appreciated. I'm sure we will have more design adventures together.

To my wonderful Beta readers, I love your brutal honesty and feedback, you always keep me pushing harder and striving to improve.

To the young voices who really helped me encapsulate the teen voice in this novel. Daisy Biciacci, Melody Fadaei and Cody Baltissen, your raw insight and honest views on teen life were invaluable. Thank you.

To my circle of friends who never ever stop believing in me, keep me on track when the self-doubt creeps in and are always the first to buy my books. Love you all to the moon and back.

Thank you to the many community members at Venus Bay who allowed me to interview them and gather research.

Thank you to my forever friend, fellow writer, problem solver and brilliant ideas lady, JoJo Leslie. I must exhaust you at times with all you help me with, from computer issues, to plot holes, and even when I need a good kick up the bum to keep going. Your creation of my website is incredible, and I highly recommend JoJo's services @creativenessdesigns.

Thank you to all the people who continue to use my services at *Wings for Grace Educational Consulting*. I love workshopping, presenting and teaching all things writing & books. Being out and about in our amazing world and meeting such a diverse range of humans energises my soul.

Thanks to Lamont Books for supporting my author career. I love the bookings and events I get to attend and share my love of writing and reading.

Thanks to all my author and illustrator friends, specifically Caz and Ben Carter. I love being inspired by you all and value your support so much. I'm so grateful to have had the privilege of interviewing many of you for your podcasts.

A HUGE thanks to Hawkeye Publishers. I had the privilege of working with Carolyn and Poppy on the structural edit of this novel. Wow, I've learnt so much and have become a much better writer after working through your insightful editing and feedback.

Finally, a big hug and thank you to my readers. Without you, none of this would be as meaningful. I love receiving your comments and reviews, and hope I encourage you all to be the best versions of yourselves.

You are worth it.

Please enjoy '*Where the Driftwood meets the Sand*'.

Kel.

@kelly.wilsonwingsforgrace.com

www.wingsforgrace.com